SPIDER-MAN 2

By Peter David
Published by Ballantine Books:

BABYLON 5: LEGIONS OF FIRE TRILOGY
The Long Night of Centauri Prime
Armies of Light and Dark
Out of the Darkness

The Hulk
Spider-Man
Spider-Man 2

Books published by The Random House Publishing Group
are available at quantity discounts on bulk purchases for
premium, educational, fund-raising, and special sales use.
For details, please call 1-800-733-3000.

SPIDER-MAN 2

By Peter David
Based on the motion picture screenplay
by Alvin Sargent
Screen story by David Koepp and
Alfred Gough & Miles Millar
Based on the Marvel comic book
by Stan Lee and Steve Ditko

DEL
REY

BALLANTINE BOOKS • NEW YORK

Spider-Man 2 is a work of fiction. Names, places, and incidents either are products of the author's imagination or are used fictitiously.

A Del Rey® Book
Published by The Random House Publishing Group
Copyright © 2004 Columbia Pictures Industries, Inc. All rights reserved.

Spider-Man and all related characters: TM & © 2004 Marvel Characters, Inc. *Spider-Man 2*, the movie, © 2004 Columbia Pictures Industries, Inc. All rights reserved.

Super Hero is a co-owned registered trademark

All rights reserved under International and Pan-American Copyright Conventions. Published in the United States by The Random House Publishing Group, a division of Random House, Inc., New York, and simultaneously in Canada by Random House of Canada Limited, Toronto.

Del Rey is a registered trademark and the Del Rey colophon is a trademark of Random House, Inc.

Excerpt on page 82 from "Four Quartets: Burnt Norton" by T. S. Eliot

www.delreydigital.com

ISBN 0-345-47054-0

Manufactured in the United States of America

First Edition: May 2004

OPM   10   9   8   7   6   5   4   3   2   1

SPIDER-MAN 2

I

Otto Octavius needed several extra arms. Certainly the two he possessed were proving inadequate.

Octavius was a darkly complexioned man, stout but reasonably muscular, hair hanging loosely about his face with very little attention paid to tonsorial trivialities. He was in his mid-forties and had an air about him that managed to be both distracted and intense. In other words, he tended to be very focused on things that had nothing to do with his whereabouts at any given moment.

He was busy trying to extricate himself from a taxicab on the corner of Sixth Avenue and Greenwich Avenue, at the edge of the university campus. He held a slide carousel in one hand; tucked in the crook of his other elbow was a folder thick with notes, and he was clutching a briefcase with his remaining free hand. This left him nothing with which to close the door except his foot, and he was having difficulty maintaining his balance. Then the cabbie informed him, with no small sense of irritation, that the twenty Octavius thought he'd handed him was actually a ten. Now he had to try to get at his wallet.

He muttered under his breath, tried to figure what he could put down where, and was extremely relieved when a familiar voice called from behind him, "Otto!"

A blondish man in a lab coat ran up to him. "Otto, we were supposed to meet at the southeast corner! This is the southwest!"

"Is it?" Octavius asked distractedly. "I'm sorry, Curtis, I'm not a ship's navigator, you know. Can you lend me a hand?"

"If the one will be sufficient, then certainly."

Octavius winced as he glanced at the flapping sleeve of Connors' lab coat, pinned at the right shoulder, underscoring the lack of an arm.

"Sorry, Curtis," Octavius muttered to Connors.

"Yo! Buddy!" snapped the cabdriver.

"I am *not* your buddy," Octavius informed him archly.

"Damn right! What about my money?"

"Curtis," said Octavius, nodding toward his right coat pocket. "Would you mind pulling out my wallet? The man needs another ten."

"Don't worry, it's my treat," said Connors, removing a roll of bills from his pocket and deftly extracting a ten.

"Curtis, I can't allow you to—"

"Don't be ridiculous. It's my pleasure, Otto," Connors interrupted, handing the money to the cabbie. "It's the very least I can do. After all, you did agree to come down here and speak to my students."

"Yes, well . . . I suppose I did," admitted Octavius. "But I insist on buying you lunch afterward."

Having paid the cabbie, Connors took Otto's briefcase to help ease his load.

"I truly am sorry about the 'lend a hand' comment, Curtis. It was insensitive of me."

"Nonsense."

"You're a genuine hero," said Otto. "Going there, to

a war zone overseas, patching up soldiers . . . then losing an arm to mortar fire. That was a hell of a thing you did."

"Yup . . . a hell of a thing that ended my career as a surgeon." Connors said it lightly, but Octavius could tell there was still sting there. "But I went where I was needed, Otto. And molecular biology has been a fascinating field . . . the students have been just phenomenal."

"Anyone with a future?"

"A few. One in particular. His name's Peter Parker. Brilliant, but lazy. If he can ever get his mind into his work . . ."

"Ah, well. Young people." Octavius shrugged. "More often than not, they have their heads in the clouds."

Spider-Man swung in a dizzying arc that snapped him around the Flatiron Building and into the middle of Broadway. He fired another web-line, and another, swooping from one side of the street to the other. Pedestrians pointed and shouted, *"Spider-Man!"* People were yanking out their cameras, but he was confident that by the time they managed to get him in their viewfinders, he'd be gone.

Even after all this time, he had to admit he got a kick out of it. What he *didn't* get a kick out of, however, was being late for class. Again.

It shouldn't have been a problem. He'd left plenty early, but then he'd wandered into the middle of that daylight holdup, and one thing had led to another and . . . well, now here he was, trying to make up for the lost time by webbing his way across town.

He had his homework and textbooks snug in his backpack, which was, naturally, on his back. It lacked a certain "coolness" factor from a Super Hero point of view. Then again, he'd never really cottoned to the term "Super Hero" that the media loved to bandy about. It was too self-aggrandizing for his tastes.

As he drew nearer to the campus, he wondered about the special guest to whom Doctor Connors had alluded at the end of last Tuesday's class. He'd been vague about it, saying only that this "special invited guest" had some intriguing thoughts and theories that Connors was certain would be of interest to the class. Peter had no idea why Connors was being elusive on the subject of the guest's identity, but he figured the doctor had his reasons.

Peter felt a pang of frustration over how things were going in class. Curt Connors had made it clear that he thought Peter had tons of potential . . . potential, Connors never hesitated to point out, that Peter consistently failed to live up to. Well, Peter was determined to turn that around, starting this very day. No more missed classes, no more being late. It was time to get his priorities in order.

Granted, he knew he had responsibilities. He had learned that lesson all too cruelly when, two years ago, he had stepped aside and allowed a thief to escape from the scene of a robbery. He had done so in a fit of pique and with a sense of poetic justice: The thief had stolen from a wrestling promoter who had screwed Peter himself over money owed him. As the thief had fled, the promoter shouted in Peter's face, livid over his lack of action. Peter had said with the sort of smug confidence that comes with being truly self-righteous, "I missed the part where that's my problem."

It became his problem hours later, though, when the same criminal—searching for a getaway vehicle to steal as police had closed in on him—had stolen the car belonging to Peter's uncle Ben, the man who had been like a father to him since his youth. Not only had he taken the car, he had also taken Ben's life, coldly shooting him and then hauling him out of the car, leaving him behind on the street like a bag of garbage.

Uncle Ben had died, right there before Peter's eyes. The tearful young man had fancied himself grabbing Uncle Ben's soul and shoving it back into his body, but naturally that hadn't happened. Then an enraged Peter had gone after the robber, tracking him down, confronting him . . . and realizing that his uncle's murderer and the man he'd smugly let run past him were one and the same.

That tragic set of events had driven home to him, in a way nothing else could, the truth of something his uncle had said to him. "With great power comes great responsibility." At first Peter had dismissed it out of hand as a cheap aphorism.

Now it was his watch phrase, his philosophy, and his reason for living, all wrapped up in a few powerful words.

He had done great good as Spider-Man. On the other hand, in some respects he had taken part in great evil. Foremost was his involvement in the death of the Green Goblin, a.k.a. Norman Osborn, father of Peter Parker's best friend, Harry. Spider-Man hadn't killed Norman Osborn himself. No, he'd simply dodged, just as the Goblin had sent a lethal, pointed vessel of death screaming through the air at him. The Goblin had been run through, by his own glider. Hanging there on the wall, pinioned like a butterfly, Osborn had gasped out his last words and his last wish. "Don't tell Harry."

Peter had honored that. Unfortunately, in doing so, he had committed an entirely *new* sin. In failing to be honest with Harry, he had inadvertently led Harry to the false conclusion that Spider-Man was, indeed, responsible for Norman Osborn's death. Not only was this naturally of great personal distress to Peter, but it meant there could be no closure for Harry so long as Peter—and Spider-Man—lived. Harry dwelled on it all the time, it seemed. Over the months it had eaten away at him, body and soul, and Peter was beginning to worry. Bottom line, Harry was his father's son, and who knew what might come of it?

After all, nobody knew better than Peter Parker the influence of fathers upon their sons. Look where the influence of his father figure, Ben Parker, had left him: dressed in garish tights, thirty stories above the ground. Harry's sanity was hanging by a thread? Peter was swinging on one.

We're all mad here, thought Peter.

That was when he heard some sort of grinding noise . . . like a tank perhaps. Naturally it caught his attention. What would a tank be doing in the middle of Greenwich Village? He hadn't read anything about an exhibition of military hardware. A parade perhaps?

Or trouble.

Spider-man increased his speed a tic, suddenly becoming concerned. He switched to Fifth Avenue because that was the area of the campus that the sound seemed to be coming from. He barreled down it, released the hold on his web-line and soared like a projectile the remaining block, landing squarely on the arch that adorned the middle of the park that served as the campus square.

Beneath his mask, his jaw dropped.

"Okay . . . *that's* different," he muttered.

*　　*　　*

"So I understand you've got some sort of major microbiological breakthrough in the works, Curtis," Otto said to him as they walked across campus.

"Right now, Otto, for me the major breakthrough would be if I could finally convince you to call me 'Curt.' Everyone else who's my friend does."

"And since when am I 'everyone else'?" Octavius demanded. "Furthermore, you're dodging the question."

"How can you tell?"

"Your eyes begin to spin counterclockwise."

Connors laughed at that. "If you must know, I'm doing some investigation into the cellular regeneration present in lizards. The way they regrow tails—"

"I know what lizards do. But this isn't about lizards, is it?" He stopped and nodded in the direction of Connors' missing arm. "Are you considering more . . . practical applications?"

Connors shrugged. "I won't say it hasn't crossed my mind."

"Listen to me . . . *Curt* . . . all I'm saying to you is: Don't do anything precipitous."

"What are you suggesting?"

"I'm suggesting nothing. What I'm telling you is that, even when I was a youth, I always detested the portrayal of scientists in Grade B horror films. I know, I know," he waved impatiently before Connors could respond, "they weren't even remotely supposed to represent reality. The problem is, those were the only portrayals most people ever saw, and perception has a disturbing habit of becoming twisted into reality. And those scientists would always be involved with some sort of wild experiment, always be in a damned hurry to test it, and the next thing you know, *bam,* they're fifty feet tall and destroying a city, or they're radioactive, or they have X-ray eyes and can see through women's clothing . . ." He paused and said, "All right, that one I never minded so much."

Connors laughed. "Lonely as a young man, were you, Otto?"

"Which of us wasn't? What you have to remember, Curt, is . . . we're scientists. To many people, even in the real world, that alone makes us monsters. And not just from the way they've seen us portrayed in movies. It stems from the fact that we challenge the most fundamental beliefs there are. They tell us that the Earth was created in a week—that man was dropped fully made into the Garden of Eden, ready to go—and we come back and say the earth took billions of years to form and, by the way, here's evolution to chew on. But we're not monsters. We must never lose sight of that, lest perception shapes the reality once more."

"My, my. You're in a mood today, Otto. Is this what you're planning to discuss with my students?"

"I could discuss a great many things. What did they say they were interested in hearing about when you told them I was coming?"

"Ahhhh," Connors waggled a finger at him. "I never told them it was you. I was purposely vague about it."

Octavius stopped in his tracks and stared at Connors. "You didn't tell them? Why on earth not?"

"Because, Otto, until you stepped out of the cab, I wasn't certain you were going to show, and I didn't want to disappoint them."

"Curtis, how could you say that?" demanded Octavius. "I made a commitment."

"You have exactly two commitments in your life that

mean anything to you, Otto," said Connors, ticking them off on his fingers. "Your wife, and your work. And not even always in that order. Tell me, how many times did Rosie have to remind you that you were supposed to come here today?"

"I have no idea what you're—"

"How many?" he prodded gently.

"Eighteen," Octavius admitted. "Maybe nineteen. But I was busy."

"You always are. Did she put you in the cab?"

"Yes."

"*And* tell the cab where to go?"

Octavius slumped his head, defeated. "All right, fine. You win. It's probably better that you didn't tell them, in case I . . ."

"Forgot?" Again Connors laughed, and he patted Octavius on the back. "Otto, if Rosie weren't in your life, you'd have had to invent her."

"Believe me, I know that all too well. If it weren't for—"

A faint vibration shook the ground beneath them. Otto looked at Connors and said, "Are there fault lines beneath Manhattan?"

"I'm not a geologist, Otto."

"Curtis!" said Otto, feigning shock. "How could you say that?"

Connors rolled his eyes. "Sorry. Seismologist."

"Thank heavens. I would have expected that—"

"Oh, my God," Connors suddenly said, his eyes widening, and Octavius turned to see what had so distressed him.

"What the hell . . . ?" breathed Octavius, no less surprised.

A vehicle that looked like nothing so much as a giant robot was charging across the quad. It had to be at least fifteen feet tall, and appeared to have stepped directly out of one of those Japanese animation cartoons. The legs, however, weren't moving independently of each other, but instead were mounted on huge caterpillar treads. People were scrambling to get out of its way, and that was fortunate, because it paid no heed to whatever or whomever lay in its path. Trees, park benches, a couple of concrete tables erected to play chess upon, all were crunched under it as it made a beeline directly toward Octavius and Connors.

Octavius stood rooted to the spot. He was able to make out a human face peering out through some sort of clear window situated in the chest area. The person appeared to be male, with a shaved head, and he had a demented grin.

"Otto, come on!" shouted Connors. "There's a giant robot coming this way!"

"I don't know that it's technically a robot," muttered Octavius. "There appears to be a human operator within. I believe that for it to be a robot, it needs to be able to function independently of—"

"*Otto!*"

"Oh! Right! Coming!"

They dashed along the sidewalk, Otto weighed down by the briefcase and teaching materials he was carrying. They were running well clear of the mechanoid's path, so Otto cast a glance over his shoulder.

"Curt . . . I believe we may have a problem. I think it's following us."

Connors turned and saw that his friend was right. The robot had changed course, and clearly was in pursuit.

Instantly, he dropped the materials he'd been carrying. Octavius looked at him accusingly. "Curtis! We're going to need those for—"

Connors didn't hesitate. He reached over with his one arm and knocked everything out of Otto's arms, sending it tumbling to the sidewalk.

"Have you lost your mind?" demanded Octavius, shouting above the rumbling.

"No, but you may have! *Run!*"

Connors immediately began running again, and Octavius had to choose between stopping to pick up his fallen materials or matching Connors' actions. He chose the latter, and within seconds the two scientists were pounding along the pavement, the robot coming right after them.

"You know . . . we can move much faster . . . now that we're not carrying my books!" Octavius called to Connors.

Connors glanced at him incredulously.

Just ahead of them was the student center, which seemed their closest chance for refuge. As they bolted for it, there was the sound of something snapping out, rather like a whip.

Suddenly Octavius found his arms pinned, and he was yanked to a halt. He looked down and discovered that a thin cable had dropped down over his torso like a lasso. Twisting his head around, he saw that it was anchored to the mechanoid that had been pursuing them. It had ground to a halt. The face in the machine was grinning widely.

"Otto!" shouted Connors, who had stopped running and turned to help his friend.

"This is intolerable treatment!" Octavius declared,

and then the cable yanked him firmly in the opposite direction. He was snapped through the air, hauled toward the mechanoid as he continued to protest.

Spider-Man's eyes widened beneath his mask as he swung down toward the campus and gaped at what he was seeing.

A giant robot—of all things—was hauling a man across the ground right toward it. A lower section had slid open, like a bread drawer, and the man was being pulled in, kicking and shouting. The moment it snapped shut, his voice vanished.

The first thing Spider-Man did was glance around to make sure there weren't any movie cameras to be seen, because it was so bizarre, he wouldn't have been surprised to find that he had wandered into the middle of a film shoot. Unfortunately there were none.

Even more astonishing, he saw Doctor Connors standing there, shaking his fist in impotent fury. The robot ignored him, pivoting on its treads and rolling away.

Spider-Man swung down toward the robot like a guided missile, released his web-line at the last moment, and landed on the robot's back. He looked for an opening, a weak spot, something he could attack, but the robot appeared seamless. He was reasonably certain, though, that he'd seen some sort of viewing port. Quickly, he scuttled around the robot to the front and found himself staring in at a bald man with a surprised expression.

"Spider-Man!" came the voice of the controller, issuing over a hidden speaker. "What do you think you're doing?" His voice sounded distinctly Australian.

"Oh, just hanging around," replied Spider-Man. "So

you coming out of this thing voluntarily, or do I have to pull out my can opener?"

The robot rolled to a stop, and for a moment Spider-man thought this was going to go easily. Then he saw the arms of the robot lift up on either side, snapping into attack position, and he realized such was not the case.

They angled toward him, huge vise grips on the end of either arm rather than fingers. Fortunately they were moving relatively slowly, and Spider-Man was able to dart between them, never losing his grip upon the robot's surface. In the meantime he kept looking for some weak spot where he could get a grip, rip the robot open, find some wiring, and tear into it. Certainly that would be enough to bring this thing to a halt.

He moved to the back of the robot once more, and the vise grips tried to get at him. But there was restriction in the arms' range of movement; the guy inside—presuming he was the designer—hadn't given them full 360-degree rotation. With any luck, that would prove to be a fatal mistake.

Looking closely, Spider-Man saw that there were, indeed, seams, but they had been welded over. *Okay. Fine. Then I'll just have to make my own fun.* He proceeded to slam the metal surface repeatedly with his fists. At first there was no sign that he was doing damage, but as the surface shuddered under the blows, dents started to appear.

"You're on the verge of making problems for me, Spider-Man!" grated the mocking voice through the speaker. "Guess I'll have to return the favor."

The entire robot suddenly began to tremble, then to shake violently, and Spider-Man felt substantial power building up at the base of the mechanoid.

"Oh, man," he groaned, "you've gotta be kidding me."

Seconds later, his worst fear materialized. The robot lifted off the ground, driven by nothing less than rocket power. Slowly at first, and then faster, it blasted skyward, with Spider-Man holding on for all he was worth.

New York City was a blur below him as his mind raced, trying to figure a way out. He was starting to be faced with the realities of drag as the high wind threatened to overcome even his incredible adhesive power.

Suddenly he felt something at his back. He'd been distracted, and the robot's arms were snapping at him again. He twisted away, and flattened himself against the robot's back.

Determined to end the confrontation, he skittered around to the front of the robot. The mechanoid began angling to the right, left, up and down, trying to shake him loose. Spider-Man moved around so that he was facing the operator once more, and he started pounding on the view port.

"No way you're getting through that!" laughed the man within. "That's triple-ply reinforced . . ." But then the laughter trailed away as cracks began to—appropriately enough—spiderweb through the view port.

Spider-Man kept pounding on it, and then his spider-sense warned him of danger. One of the vise-grip arms was descending right toward him. The world seemed to slow around him and he waited, waited for the right moment. Just as the vise grip was about to grab him, he twisted clear, stood, and grabbed it. Using the arm's own momentum against it, he slammed the claw down with all the strength he had.

The grip drove down and shattered the view port. The man inside let out an alarmed scream as Spider-Man reached in a gloved hand and grabbed him by the throat.

"Do you remember being born?!" demanded the web-slinger.

"W-what?!?"

"Do you remember being born!"

"No, you lunatic! Of course I don't remember—!"

"Fine, then! It went something like this!" And he started to pull the man out through the narrow space, headfirst.

The man screamed at the top of his lungs. "Don't! Don't! I'll set us down! I'll set us down!"

"Back at the university!"

"All right! Yes! All right!"

Spider-Man released his grip on the man and glared at him balefully . . . which, naturally, the guy couldn't see because of the Spider-Man mask.

The thoroughly cowed pilot was as good as his word. Within minutes, the robot was coming in for a landing back at the central quad. When people saw that Spider-Man was astride the robot, they began shouting and cheering, waving fists in appreciation.

"Let the guy out! Now!" ordered Spider-Man. The pilot nodded numbly, manipulated some controls, and the hatch snapped open. A man stumbled out of it, gasping for breath, looking around in confusion.

Spider-Man, meantime, had gotten a solid grip on the front of the robot now that it wasn't moving. He pulled, with a grunt, and the front section of the mechanoid ripped away. Sparks flew and the robot shuddered violently, then shut down. Gripping the pilot by the front of his shirt, he pulled him close and snarled, "We're having words, you and I." He fired a web-line and, seconds later, he was hauling the squirming pilot upward.

The man let out a satisfying screech of terror as he swung higher and higher, tucked under Spider-Man's arm, his arms and feet flailing wildly.

"I wouldn't thrash much if I were you. I might drop you," Spider-Man pointed out to him, whereupon the man promptly went limp.

Octavius sagged against the side of the fallen robot, breathing heavily. The air had been getting stale inside that insane mechanism. People were clustering around him, shoving in close, all asking him if he was all right, and what was up with the robot, and a hundred other questions. He flinched back, trying to ward them off.

"One side!" came the angry voice of Curt Connors. "Move! Any student within the sound of my voice who doesn't get out of my way is going to see his GPA go down the toilet. I guarantee it!"

That was more than enough to cause the crowd to part, and Connors reached his grateful friend. "Oh, thank God," muttered Octavius.

"Otto, are you all right?"

"Truth to tell, I've had better days," admitted Octavius. "Curtis, do you think we might be able to postpone my talk with your students? I don't exactly think I'm up to it right now."

"Yes, yes, of course," Connors assured him. "Some people helped me gather your belongings. I . . . was going to send them to Rosie . . ."

"In case I didn't make it back? Very considerate." He patted Connors on the shoulder. "And very well-ordered priorities. We'll make a scientist of you yet, Curtis, even if you don't know the difference between a geologist and a seismologist."

Connors looked at the robot in amazement. "But . . . who was this person? What did he want *you* for?"

"Not a clue. And—not that I'm knocking it—but what am I doing back down here?"

"It was Spider-Man, dude!" said one of the students nearby, and others were nodding their heads.

"Spider-Man?" Octavius asked Connors. "That lunatic who goes about risking his life helping people?"

"Apparently so."

"Hunh," said Octavius thoughtfully. "Apparently it takes a crazy man to stop a crazy man."

"You're crazy, man!"

The former robot pilot was dangling upside down as Spider-Man looked down at him, casually holding a web-line that was attached to the pilot's right foot. *"You're crazy!"* he howled again.

"You have *no* idea," replied Spider-Man. If there was anyone he'd ever considered dropping from this height—ten stories high as he stood on the edge of the rooftop—it was this guy. Clearly he wasn't going to make it to class, which wasn't going to endear him to Doctor Connors.

He was supporting the dangling man's weight with one arm, and now he started rubbing that arm's bicep and saying, "Y'know, I think I may have strained this muscle while you were trying to smack me around on Gigantor back there. Not quite sure it has the strength it normally does."

"Please let me down!"

"Down isn't your problem," Spider-Man reminded him. "Staying up is the problem. And you'll only be doing that for as long as I feel like keeping you here. The speed with which you go down is dependent entirely on how reasonable you're prepared to be."

"Anything! *Anything!*"

"Oh, good. Okay. Question number one: Who are you?"

"Jack! Jack All!"

Spider-Man just stared at him. "You can't be serious."

"Full name's Albright! But I go by Jack All! It's my alias, okay?"

"Brilliant. *There's* a name that'll strike fear into the hearts of millions."

"Hey! Hey!" The guy sounded annoyed. "Like 'Spider-Man' is any great shakes! How long did'ja have to think to come up with *that* one, eh? Why not something *really* creepy, like the Human Spider?"

"I thought of that, actually," Spider-Man said a bit too defensively. "But there was this guy, and he—"

"Not caring!"

"Okay, fine!" Spider-Man shook him a little to regain control of the situation and was rewarded with a terrified yelp. "Who was that guy you grabbed?"

"Otto Octavius!"

Spider-Man kicked himself mentally. Of course. How could he not have recognized him? He'd been following the man's work for ages, discussed him at length with friends who, more often than not, were just pretending to understand what he was talking about. In this case, he supposed he could be forgiven, since he'd only gotten quick glimpses of the man in all the confusion. But certainly he'd seen his photo enough times in *Scientific American.* Nevertheless, he decided to respond in a guarded fashion. No sense letting upside-down boy know that Spider-Man was a science guy.

"Who?"

"Octavius! Otto Octavius! He . . ."

And then Jack All passed out.

At first Spider-Man thought the guy might be faking it. He shook him a little, even mimed releasing the web-line. There was no reaction.

"Man, they're just not making criminal masterminds the way they used to," he said to himself as he hauled the guy up to the roof. He dumped the limp body there, then lightly slapped his face a couple of times while saying, "Wakey wakey."

The guy stirred and then gasped as he found Spider-Man staring down at him. He looked around frantically, thoroughly disoriented.

"Otto Octavius," prompted Spider-Man.

"Oh . . . right," grunted Jack All. He sat up, running his hand over his bald pate. "He's a scientist. Doing research. I figured he could be of use to me."

"Waaaaiit a minute," Spider-Man said, acting as if he were trying hard to recall something, rather than knowing it off the top of his head. "I read about him somewhere, I think. Something to do with some sort of energy source?"

To his surprise, Jack All let out a dismissive snort. "If you think I care about that, Spider-Man, then you don't know Jack All."

"You've probably been waiting this whole time for a chance to say that," accused Spider-Man.

"Well, kinda. Yeah," Jack admitted.

"All right, so if it's not an energy source . . ."

"It's the other thing."

"What other thing?"

Jack glowered at him. "The weapon."

"Octavius isn't a weapons-maker."

That seemed to amuse Jack tremendously. "No, he's

not. And he's not intending it as a weapon. But he's working on something that *could* be one. Stupid bugger probably doesn't even realize it." He pulled a battered packet of cigarettes and a lighter from his pants pocket. "Lucky these buggers didn't fall out, what with all that dangling. Do y'mind?" he said.

"Go right ahead, kill your lungs. See if I care."

Jack nodded and lit up a cigarette. Then he tucked the pack in his shirt pocket.

"How do you know about it?" Spider-Man asked him. "This 'weapon.' "

"Heard tell through the grapevine. I would've tried to snatch Octavius at his lab, but I didn't want to take a chance of messing with what he's cooking up in there. It's got that much potential, is what I hear." He nodded his head in the direction of the university. "Bottom line, mate, I'm a merc. Strictly freelance. And I'm a techno junkie. Whipped up that little battle shell there, and it ain't bad. Not at all. But Octavius, without even trying, may well have outdone me. So I nabbed him 'cause I wanted to pick his brain. Find out the details, find out how it works."

"How *what* works?" Spider-Man said in exasperation.

"The arms, mate. The arms."

"What arms? What are you—?"

Suddenly Jack All flipped the cigarette in Spider-Man's direction. His spider-sense screamed a warning at him, and he desperately back-flipped to get out of the way. He didn't entirely make it, and the cigarette exploded in a fireball. It knocked him clear to the other side of the roof.

As he scrambled to his feet, he heard screaming.

Jack All was staggering around on the rooftop, slapping at himself frantically. He was completely aflame. Apparently all of the cigarettes he'd had on him were likewise incendiary devices. A stray flame from the one he'd just set off had struck his chest and ignited the rest of them. His screams were horrifying, and Peter mused that burning to death had to be just about the worst, most painful way that someone could die.

Fortunately enough for Jack All, that wasn't to be his fate. His back leg hit the edge of the roof and he toppled over. Spider-Man fired a web-line and it snagged him just before he went, but the heat of the flame promptly sizzled through the gossamer threads and Jack fell off the roof.

Spider-Man vaulted from one end of the roof to the other, but knew even before he reached the other side that he was going to be too late. He was right. He peered over the edge of the roof and saw the burning and motionless body of Jack lying on the ground. People were backing up, some screaming, and someone was running at Jack All with a fire extinguisher that wasn't going to do a bit of good.

Then people started pointing upward at him, shouting things. Even at this distance, he was able to discern what they were saying.

"Spider-Man! What the hell did you think you were doing!"

"Why didn't you save that guy!"

"Maybe he pushed him!"

"Someone down here could'a been killed, y'freak!"

He sighed heavily, fired a web-line, and swung away. As he did so, his thoughts kept wandering back to Otto Octavius. What had Jack been talking about? Arms? Was Otto Octavius becoming some sort of weapons developer? Had he taken on some contract for the military? That didn't sound like him, though. Certainly not based on anything that Peter had read.

Peter felt adrift. There was no one he could ask about it, and he had no way to follow it up. This Jack guy had obviously been deadly serious, but Peter just couldn't fathom what any of this was about.

Perhaps he should ask Doctor Octavius.

And how, precisely, was he supposed to do that? Stroll up to the guy and say, "Excuse me, are you involved in some sort of arms program that would attract the interest of mercenaries? No offense." Yes, definitely, that was sure to work. Crackerjack plan.

Inform the authorities? They'd want to know how he knew what he knew. If he contacted them anonymously, they'd likely pay him no mind. If he went in as Peter Parker, they'd ask him all sorts of very uncomfortable questions. And if he went as Spider-Man . . . well, thanks to J. Jonah Jameson's constant diatribes in the *Daily Bugle,* he had the credibility of a dirty politician, a terrorist, and a shyster lawyer all rolled into one.

Still . . . reading up on Octavius, doing a little digging . . . that might not be such a bad idea after all. If nothing else, he might be able to find out just what sort of arms might be worth dying for.

"The first time I found myself in your arms, I thought I was going to die," said John Jameson.

John was a tall, strapping young man, with a square jaw and closely cropped brown hair. His eyes spoke of quiet intelligence, and his entire demeanor conveyed someone whose nature was to remain calm and collected no matter how stressful the situation. It made him the polar opposite of his father, who could be counted on to fly off the handle at the slightest provocation.

He was sharply attired, having chosen to wear his air force dress uniform for the occasion. The circumstances were right for it: lunch at an extremely fashionable and, frankly, snooty men's club. His father loved to make a fuss over the uniform, especially the medals that gleamed on the chest, and he wanted his dad in a good mood.

Whereas the club itself was men-only—one of the last bastions of such gender segregation—they had opened the main dining room to women, provided they were accompanied by a club member, of course. This had been done to prove that the club was willing to change with the times—which it wasn't, really, but the management had done so at the strident advice of its attorneys, in order to avoid lawsuits.

The change in policy was fortunate for John, since he had his girlfriend with him today. She sat next to him in the back of the limousine that had been sent for them. She had long red hair, a round face, and eyes that sparkled with laughter. "Is that supposed to be a compliment?" she asked of his declaration.

"Well, of course. It meant that I was so filled with joy that it was all I could do to keep myself from dropping dead with ecstasy."

"Ah. That's good. Because, I don't know," she said, and her voice was slightly singsong, "see, to me, it made it sound like I was some sort of vampire or something. That the moment I had my arms around you, that's when you spotted the fangs and knew that you were in a world of trouble."

He shook his head. "That's quite an imagination you've got there. How is it that someone so fundamentally upbeat is able to come up with a worst-case scenario out of thin air, no matter how positive the inspiration?"

"Practice. Years of practice."

With that, her voice had become uncharacteristically somber and he leaned over toward her, nudging her shoulder with his own. "Something bothering you?"

"Nah. It's nothing."

"Honey, what's wrong?"

"I told you, it's all good."

"Yes, you told me that," he said firmly, "and you can see by the look on my face that I'm not buying it. Now spill."

" 'Now spill.' Sounds like some old crime drama where the—"

"*Honey.*"

The sharpness in his tone brought her up short. "I'm just a little nervous, that's all."

"About what?"

"Well," she shifted uncomfortably in her seat, smoothing the front of her skirt, "it's just that . . . I've never had much luck with fathers. My own father was . . ." Her voice trailed off.

"I thought you'd sorted out things with your dad," he said gently. "That he'd changed, at least a little, after he and your mom broke up."

"He has. A little. I mean, we can actually, y'know, spend time in the same room now. But he still acts like a jerk sometimes, and those eighteen years when he was doing it regularly, berating me, beating me down . . . it takes a toll, y'know?"

"Yeah, I know."

"Plus there's the fact that the last time I met a boyfriend's father, it didn't exactly go well. He was . . . well, he was kind of mean. So mean it wound up killing the relationship, because my boyfriend took his dad's side, and, well," she shrugged helplessly, "that was kind of that."

"If the relationship was so fragile that it couldn't withstand a disapproving parent, then it wasn't that strong to begin with, honey. Ours is made of sterner stuff than that."

"You think?"

He squeezed her hand firmly. "I'm sure of it." Then he grinned encouragingly. "Besides, don't worry about it. See, my dad has yet to approve of a single girlfriend of mine he's ever met, and never once has a relationship gone bust because of it."

She rolled her eyes. "Oh, well, that's great, John. If it

wasn't his disapproval that killed the relationships, what was?"

"Well, jealousy, for one thing. See, I was so much prettier than they were . . ."

"Which isn't a problem in our case," she assured him teasingly.

"Of course. Plus I wouldn't leave the space program for them."

She turned and stared at him with genuine surprise. "Really?"

"Really."

"But why . . . ? I mean, to me, that's so amazing, what you do."

"And dangerous. They'd hear about the accidents and be worried I was going to be blown to bits due to some malfunction. Because, you know, as soon as something goes wrong, millions of Americans listen to CNN and suddenly everyone's a rocket scientist, capable of second-guessing everything NASA does." He studied her thoughtfully. "So it doesn't bother you? What I do for a living?"

"Of course not. I know it's dangerous, but it's part of who you are. So much a part of you that I have to accept it."

"You know what, honey? Just say that to my father, and I guarantee you, everything's going to go just fine. And by the way, anyone who would toss you aside just because his father acts like a jerk *deserves* to be your former boyfriend. Oh!"

"Oh what?"

"We're here," he said, leaning forward and peering out the window.

The limo pulled up in front of the Ascot Club, situated in a neatly adorned brownstone on Lexington Avenue. The chauffeur came around and opened the door next to John's girlfriend.

She sat there, hands on her lap. Then, to John's confusion, she reached over and pulled the door shut.

"Honey!"

"Okay, one other thing," she said. "In the interest of, y'know, total honesty."

"Yeah?" he prompted warily.

"I have a friend and . . . well, he sort of works for your father."

"Peter Parker?"

She blinked in surprise. "How did you know—?"

"I've seen his photo credits in the paper, and you've mentioned him by name a few times. Like, 'As my friend Peter Parker always says . . .' That kind of thing. So I made the connection."

"Oh. I didn't know . . . uh, this is kind of awkward, then . . . I didn't want you to know that it was Peter who . . . um . . ."

"Let me guess," John grinned. "He's had less than flattering things to say about my dad. Horror stories, in fact. And you don't want to get him in trouble because he was the one who said them. But because of what he's said, it makes you nervous about meeting Dad. Is that in the ballpark?"

"Right down the middle of home plate, actually."

"Honey." He shook his head. "You think I've known my father all these years and remained unaware of how he can be with people? Not just girlfriends who he thinks aren't good enough for me, but everyone? He can be bellicose, bombastic—"

"And many other 'b' words whose definitions I'm shaky on," she said.

"The point is, you shouldn't think that's all there is to

him. Because he's still my father, he wants me to be happy, and deep down he's a caring, affectionate guy." When she just stared at him, he added, "Deep, *deep* down. Way deep. Marianas Trench deep."

"Terrific."

"Honey, do you trust me?"

"Yes, of course," she said impatiently.

"Then shouldn't that be all that matters?"

"I guess."

"You *guess*?"

She steadied herself and obviously forced a smile. "You're right. It's just me and my baggage. It'll be fine. Oh," she added urgently, "you won't mention what I said about Peter, right?"

"What, mention to Dad that he's pissed off one of his employees? Boy, is *that* the worst-kept secret of the year. But yes, don't worry, not a word."

Thus assured, she opened the door of the limo. The chauffeur, now confident that she was going to emerge, caught the door as it swung, and opened it the rest of the way, helping her to step out onto the curb.

Together, their arms linked at the elbow, they entered the main foyer. J. Jonah Jameson was waiting for them, looking pointedly at his watch. "Our reservation was for ten minutes ago!" he said, his mustache bristling.

"Traffic, Dad."

"Traffic!" bellowed Jonah, approaching him. "How could traffic possibly be a bother to you! My son, the astronaut? Traffic is for mere mortals! You should be able to leap over it in a single bound!"

"I could have if I'd remembered to wear my tights and cape. Sorry."

"Don't let it happen again," said Jonah, embracing

his son warmly. Then he looked at John's companion. "And who is this?"

"Dad, may I present Miss Mary Jane Watson. Mary Jane, my father, J. Jonah Jameson."

"What's the 'J' stand for, Mr. Jameson?" she asked.

"Jolly," deadpanned Jonah. "And please, 'Mr. Jameson' is so formal. Call me . . ." He stopped, considered. "No, on second thought, 'Mr. Jameson' will do. Now come on: We're eleven minutes late and counting."

They followed in his wake, walking briskly through the corridors, and arrived at the dining salon less than a minute later. The walls were deep, rich oak, lined with scowling paintings of famous members of the club going back centuries. If even one of them could have seen women eating there, they'd have died a second time.

Once seated, menus in front of them, Jonah stared at Mary Jane, his eyebrows furrowed. "You look familiar, Miss Watson. Have we met before?"

"I don't think so."

"I've seen you, though. I never forget a face."

"Mary Jane's an actress, Dad," said John helpfully.

"Oh! And there's my billboard!"

"That's got to be where you know her from, Dad," John assured him. "There's this billboard out, twenty times bigger than life, with her face plastered all over—"

"Osborn's kid. Harry," Jonah said abruptly.

Mary Jane paled visibly. "W-what?"

"You used to go out with Norman Osborn's kid, Harry," said Jonah, pointing at her. "Isn't that right?"

"Y-yes." She glanced at John to see his reaction. "How did you—?"

"*Hah!*" and Jonah thumped the table triumphantly. "Sherlock Holmes lives. Can't slip anything past me."

"Mr. Jameson," Mary Jane said cautiously, "I wasn't

trying to slip anything past, I just . . . How did you—?"

"Saw photographs of you with him. Parker snapped them during that whole World Unity Festival debacle. Right before that armored nut attacked."

"Parker," John said, taking exaggerated pains to explain, "is one of Dad's photographers. Peter Parker, I think his name is. Right, Dad?"

"That's him. And I remember looking at that photograph and thinking, I wonder if young Osborn is paying for her time."

"Dad!"

Mary Jane's jaw dropped, but before she could say anything, Jonah added, "Believe it or not, young lady, that was intended as a compliment."

She found her voice, although it wasn't easy. "I was leaning toward 'or not,' actually."

"All I was saying," Jonah informed her, "was that considering how weak-kneed and unpromising a man young Osborn was—his own father's assessment, by the way—I was amazed he was able to engage the interest of such a striking young woman."

"Well, thank you . . . I guess," she said uncertainly.

"What *were* you doing with young Osborn, though?" Jonah demanded.

"Dad, I don't see how it's any of your business."

"She's dating you. That makes it my business."

"John," Mary Jane put up a hand, "your father's right. It is his business. The fact is, Mr. Jameson, there was more to Harry than his father gave him credit for. Maybe I just saw things in him that his dad didn't, but might have eventually, if he'd lived long enough. And let's face it, not every son is as lucky as John, to have a father who's perceptive enough to see all his potential. I mean, you had to have been supporting John for many years for him to get to where he is today, true? A son like this doesn't just spring up out of nowhere. He's molded and shaped by a father with vision."

Jonah considered that, rubbing thoughtfully at his chin. "That's very true," he said at last.

John brought his hand up, covering his mouth to hide his grin.

Mary Jane leaned forward, warming to her topic. "The fact is, sometimes I think John doesn't realize how lucky he is, to have a father like you."

"See! *See there!*" Jonah demanded, thumping John on the arm. "How many times have I told you that, eh? And you, you ingrate! You never believe me! You just smile that perfect smile—which is only there thanks to the braces I funded, thank you very much."

"You wore *braces*?" Mary Jane stifled a laugh.

"Don't start," John warned her.

Jonah continued, "And you say to me, 'Of course, Dad. Whatever.' What is this 'whatever' young people are always spouting about these days?" he asked Mary Jane.

She propped up her chin and gazed at him doe-eyed. "As far as I'm concerned, it's what they say when they realize their parents have pretty much won an argument and they just don't want to admit it."

Jonah Jameson thudded the table with such vehemence that he almost knocked over the centerpiece. John quickly grabbed for it, and just managed to prevent it from toppling over. Oblivious, Jonah bellowed so loudly that heads turned throughout the room. "*By thunder, John, this girl is a treasure! A treasure!*"

"By the way, Mr. Jameson," said Mary Jane, clearly deciding to push her luck, "I hope I'm not being too forward here, but I simply have to say, that's *very* exciting hair you have."

"Really!" Jameson grinned broadly. "Who says you can't get a good two-dollar haircut anymore?"

"Not me."

"I trust my barber," he said sincerely.

"It's trust well placed, Mr. Jameson."

He displayed his teeth, stained yellow from cigar smoking. "Call me Jonah."

For the second time in the afternoon, John Jameson went slack-jawed. His father fired him a look. "What are you gaping at? Haven't you ever seen two people bonding before?"

"Yes," said John cautiously. "It's just . . . you were never one of them."

Jameson waved him off dismissively and turned his attention back to Mary Jane. "Where did you two meet?"

"Well, actually, I bet you can figure it out, Jonah," Mary Jane said challengingly. "You know I'm an actress. So what do most actresses spend most of their time doing to make a living?"

"Waiting tables," Jonah replied instantly. He glanced from one to the other. "You met her when she was working at a restaurant?"

"You're amazing," Mary Jane said, and turned to John. "Isn't he amazing, John?"

As far as John was concerned, Mary Jane was the amazing one.

"Actually," Mary Jane continued, "it was more than just 'meeting.' John bailed me out of a rather dicey situation . . .

Mary Jane had had it.

It was bad enough waitressing at a dive like the Moondance, knowing that only the money passed un-

der the table was keeping the Board of Health from closing the place down. Bad enough that the food was for crap and that the boss, Enrique, was constantly on her case.

But when the burly trucker reached over and pinched her backside for the third time in five minutes as she went past, that was it. Mary Jane spun, glared at him, and dumped a plate of spaghetti into his lap.

The guy leaped to his feet with a strangled yelp, and Enrique bolted out of the kitchen in response to the shout. Mary Jane stood in front of the trucker, arms folded, looking defiant.

"You did that on purpose!" he bellowed.

"It slipped," Mary Jane said, but she didn't sound convincing, nor was she trying to.

"You apologize to the man, right now!" Enrique told her. When she hesitated, he shouted in her face, "Do it, or you're out of here!"

She hesitated, her resistance beginning to slip. And then a calm, commanding voice said, "Don't do it."

Mary Jane looked in the direction of the speaker. He had been sitting on a stool at the counter, sipping a cup of coffee. But now he was standing and walking toward the situation with a confident grace. "Don't apologize. He had it coming, and if you say you're sorry when you know you're not, you'll only regret it."

"How'd you like to have a big piece of regret?" challenged the trucker. He took a step toward the man who had spoken. "This ain't your business."

The man reached into his jacket, pulled out an official-looking I.D. and flipped it open. "Threatening an agent of the FBI is a federal offense, friend." Then he snapped it closed.

The trucker promptly seemed to wither as he stepped back and said, "Yeah, well . . . whatever. Forget the apology."

"And forget this, too," snapped Mary Jane, yanking off her apron. "Take this job and shove it, Enrique."

She tossed him the apron and stormed out the door as Enrique called after her, "Don't bother using me for a reference!"

Mary Jane stomped into the street and, a moment later, the man who had intervened was at her side. "You did the right thing," he assured her.

"Yeah, well, we'll see how right it is when I don't have money for the rent. Nice of you to jump in, though. What were you doing in there? You're a lot classier than the guys we usually get."

"Actually, I was just killing time waiting for the Auto Club. My car battery died . . . Ah!"

Mary Jane looked where he was pointing. A tow truck had come around the corner and was pulling up in front of a red sports car that was parked at an angle at curbside. "I can give you a lift as soon as the car's up and running," he said.

"That'd be great, actually. So . . . being a Fed must pay pretty well if you can afford such a nice car."

"Hmm? Oh . . . Lord, no. I'm not a Fed. I just asked him if he knew threatening an FBI agent was a federal offense. I never said I was one."

She gaped a moment, and then laughed. "Then what did you flash at him?"

"My pilot's license."

"You're a pilot?"

"Occasionally. Actually, I'm an astronaut."

"Wow. That's even cooler than being a Fed."

"I've always thought so," he said. He extended a hand. *"John Jameson."*

"Mary Jane Watson," and she shook his hand firmly.

Jonah Jameson was laughing at his son's audacity. M.J. thought he had a very strange laugh, like a seal barking. "That's my son. Never afraid to jump to the rescue of a lady fair. And frankly, you didn't need that job. I'm sure you could do far better."

"Actually, she's done much better," John assured him. "There's not only that billboard ad she told you about, but she's starring in a play."

"It's not one of these new-wave things that you have to take your clothes off for, is it?" Jonah asked suspiciously. "Trash like that is what's killing the theater."

"It's pretty old wave, actually," she said.

"Dad, it's *The Importance of Being Earnest.*"

"Of course!" said Jonah. "By what's his name. Thornton Wilder."

"Oscar Wilde," she corrected.

Jonah looked at her suspiciously. "He was the fruit, right? Ah, well." He shrugged. "British. What else do you expect, right?"

"You said it, Jonah." Mary Jane smiled, deriving endless amusement from watching John put his face in his hands and moan as quietly as he could manage.

Jonah glanced at him. "What's your problem?"

"I don't think he liked the jumbo prawn appetizers."

"Yeah, that tasted a little off to me, too," agreed Jonah.

They'd made it all the way to dessert before Mary Jane finally decided to step deep into the fire and see just how burned she came away. "Jonah," she said, leaning forward with her fingers interlaced, "there's something I'm curious about."

John looked at her with a trace of concern, sensing something was up. Jonah stopped sipping his coffee and leaned back, looking to be in an expansive mood. "What would that be, my dear?"

"Spider-Man."

"Arrhhhh!" Jameson moaned, and put the coffee down. "While I was eating, you brought him up?"

"Spider-Man's kind of a sore subject as far as my dad is concerned," John said, obviously hoping Mary Jane would drop it.

But she had no intention of doing so. "Well, I was just curious, that's all. I've seen all the articles, the editorials. And I was just wondering, y'know, what he ever did to you."

"What makes you think he ever did anything to me?"

"Well, you write about him so much . . ."

"He sells newspapers, Mary Jane," Jameson told her. "That's the single and sole reason he's occupied as many column inches as he has."

"But . . . the slant . . . your editorials . . ."

"I call them as I see them."

"I just . . . I guess I wonder why you see it that way." Mary Jane saw that John was making throat-cutting gestures, mutely pleading with her to end the discussion. "But if you don't want to talk about it, I understan—"

"Mary Jane," said Jameson, "you can search high and low for the rest of your days, and you will never, ever find a topic I don't want to talk about. You see that son of mine?" and he pointed at John, "he's a hero. A real hero."

"Dad, I'm just a guy doing a job."

"You're a hero," Jonah said firmly. "Policemen, firemen, they're heroes. Men who follow the president around day after day, ready to take a bullet for him, they're heroes. And you know why, Mary Jane? Because they lay it . . . on . . . the . . . line . . . " He thumped his forefinger on the table with each word for emphasis. "And my reporters? They lay it on the line. So do I. Every time we go after crooks or double-dealers or power-mad politicians in the *Daily Bugle,* the name of the person or persons who wrote the piece is right there, in black and white. You know what that's called?"

"The byline?"

"No. Well, yes, but no, what I meant was, it's called 'personal responsibility.' Taking responsibility for your actions and standing up for what you do. Spider-Man doesn't do that."

"He doesn't?" she asked, wide-eyed.

"No. He's no different than these idiots who creep around on the Internet, writing vicious attacks and then hiding behind fake names."

"Well, I think he's a *little* different," Mary Jane pointed out. "I doubt a lot of those Internet guys go swinging around Manhattan on webs."

"The principle's the same. The fact is that he goes around doing whatever he wants, wherever and whenever he wants—getting himself involved in situations best left to trained professionals such as policemen or firemen—and hides from any mistakes he might make in doing so behind a red mask! The way society manages to survive is through checks and balances. Policemen, for instance, are answerable to boards of review, internal affairs, systems set up to make sure they don't abuse their power. You know why? Because as Chairman Mao said, power corrupts, and absolute power corrupts absolutely."

"Actually, it was Lord Acton," Mary Jane delicately corrected him, "and what he said was that power *tends* to corrupt. It doesn't always. I mean, look at all the power you have, Jonah. A newspaper, millions of readers who are influenced by every word you write. You shape opinion for the majority of people in this city. Are you saying that you've become corrupted by that power?"

"There are checks and balances on my power, as well," Jonah pointed out. "Laws against libel, for instance."

"Which Spider-Man could never make use of, since he's a public figure and you're just stating opinion. Plus he'd have to reveal his identity in order to sue you, which you know he won't do. Really, there's no check or balance on you at all. So I'm asking again, do you think you might be corrupted by the power you wield as publisher of the *Bugle*?"

"I have forty-seven years as a journalist, young lady," Jameson said slowly, "going back to when I was a paper-boy. That's a lot of years learning how to be fair and balanced. So no, I don't believe power has corrupted me."

"Then isn't it possible that the same goes for Spider-Man?" she asked.

There was a long silence at the table, and then John said softly, "Still think she's a treasure, Dad?"

"Maybe he's thinking about burying me," said Mary Jane.

"No, no," Jonah assured her. "Actually, I like a challenge. Keeps me on my toes. I've been answering a lot of questions for you, young lady. Now you answer one for me: What's your personal interest in Spider-Man?"

"What makes you think I have any?"

"Because you've got a fire in your belly sadly lacking

in much of today's youth, and I'm thinking it's there for a reason. As I said, forty-seven years of journalism. You seem to think you've got a better handle than I do on Spider-Man. Why?"

"Maybe because he saved my life."

John turned and gaped at her. "You never told me that."

She shrugged. "You never asked."

"Who asks something like that?"

"Of *course*!" Jameson said abruptly. "If you were with young Osborn when the Green Goblin attacked, Spider-Man showed up for that."

"And stopped me from falling to my death when the balcony collapsed, yes. And . . ."

Some instinct stopped her then, preventing her from talking about the other times Spider-Man had saved her. That time when she'd almost been mugged, or from the dizzying heights of the 59th Street Bridge. Somehow he'd always been there when she needed him . . . and she was wary enough not to want a journalist curious as to exactly why that was the case. She was concerned that it might lead to questions she couldn't answer, and answers she might not appreciate. Hell, she could just see the headline: "Masked Menace Stalks Actress!"

"And what?" prompted Jonah.

"And I was grateful," she said.

"Tell me this, then, Mary Jane," said Jonah. "Did it ever occur to you that maybe, just maybe, Spider-Man might have been working *with* the Green Goblin?"

"That's ridiculous."

"Why? Oldest con game in the world. Mr. Smith threatens the mark, Mr. Jones steps in and stops Mr. Smith and collects the monetary gratitude of the grateful mark . . . and then turns around and splits it with his partner, Mr. Smith."

"Spider-Man doesn't take money."

"How do you know that? Check his bank records? His tax returns? Furthermore, at the very least, he's a material witness to the Goblin's crimes. Did he cooperate with police investigations as any good citizen would? No. He hid. He hides because he has something *to* hide, Mary Jane."

"Maybe he's just worried about recriminations against family and friends."

"A risk taken by every district attorney who ever prosecuted a powerful felon. And yet they don't feel the need to operate outside the law. Spider-Man does. And as long as he feels that need, the *Daily Bugle* will point it out." He paused and then, to her surprise, rested a hand atop hers in a manner that actually seemed conciliatory.

"Understand something: You obviously make my boy happy. And because you make him happy, that goes a long way toward making me happy. And I'm willing to accept the notion that Spider-Man is responsible for your surviving to make my son happy. In that respect, I fully understand your point of view regarding him. But that's not going to change the fact that when it comes to making people aware of Spider-Man's potential for nefarious designs, I have a job to do, and nothing can stop me from doing it."

"I understand that, Jonah," she said amicably. "Then again, maybe you have more in common with Spider-Man than you think."

"How do you figure that?"

"Well, maybe he likewise feels he has a job he has to do . . . and nothing can stop him from doing it."

III

Spider-Man hated his job, and wished for the hundredth time that day that he didn't have to do it.

It had been two weeks since he'd rescued Otto Octavius from his airborne kidnapping, and his life had settled back into its standard abnormal pace. Actually, it wasn't Spider-Man having the job-related frustrations so much as it was the costumed Peter Parker, swinging in midair through the concrete canyons of New York City.

He pondered the many uses to which he'd put his miraculous spider-powers. With such abilities as his strength, his speed, his spider-sense, the webbing that shot from his arms—why, he had stopped madmen in their tracks. Saved plummeting tram cars. Rescued countless people from falls or from being crushed by gigantic oncoming objects, or from fires, or from bank robbers, or bullies, or rapists.

The fact that he had accomplished so much wasn't what daunted or haunted him. It was that he couldn't get movies out of his mind.

In movies, as sequels progressed, the hero always found himself facing greater and greater obstacles. Not that Peter thought of his life as a movie: He wasn't insane. He knew better than that. He knew that his life, however over-the-top it had become, was still his life.

But, what if life imitated art? Sometimes he would lie awake, imagining the stakes rising like floodwaters. What new dangers awaited him? What tremendous new challenges would be hurled at him? What dazzling new exploit would the amazing Spider-Man be required to pull off next?

Somehow, in all his midnight ruminations, delivering pizza at web-slinging speed never cropped up.

Life is what happens while you're busy making other plans. The John Lennon line flitted through Peter's mind with the same alacrity that he torpedoed across the skyline, deftly balancing a distressingly high stack of pizza boxes in one hand. He'd taken the precaution of webbing the boxes together so they wouldn't skid off, but it was still a superhuman feat keeping them flat as he bounded from building to rooftop to building again. Then again, "superhuman" was pretty much his stock-in-trade.

It had certainly been his stock-in-trade less than an hour ago, when he'd been sporting this very costume and swinging up toward a dangling construction worker. As rescues went, it seemed as if it was going to be pretty tame, spiraling gracefully upward and snagging the worker who was clinging to an I beam, holding on for dear life. It was only upon Peter's high-flying arrival that matters took an abrupt turn for the worse as it turned out the I beam wasn't properly anchored.

It slipped from its moorings and the construction worker tumbled off. As a result, Peter gaped in horror through the lenses of his Spider-Man mask as the worker went falling in one direction, and the I beam went tumbling in another. The crowd below, screaming, didn't know which way to run. Those who weren't crushed by the I beam would be trampled in the stampede of frightened humanity.

Maybe that spider bite should've given me extra arms, as well, he thought grimly, and then regretted even coming up with the notion. It would be just his luck if Fate overheard the passing thought and said, "You want it? You got it." Ba-bing, ba-boom, next thing he knows, he's toting around four extra limbs to give him a grand total of eight. Go try to hide *that* under a windbreaker, why don't you.

His straying thoughts didn't slow his movements one bit. Anyone watching would have seen Spider-Man course-correct without hesitation, swinging on his web-line, angling toward the falling I beam. A huge glob of webbing fired from his wrist, enveloping the beam, and then Spider-Man's trajectory took him feetfirst right into the beam. He struck it squarely, sending it bounding back toward the skeleton of the building under construction. The I beam slammed against the structure, the webbing adhered to the surface, and there the beam stuck.

It was only a temporary fix, but it was all he needed. Once the construction worker was squared away, he could come back and properly attend to the I beam.

However, at that moment he was in a hurry.

Using the momentum from impacting the I beam, Spider-Man hurtled down toward the falling construction worker. The man was thrashing about, screaming. He'd only been plummeting about two seconds, but the way he was flailing around, he wasn't going to last much longer. The free fall would cause him to snap his spine or neck before he dropped another hundred feet.

Having already released his hold on his web-line,

Spider-Man straightened his body, dropping like a missile, and fired a cocoon of webbing at the worker. His aim was pinpoint and perfect. In a heartbeat, the man was wrapped top to bottom in webbing. Unfortunately, he was still falling.

So was Spider-Man. But that was quickly attended to as he tightened his strands upon the falling worker, even as he fired another web-line. It snagged on the front of a billboard and he swung toward it. As he did so, he snapped the trailing web-line, and the worker rolled up toward him like a yo-yo. With a *thump*, Spider-Man landed on the billboard, with the worker—still screaming, not yet realizing that he was safe—tucked under his arm.

He stared at the billboard.

Mary Jane Watson stared back at him.

He couldn't believe it. Beneath his mask, Peter Parker wanted to guffaw. But this was hardly the time. Instead, ignoring the irony, he crawled over Mary Jane's face and settled the worker onto the rooftop. The man had finally stopped screaming, and had passed out.

It was a huge billboard. Mary Jane, her eyes literally gigantic, was gazing out at an undeserving populace. The logo read, "Emma Rose Parfumerie."

As Spider-Man began to unwind his webbing from the unconscious worker, he felt a wave of almost Shakespearian melancholy falling upon him. Adopting the appropriately grave demeanor, he turned to the senseless worker and intoned, "I have been stung by fate. I am its prisoner. A prisoner of my own conscience. My love for the girl I want, always to be locked within me." He glanced once more at the billboard. "With me, she's always in danger from those who fight against me. Without her, I travel a lonely road. My story will always be about the loss of a girl." He ceased his work and pointed at her. "That girl. Mary Jane Watson. And every day I ask myself, how long can I endure this loneliness?"

He stopped talking and exhaled a heavy sigh. "I know, I know. More lachrymose than you'd expect from your friendly neighborhood Spider-Man. Guess we all have our off days, though. So never you mind. Just keep on sleeping. I have an I beam to get squared away."

And with that, Spider-Man fired a web-line and swung over toward the still-precarious girder.

All of that had transpired a little more than half an hour earlier. Consequently, when Peter pulled up in front of a seedy rat-trap of a restaurant called Joe's Pizza over on MacDougal Street in the Village, his mind was elsewhere. Specifically, it was on another one of those same billboards with M.J.'s face adorning it, staring down at the pizza place in a manner that Peter might almost be inclined to call "protective," if he were given to flights of fancy.

Now dressed in his "civilian" clothes, Peter sat astride a small motorcycle. His aunt May had had a fit when she'd first learned he was tooling around on such a "death trap." He'd sworn to her he'd always drive responsibly, and *never* over twenty miles an hour. He suspected she didn't believe that last part, but they maintained an unspoken agreement to let it stand.

Peter was rolling up to curbside, staring up at the billboard, reflecting on the things he'd said earlier to the unconscious construction worker. *Is this what I'm re-*

duced to? Peter wondered. *So desperate to have someone to talk to that I chat it up with people who can't hear me? But really, what other choice do I have? There are things I have happening in my life, and no one I can talk to about them. That's just the way it is when the world knows you as Spider-Man but everyone you love only knows you by the name of Peter—*

"Parker!"

Peter nearly toppled off his cycle, but instantly righted himself. Standing outside the pizza parlor was the owner, one Rahi Aziz. Dark-haired and of indeterminate Middle Eastern descent, Aziz was flustered and frustrated and didn't hesitate to make Peter aware that he was the cause. With one hand he was pointing angrily at Peter; with the other, he was waving to the banner over the front wall that said, "Our Oven to Your Door. 29 Minutes or It's Free!"

"Parker!" he shouted a second time. "You're late again! Always late!"

"Sorry, Mr. Aziz," said Peter. "There was a . . ."

Man about to die, and he was going to take a sizable portion of a crowd with him, and I saved him, me, with the strength and powers in these two arms. Whose life have you saved today?

Yeah. That would help the situation, big-time.

". . . disturbance," Peter finished, displaying far less conviction than when he'd started.

Aziz stared at him, giving him as much credence as if Peter had just said the dog ate his homework, or that his grandmother had died for the fifth time. "Another disturbance? Always a disturbance." His expression warred briefly between amused incredulity and unfettered annoyance. Unfortunately for Peter, the annoyance won out.

"One more chance," Aziz said, waving a finger in the air. "Twenty-one minutes ago, in comes an order from Harmattan, Burton, and Smith. Woolworth Building. Seventeen extra-large deep-dish pizzas."

Peter's heart was sinking with every new tidbit of information. He'd delivered to HB&S. They were cranky and demanding customers. The Woolworth Building was many blocks downtown. *Seventeen?* How could this possibly get worse?

"In eight minutes," continued Aziz, answering Peter's unspoken question, "I am defaulting on Joe's twenty-nine-minute guarantee. Then not only will I be receiving no money for these pizzas, I will lose the customer forever to Pizza Yurt."

"Why didn't you send Salim?" Peter asked, trying to find a way around the onerous task.

Aziz was already in motion, grabbing pizzas being brought out to him by sweating chefs from the restaurant. "Salim was deported yesterday," said Aziz briskly, shoving the pizzas into Peter's arms. "I have no hope but you. You must make it in time."

He kept stacking pizzas to the point where Peter couldn't see over the top of them. All the while he kept talking. "You are a nice young man, Peter, but you are not dependable. This is the last chance I can give you. You must cross forty-two blocks in seven and one half minutes. Or your ass is to be fired."

Not entirely sure why he was even bothering, Peter shot a glance at the clock on the wall of Joe's Pizza. It read 1:52. The banner with the twenty-nine-minute guarantee on it flapped in the wind.

Peter couldn't help but feel that since it was Joe's bright idea to issue that guarantee, why shouldn't he be the one to undertake the impossible task that had just been set out? He'd met Joe once. Huge, beefy guy, could barely move his arms anymore because of all the flab hanging from them. Picturing that guy trying to dash forty-two blocks in less than eight minutes was an extremely entertaining mental image.

It did not, however, bring Peter all that much amusement. Not when he was weaving his way through bumper-to-bumper Midtown traffic. He wasn't in danger of falling off his cycle: Someone whose balance was so precise that he could walk across a web-strand stretched fifty stories high wasn't about to take a header off a motorbike. But buildings didn't try to hit you. They were comfortingly steady. In this case, Peter had to remain hyperaware of taxis, crazy New York drivers, and even crazier out-of-state drivers, all of whom seemed determined to cut him off whenever possible. Plus he had to watch the angle of his turns; although the pizzas were strapped to a rack behind him, they could still slide within the boxes. He didn't want to deliver seventeen pizzas, all of them with the cheese piled to one side.

All the while he knew that he was hemorrhaging time.

He darted between two cars, zipped around a hesitant truck, and suddenly he was out in the open, ahead of the traffic jam. His heart soared.

Naturally, that was when his bike stalled out.

He couldn't believe it. And yet—depressingly—he somehow *could* believe it, all too readily.

He kicked wildly at the starter, hoping against hope that he'd catch one of those most ephemeral and hard-to-snag things of all: a break. Didn't happen. The bike didn't even cough or sputter. It just sat there under him, affording him as much transportation as a paperweight.

Peter's head snapped around and he looked up at a large digital clock outside of a bank. It read 1:57. He didn't know if the clock was in sync with the one at Joe's, but he couldn't take the chance.

With a quick yank, he snapped the cord holding the pizzas to the back of the motorbike. Then he ran down a nearby alleyway, moving as fast as he could considering the circumstances. Once inside the alleyway, he yanked off his outer clothing. Then, having webbed the pizza boxes together, he fired a web-strand to an overhanging ledge. It snagged on the underside. An instant later, he was drawing himself up the web-line as fast as he could go.

From behind him, he heard shouts. "It's Spider-Man!" called out one person, and another called out, *"He stole the delivery boy's pizzas!"*

He didn't know whether to laugh or cry. At least no one had I.D.'d him. They'd apparently been too dense for that, missing the obvious conclusion in favor of a determination that made him—Spider-Man—look bad. The problem was that these days people always seemed more than willing to believe the worst of him, mostly thanks to J. Jonah Jameson and his incessant attacks in the *Daily Bugle*.

No time to dwell on it, though. Instead, he was too busy enjoying the convenience and freedom that his Spider-Man persona provided him. All the people crammed onto the sidewalks, all the cars lined up waiting for interminable red lights and scores of jaywalkers . . . When he was Spider-Man, it was almost as if they were a different species. Or maybe *he* was.

Well, that would explain the incessant suspicion, now, wouldn't it.

He pulled his mind away from such depressing notions to concentrate on the business at hand. As opposed to his first tentative and frankly catastrophic efforts, web-swinging had become so second nature to him now that he didn't need to pay attention to what he was doing. That was under ordinary circumstances, though, and these were hardly ordinary. Here he had one hand occupied, the other attending to the pizzas. So he had to swing in an arc, release the web-line, and then free fall until he could fire another web-line and anchor it once more. Swinging in such a manner couldn't help but slow him down, at a time when he needed speed more than ever. But he had no choice.

Something he noticed out of the corner of his eye snagged his full attention. A couple of young boys had been practicing dribbling a basketball on the sidewalk while preparing to cross the street to a basketball court on the other side. One boy had tried to snag the ball from the other and it had rebounded into the street. With the feckless belief in their own immortality that characterized the typical eight-year-old, they dashed after the ball, heedless of the Mack Truck that was bearing down upon them.

High above, Peter didn't hesitate. He tossed the pizzas in the direction of a nearby rooftop, not even wanting to think about what the condition of the pies was going to be when he retrieved them. But he had no choice. Having divested himself of his cargo, he aimed a web-lasso at the kids even as he angled down toward them. The web-line fell around them, snagging them, and the startled kids were yanked to the opposite side of the street as the truck shot past them, horn blasting.

The kids lay on the sidewalk, bewildered, and then they looked up to see Spider-Man crouched atop a lamppost. He waggled a scolding finger and said, "No playing in the street."

Numb, the best they could manage was a "Yes, Mr. Spider-Man." But Peter barely heard it, because he was already off, swinging up toward the roof, where he prayed the pizzas were intact.

As it so happened, they almost weren't.

Miraculously, the boxes had survived the drop. Peter chalked that up to the durability of Joe's boxes, so heavily corrugated that a panzer division could roll over them and do only minimal damage. A moocher had made the scene, however. It was a heavyset man, apparently hanging up some laundry, who had dropped what he was doing and made a beeline for the heaven-sent pies. He'd pried open the top box and was holding a slice of plain cheese pizza in his thick hands, about to shove it into his mouth.

Then his eyes widened at the sight of a lithe blue-and-red form descending from on high and heading right for him. He managed a strangled gasp and then Spider-Man snagged the pizza boxes with a web-line and hurtled skyward. The man watched him go, his mouth still wide, thanks to the fact that his jaw had gone slack. Finally, he looked at the slice still in his hand—except a web-line zipped in, snagged the sole remaining slice by the crust, and whipped it from his hand.

Pausing only long enough to toss the slice back into the box and web the container shut, Peter covered the remaining distance to the Woolworth Building at such breathtaking speed that he thought he was going to out-fly his own costume. His destination loomed in front of him, and he snagged the pinnacle of the building with a web-line. He arced around it, the world blurring past him, and then landed on the roof.

He didn't know what time it was. He didn't want to know. He eschewed the idea of changing back to his clothes right there; it was too narrow, and it would be just his luck if some idiot tourist with a telescopic lens wrecked his secret for him.

Instead, he went directly to the maintenance panel on the roof that was used to gain access to the elevator shaft. From that point it was a quick slide down the cables and through the trapdoor in the top of the waiting elevator car. Pushing the button for the twenty-fifth floor, he clung to the top of the car, keeping the pizzas close to him. The instant the doors opened, he moved like a literal blue streak, scuttling across the ceiling while the bewildered receptionist stared into an empty elevator and scratched her head.

Moments later, Peter Parker—back in his regular clothing—emerged from a janitor's closet. He held the pizzas aloft and called out, "Pizza time!"

The receptionist stared up at him like a dead fish as he brushed away strands of web. Then she said nothing, but simply glanced in the direction of the clock over her head. It read 2:03.

He forced his smile wider. It was in inverse proportion to the degree of happiness he felt. "Hey, c'mon," he said wheedlingly. "What's five extra minutes between friends, huh?"

As it turned out, the receptionist was not his friend.

"Joe's twenty-nine-minute guarantee is a promise!" an apoplectic Aziz was shouting in Peter's face. "I know a promise means nothing to you, Parker, but to me it is serious!"

Aziz wasn't even trying to keep his voice down, and passersby were glancing in Peter's direction as the manager stood on the sidewalk outside the pizza parlor and chewed him out.

His words stung Peter. If there was one thing he believed in strongly, it was promises. A promise had shaped the course of his life: The promise he had made at the grave site of his uncle, Ben Parker, never to allow through inaction an innocent to come to harm. The sacrifices he'd had to make because of that promise, the risks he had taken, the danger he faced on a daily basis—in comparison, pizza delivery was an inconsequential pastime.

Unfortunately, it was an inconsequential pastime that paid the bills.

Peter bit back the anger he felt and managed to keep his voice even as he said, "It's serious to me, too, Mr. Aziz . . ."

Aziz wasn't even listening to him. "You're fired!"

"Give me another chance," Peter said, knowing already what the answer was going to be before it was spoken.

"No more chances!" Aziz thundered. "You're fired! *Fired!*"

At least this day can't get any worse, Peter thought bleakly, and promptly he mentally kicked himself.

"You're fired!" J. Jonah Jameson informed Peter Parker at his customary decibel level.

Unlike the passersby at the pizza place, not a single *Bugle* staffer bothered to glance in the direction of Jameson's office. Not only were they busy at their own jobs, rushing to meet their deadlines before the late edition went out, but they'd simply learned to tune out Jameson's tantrums. It was much the same as people living under a busy elevated train track who learned not to notice the train thundering overhead every five to seven minutes.

That didn't stop Peter from feeling as if he were under a microscope. His head slouched, his shoulders practically collapsed in on themselves. He looked so withdrawn that Jameson must've thought for a moment that he'd let his attention wander. "Hello! Parker!" he bellowed, and when he was sure once again that he had Peter's undivided attention, repeated, "You're fired!"

"Why?" demanded a frustrated Peter. The truth was, he suspected he knew what Jameson was going to say. But he was stalling for time, hoping to come up with a handful of pithy rebuttals.

Unfortunately for him, Jameson opted for the truism that a picture was worth a thousand words. And he chose to use Peter's photos to pile on the words.

Peter had been "lucky" enough to be in the right place at the right time and snap pictures of Spider-Man in action. But the situation had palled for him, and he had tried his hand at other photo subjects.

Jameson didn't appear interested. He was motoring through the stack of photos on his desk, ashes falling on them from the cigar he had clenched between his teeth. "Dogs catching frisbees . . . pigeons in the park . . . couple'a old geezers playing chess . . ."

Betty Brant, Jameson's secretary, stuck her head in. Reflexively her nose wrinkled at the cigar smell. The stench wafting through the air rendered Jameson's office very uncomfortable to anyone who still happened to possess olfactory senses, or even lungs. "Boss," she said.

"*What?*" snapped Jameson, peering through the haze of smoke, obviously uncertain as to where the voice had originated. His eyes narrowed as he spotted her. "Not now!"

Jameson's preoccupation with shredding Peter's hopes of a sale was once again stymied, however, as city editor Joe "Robbie" Robertson strode into Jameson's office, with advertising manager Ted Hoffman practically nipping at his heels. Hoffman started to open his mouth, but Robbie cut him off with a brusque, "I said I'd take care of it," and turned to Jameson in an endeavor to keep Hoffman silent. "We've got six minutes to deadline, Jonah. We need page one!"

Hoffman took a fast step around Robbie and said in a reedy voice, "The university president's furious."

Robbie fired him an annoyed look. Jameson just looked bored. "Why?"

"Your editorial says he's not even fit to teach kindergarten," Hoffman explained, glancing nervously in Robbie's direction.

"Print a retraction!" barked Jonah Jameson, and Hoffman looked clearly relieved, until Jameson continued, "He *is* fit to teach kindergarten!"

Hoffman moaned softly and walked out of the office. No doubt he was envisioning the university's regular full-page advertising going the way of the dodo. Jameson, meantime, appeared to have forgotten Hoffman. Instead, he turned his energies and diatribes back upon the hapless Peter. "Parker, I don't pay you to be a sensitive artist!"

Betty looked helplessly at Peter, obviously wanting to get him off the hook somehow. "Boss—" she said more forcefully.

She would have required the force of a wrecking ball to get Jameson off track. "*Still* not now," he said. Betty shrugged helplessly and walked out. Peter desperately wished she'd stayed. He could use whatever support he could get, even if it was the mute, moral kind. Jameson, meantime, hadn't paused. "I pay you because for some reason that psycho Spider-Man will pose for you!"

"Spider-Man won't let me take any more pictures of

him," replied Peter. "You've turned the whole city against him!"

Jameson leaned back in his chair, his hands behind his head. His cigar migrated from one side of his mouth to the other, apparently on its own. "A fact I'm very proud of! Now get your pretty little 'portfolio' out of my sight," he swept the pictures aside with one hand, "before I go into a diabetic coma!"

The intercom buzzed. Reflexively Jameson hit the button and Betty's voice filtered through. "Boss, your wife's on line one. She says she can't find her checkbook."

"Thanks for the good news," replied Jameson, and shut off the intercom.

Peter used the brief pause in Jameson's diatribe to jump in and try to appeal to Jameson's very likely non-existent compassion. "Mr. Jameson, please! Aren't there any of these shots you can use? I really need the money."

Jameson responded pretty much the way Peter had expected: "Awwww . . ."

Obviously dissatisfied with the outcome of her intercom end-run, Betty strode back into the office. Before she could get a word out, Jameson swiveled in his chair and said, "Miss Brant! Get me a violin."

Robertson, who hadn't budged the entire time, simply stood there with his arms folded, maintaining patience honed through long years of practice. "Five minutes to deadline, Jonah."

Jameson turned to Robbie, and then noticed that Peter hadn't left. "What? What? Why are you still here? Oh, devil take it! Anything so I don't have to look at that clubbed baby seal expression." He grabbed one of the pictures at random and flung it at Robertson, who caught it. "Stick this in an empty space in the paper! Toward the back! On the obits!"

"Two old men playing chess in the obituaries?" asked Robertson.

"With any luck, one or both of them are dead by now," Jameson said, scribbling out a voucher. "Besides, it's symbolic, like in that Ingrid Bergman film."

"Ingmar," said Peter.

Jonah was holding up the voucher he'd just filled out and he glared at Peter. "You want this?"

"Ingrid Bergman is my favorite director," Peter said immediately, and snatched the voucher from Jameson's outstretched hand. He was out of the office before Jonah could rethink his actions.

Quickly, he went to Betty's desk and handed her the voucher. "Hi," he said, waiting for her to open the cash drawer.

Betty barely had to glance at it. "Sorry, Pete. This doesn't even cover the advance you got two weeks ago."

His heart sank. He'd forgotten about it. "Oh, right," he sighed. Then he glanced at the clock on her desk and his stomach sank somewhere into his shoes. Jameson had kept him waiting so long that he'd totally lost track of time, and now he was running terribly late. "Thanks anyway. Gotta go."

And he was out the door, down in the street, and literally motoring toward the university campus. Briefly he'd considered web-swinging over there, but lately it seemed every time he crawled into the costume, disaster struck. Better to just stick to normal means of getting around for the time being.

Upon arriving at the campus, he parked his motorbike and sprinted across the grounds. From the way people were gaping at him, he realized that he was moving far faster than any normal person should be going. But he didn't have time to slow down. If anything, he sped up.

He hurtled around the corner of the science building, backpack flapping against his spine, and at the last split second his spider-sense warned him that there was an obstruction in his path. His instinct was to somersault over it, but he fought it, and instead managed to break to a halt at the last instant. It wasn't enough to avoid impact, however, because the "obstruction" had kept moving. Consequently, they collided, sending papers and books flying everywhere. Peter pulled himself together quickly, looked up, and saw that he had slammed into the very last person with whom he'd want to have such a violent encounter.

"Oh, hey . . . wow! Doctor Connors! Sorry!" Peter immediately bent down to help the one-armed professor gather his fallen study materials.

"Where were you headed, Parker?" demanded a clearly annoyed Connors.

"To your class."

"My class is over. See? See me," and he pointed at his own head, "standing here?"

Peter felt his face burning with embarrassment. "I'm sorry, Doctor Connors. I lost track of time."

Connors shook his head, and when he spoke it wasn't scoldingly, but more with an air of disappointment. "I don't think it's time you've lost track of. I think maybe you've lost track of your life." He held up individual fingers, counting off the instances as he went. "Your grades have been steadily declining. You're late for class. You always appear exhausted. That paper on fusion is still overdue . . ."

At that moment, Peter saw a chance to solve two problems at one time. He'd given no thought whatsoever to the paper on fusion, but he knew who was doing the most breakthrough work on that most elusive of energy sources: Otto Octavius. Octavius, whom a now-dead merc had accused of being involved in the production of some sort of dangerous armament. Here was an opportunity to legitimately take time to explore whether Octavius was really up to something untoward . . . and get graded for it! It was like one of those schools where you get credit for life experience.

"I'm planning to write it on Doctor Otto Octavius . . ." he told Connors.

" 'Planning' is not a major at this university. Finish that paper or I'm failing you." He started to turn away, then paused and glanced at Peter with a reflective look. "The great Octavius. He's a friend of mine. Better do your research. Get your facts straight, Parker!"

That final admonition left Peter wondering just what the hell he was doing to himself, and why he was doing it. It wasn't that he'd lost track of his life. It's that he was trying to live a second life, and it wasn't exactly meshing with the first.

But before he could dwell on it further, he noticed that the clock tower said it was one minute to six.

"Shoot!" he yelled.

And he was gone. If it had seemed to the casual observer that he was running with amazing speed before, that was nothing compared to the burst he displayed now. Anyone seeing him wouldn't have "seen" him, so much as notice something out of the corner of their eye and then wonder where it had gone.

He vaulted onto his motorcycle and ripped out into

Manhattan traffic, barreling between cars, using every ounce of his spiderlike agility.

He made it to Forest Hills in twenty-one minutes flat, which was twenty minutes later than he'd promised Aunt May he'd be there. He glided the cycle to a stop, jumped off, and moved quickly to the front door. He threw it open and stepped into the living room. And that's when, screaming, they leaped out at him.

IV

"*Surprise!*"

Peter did everything he could to maintain a startled expression, even though he'd long-ago figured out that his aunt, May Parker, was planning this party for him. She was a dear woman and skilled at many things, but duplicity wasn't her strong suit. She'd telegraphed her plans in a hundred different ways. The only thing Peter was left wondering was who the heck she'd invite, considering he hardly saw anyone these days unless he was either rescuing them or webbing them up to be left for the police.

So there was a genuine element of surprise for him as his former roommate, Harry Osborn, and . . . Mary Jane . . . leaped out at . . .

Mary Jane.

It was all he could do not to melt at the sight of her, with that gorgeous grin and the flaming red hair that danced around her face. From near his shoulder, Aunt May was urging him, "Well, say something!"

"Uh," was all he could manage, and then he forced his attention away from Mary Jane, itself a Herculean feat. He smiled broadly. "What's the occasion?"

"Really, Peter," said May with an affectionate scold. "It's your birthday, whether you wish to remember it or not."

"Peter lives in another reality, don't you, Pete?" Mary Jane asked coyly.

Yeah, I think living in a reality that includes scrambling up the sides of buildings and swinging from threads could qualify as "another" in the reality biz.

Oh, yeah. That was just the thing to say.

Mary Jane cocked her head slightly as if sensing the thoughts tumbling through his mind. "Long time no see."

He managed a nod. "Hi, M.J."

"Peter's also a photographer," Harry said with an almost fraternal pride as he draped an arm around Peter's shoulder. But when he spoke again, his voice was infected with an obviously false cheerfulness. "Spider-Man's photographer. How is the bug these days?"

"Haven't seen him lately," Peter said, feeling very uncomfortable. And why shouldn't he have felt uncomfortable? After all, Harry was convinced Spider-Man had killed his father, and Peter had no way of convincing him otherwise. None that wouldn't compromise his secret, at any rate.

Aunt May made a dismissive wave of her hand. "The less you see of a man like that, the better. Peter, let's have some punch." She had moved to a punch bowl and was ladling out her famous fruit drink. "Let's celebrate all the good. M.J. is in a Broadway play."

"Off-Broadway," Mary Jane corrected her. "It's just a little part. Harry sent me roses," she added, clearly grateful. Harry bobbed his head in acknowledgment. M.J. had been his girlfriend in the past, so it was nice to know they were still getting on, even though the relationship had ended.

"How lovely, Harry," May said approvingly, and handed him a glass of punch. "And you're at OsCorp, doing things that would make your father proud, rest his soul."

"I'm in charge of Special Projects," Harry said. "We're funding one of your idols, Pete. Otto Octavius."

"I'm writing a paper on him," said Peter, taking a glass of punch.

"Want to meet him?"

Peter could scarcely believe it. This was just simplifying matters so much that it could completely wreck his hard-won, hard-luck image. "You'd introduce me?"

"You bet," said Harry as if it was the simplest thing in the world. "Octavius is going to put OsCorp on the map in a way my father never even dreamed of."

"What a lovely birthday present!" May said. "Okay, somebody want to help me in the kitchen? M.J.?"

Mary Jane looked slightly startled, as if her thoughts had been elsewhere. On me? Peter wondered. As if. He had told her in no uncertain terms that all they would ever be, could ever be, was friends. And M.J. was far too much the free spirit to hear no for an answer more than one time. Peter was sure she was back on the dating scene, with no looking back.

As M.J. followed May into the kitchen, Peter's gaze followed her. There was so much he wanted to say . . . and knew he couldn't. Harry leaned against the banister, serenely confident. "She's waiting for you, pal."

Peter was walking over to the desk to see if there was any mail for him. "What do you mean?"

"The way she looks at you, or doesn't look at you, however you want to look at it."

At that, Peter chuckled. Harry certainly had all the angles covered. If she looked at him longingly, or didn't give him a second glance, it meant the same thing. "Don't have time to think about girls right now."

As he said that, he paused. An envelope not addressed to him had caught his notice. It was from the mortgage company. Aunt May's mortgage company. The words "Pre-Eviction Notice" were visible through the plastic-covered window in the envelope.

"Why? Are you dead?" Harry asked skeptically.

Peter wasn't even looking at him, his attention fully engaged by the less-than-sterling news in the envelope. "Been kinda busy."

"Taking pictures of your friend?"

That brought Peter's thoughts back to Harry. The ongoing topic of Spider-Man had already gone a good ways toward poisoning their relationship, and Peter had hoped that Harry would—at the very least—be able to rein himself in for this gathering. Obviously, that wasn't going to be the case. With more anger in his voice than he'd have liked, Peter said, "Could we get off that subject!" Taking a breath, trying to get back to being calm, he continued, "I want us to be friends, Harry. I want us to trust each other."

"Be honest," said Harry levelly. "If you knew who he was, would you tell me?"

Peter's tone was hollow. "You'd only want him dead."

"Of course I would!" Harry told him, having no idea how his words were wounding. "The same way you'd want the man who killed your uncle Ben dead. My father loved you like a son, Pete."

Harry paused and then seemed to remember where he was and the fact that they were supposed to be celebrating Peter's birthday. He draped an arm around Peter's shoulder. "Hey, I don't mean to rag on you. You're my buddy. You know that."

"I understand."

"Call me tomorrow. I'll arrange for you to visit Otto."

Peter looked at him askance. "You call him 'Otto'?"

Suddenly the lights went out and for a moment Peter tensed. Then Aunt May and Mary Jane came shuffling in from the kitchen, walking slowly as if in a processional, May bearing a birthday cake with "Happy Birthday, Peter" etched on it. May, Mary Jane, and Harry launched into a deliriously off-key rendition of "Happy Birthday to You."

My friend who hates me but doesn't know it, the girl who loves me but I can't afford to truly let her into my life, and my aunt who's being evicted. Oh, yeah. Life is good.

Happy birthday to me, he thought glumly.

Mary Jane had excused herself early from the party, leaving not long after the presents had been opened. Peter hadn't known how to feel about her departure. He was relieved because in some ways talking to M.J. was like a knife in his heart. But he was depressed because it was the sweetest pain he knew.

So those same mixed feelings resurfaced later, after Harry had left, when Peter was hauling a bag of trash from the party into the back and discovered Mary Jane standing on the other side of the fence, in the backyard that belonged to the Watsons, M.J.'s parents. On the one hand, he felt as if she'd been waiting there for him; on the other, he was concerned he'd wandered into her private musings. Well, if she wanted privacy, she always could have been inside her folks' house.

She smiled awkwardly at him. It made him feel like he

was back in high school, and that any conversation they had would be interrupted by Flash Thompson pulling up in his car and honking, drawing her away from him.

"Hey," she said.

"Hey." He paused, and then told her, "Saw your billboard on Bleecker." He'd also seen it uptown when he'd landed on it, but he saw no reason to add that nugget of information.

"Isn't it funny? I'm really kind of embarrassed."

"Don't be. It's nice." He smiled. "I get to see you every day now."

Well, doesn't that sound pathetic. The only reason you don't see her every day in person is your own stupid choice.

Mary Jane was compassionate enough not to point that out. Instead, she shrugged and said, "Photographer liked my face. I was only supposed to be in a catalog. Then I got this part in the play. Everything at once."

"Dreams come true."

"How about yours?"

"I'm fine," he said in that guarded way that had become second nature to him.

"I wish you'd come see the play. You're the one who always encouraged me," she said.

"I plan to."

She paused, and Peter braced himself. He knew it was coming: She was going to tell him how hurt she was that he'd shut her out of his life, about the frustration, the resentment. How even being with him tonight was torture and a huge mistake . . .

"I liked seeing you tonight, Peter."

He was so filled with relief, he could barely stand. "Oh, boy . . . yeah . . ."

"Oh, boy, yeah, what?"

A hundred responses filled his mouth, but all he came out with was, "Nothing."

Her blue eyes were locked on him. "I know the feeling. Sometimes you want to say something but it won't come out." It was as if they were both onstage and she was trying to guide him toward forgotten lines. "Do you want to say something?"

"Do you?" he replied.

"You first."

It was insane. He'd thought he could keep them apart through sheer force of will, but it was like two magnets being drawn inexorably toward each other. "I . . . uh . . ."

Then Uncle Ben came to him.

Not literally. But the mental image that haunted him day and night flashed through his thoughts, just for a heartbeat. It was enough, though. That in turn opened the door to his view of her falling away from him, tossed off the top of the 59th Street Bridge by the Green Goblin. Once again it strengthened his resolve. Anyone close to him could be at risk, and maybe—just maybe— he didn't really deserve to be happy in the first place because of his great sin of omission. Because Uncle Ben was dead, and he was responsible.

"I was wondering . . . if . . . uh . . . you're still in the Village?" he asked.

She stared at him, as if she'd been able to see the pictures running behind his eyes, and was trying to make sense of them. "You're such a mystery," she said. "Sometimes I just want to punch you and wake you up."

He offered a shoulder to her. "Go ahead."

She took a step closer and gently threw a tap to his

jaw that couldn't have knocked over an origami swan. Then she said, "I gotta go. My mom's sick. Y'know, my dad left."

"Yeah, I heard. I'm sorry."

"Don't be," she said, her voice turning harsher. "He was abusive and nasty and wasn't happy unless he was tearing me or my mom down."

"I know. That's what I'm sorry about."

She shook her head and, sounding frustrated, said, "Oh, Peter Parker . . ."

"What?"

M.J. was right up against the fence, and she reached over and brushed his hair back. He thought she was going to kiss him and realized that, right then—despite all the reasons it would be a bad idea—it was what he wanted more than anything. Instead, all she did was say, "Happy birthday."

She moved away from him then and started for the house. But she paused on the steps and, without turning, said, "I'm seeing somebody now."

Thinking that she was still dwelling on unresolved issues with her father, Peter said, "Oh? Therapy?"

That prompted her to turn and look at him suspiciously, trying to determine if he was making fun of her. When she saw the open curiosity on his face, she apparently realized that he was honest in his confusion. "No. A person. A man."

Peter's heart started racing. *Well, that's what you expected. She wasn't going to wait around for the guy who made a point of keeping her at arm's length.* "You mean like a boyfriend?"

"Well . . . I like him," said Mary Jane.

"Oh."

"What?"

Keeping his outward cool, Peter said, "No. No . . . it's good. Companionship."

"Maybe more than that."

"More?"

Her lips twitched. "I dunno."

Suddenly it was desperately vital to Peter that he let Mary Jane know how important she was to him. "Hey, I'm gonna come see your play tomorrow night."

"You're coming?" She was visibly surprised.

"I'll be there."

"Do you want me to put a house seat aside for you? Third row center? Prime spot?"

"Absolutely."

She seemed gratified. "Don't disappoint me."

"I won't," he assured her.

What the hell are you doing? Peter demanded silently of himself as Mary Jane walked back into her former home, while Peter walked into his. *She's getting involved with someone else. It's what you wanted. She's moving on with her life, and now you're trying to insert yourself back into it? You push her aside, and suddenly you can't let her go? What's your problem?*

And out loud, so far under his breath that no one could hear him—so softly he himself could barely hear—he said, "I love you, Mary Jane."

He walked into the dining room and saw that Aunt May had fallen asleep in a chair, a dish towel clutched in her hand like a security blanket. He watched her for a moment, then moved to the table and sat in a chair across from her. She seemed so peaceful, but he knew he couldn't just leave her there; her back would never forgive her in the morning. He rested a hand atop hers and she awoke with a start.

"What . . . Ben?" she gasped out, and in her confusion didn't see Peter flinch when she said it. She tried to focus on her surroundings. "Oh, my, I'm . . . wait . . ."

"Aunt May?"

"Peter?" Then she laughed at her own bewilderment. "For a second there, I thought it was years ago. Everybody's gone, aren't they?"

He nodded. "Party's over. They both went home."

She stood up with great certainty, as if she had many things she had to attend to. "Well, now, it was a very nice little birthday get-together," she said. Her voice sounded slightly singsong, as if it wasn't quite connected to the world around them. "Did they have a good time?"

"I'm sure they did. You okay?"

"Of course I am. But you go on home," she said, patting him on the upper arm. "And be careful. I don't like that scooter thing you drive around."

"I'm worried about you," he said, making no effort to leave. "You're alone, maybe too alone sometimes, and . . ." He hesitated, and then admitted, "I saw the letter from the bank."

She shrugged. "So I'm a little behind. Everyone is."

As if that settled the matter, she moved toward her purse on the counter, situated between the birthday candles and a quart container of milk that was sitting open and mostly empty. As she put the remains of the milk away, her hand darted into the purse at the same time, sneaking something from it. She probably thought Peter didn't see the movement. She was mistaken. Then again, she couldn't know the difficulties of trying to elude the notice of someone with spider-sense.

"Anyway, I don't wish to talk about it. I'm tired now and you'd better start for home."

Then she turned to him and stuffed into his palm what she'd taken out of the purse: a crumpled twenty-dollar bill. "Here," she said, "you need this more than I do. Happy birthday."

"Aunt May, I can't—"

And with a ferocity that startled Peter, she shot back, "*Yes, you can!* You take this money for me! For God's sake, it's not much, it's a measly twenty dollars, now take it! Don't you dare leave it here!"

Her anger was akin to an intense downpour. It wasn't capable of sustaining itself for long. She seemed to shrink at the end of the outburst and said, in a much lower voice, "Sorry. Lost my temper."

She was clearly fighting tears. Peter wanted to reach out to her, embrace her, but he sensed she would consider it . . . patronizing, somehow. Thin tears worked their way down the crags of her face as she said, "It's just that I miss your uncle so much sometimes. Can you believe it will be two years next month that he was taken?" She didn't wipe away the tears then. She just appeared to shut them off through willpower alone. "I think to myself at times, were I to face the one responsible for what happened, I . . . I don't know what I would do. I hate to think what I might be capable of."

Peter tried to keep the guilt from his eyes. Aunt May had found no closure at all for the death of Uncle Ben. The frustrating thing was, he knew perfectly well that the man responsible was dead. He had seen him fall to his death from the window of that warehouse down by the docks. But there had been no eyewitness to the car-jacking that had cost Ben Parker his life. And when the police had arrived, they'd seen two distinct individuals moving in the windows of the warehouse that night. They didn't know for sure that the man who ended up a crumpled heap on the dock was the perpetrator of the crime. They suspected it, but couldn't prove it beyond a shadow of a doubt. There was always the possibility that the man whom they had spotted, but who had escaped, might have been the actual robber and killer.

And Peter was hardly in a position to say, "No, that was me, dressed in my wrestling costume. I avenged my uncle's death. You can close the books on this one."

So the books remained open. And May Parker continued to suffer.

He was about to say something to her, something to alleviate her pain. What it was, he didn't know. It might have been the last thing she needed to hear. As it turned out, he didn't get to say anything, because Aunt May intercepted it. "Oh!" she exclaimed as she wiped her eyes with a birthday napkin. "You'd better take some cake home."

There was always room for cake.

It was late at night and Peter was feeling completely drained. He felt as if he'd started the day a hundred hours ago. He locked up his bike and trudged up the stairs to the apartment he rented above a television repair shop.

He walked past the slightly open door of his landlord, Mr. Ditkovitch. Had he chosen to do so, he could have moved with such stealth that Ditkovitch would never have detected his passing. But considering the array of ups and downs—mostly downs—he'd experienced on this, the crappiest birthday ever, he simply strode in knowing that he would hear exactly what he did:

"Rent!" Ditkovitch's voiced thundered down the corridor. Peter stopped in his tracks as Ditkovitch kicked the door open wider. His TV was playing some reality programming involving sex-crazed couples. Ditkovitch's young daughter, Ursula, was visible behind him.

Whereas her father was heavyset and jowly, Ursula—who was in her mid-twenties—must have taken after her mother. She was tall, lanky, and rail thin, and when she looked at Peter, it was with an open interest that always served to make him feel uncomfortable.

"Hi," muttered Peter.

"Hi? What's hi? Can I spend it?"

"I have a paycheck due this week," Peter lied.

Ditkovitch didn't appear impressed. "You're a month late again. *Again*."

"I promise to—"

His landlord blew air dismissively between his cracked lips. "If promises were crackers, I'd be fat!"

You are fat, you slob. "I'm really sorry, Mr. Ditkovitch." Reasoning that it was just another case of easy come, easy go, Peter pulled out the twenty dollars from Aunt May and proferred it. "I can give you twenty until next week."

With the speed of a striking lizard, Ditkovitch snatched it from his hand. "Sorry doesn't pay the rent. And don't try to sneak past me. I have ears like a cat, eyes like a rodent."

"Thanks, Mr. Ditkovitch," said Peter, even though he didn't know what he was thanking the man for, and closed the door of his apartment behind him.

He flopped onto the bed in the one-room dump, looking around at the still-packed boxes, the radiator, the secondhand desk. The starkness of the place was spruced up only by the array of photographs on his dresser. He missed the far nicer digs he'd shared with Harry, and would have continued to share had Harry not moved back into the town house now that his father was gone. It was a huge place, and Harry had invited Peter to move in, as well. But Peter had declined.

Harry's obsession with Spider-Man was already making things uncomfortable. Being subjected to it every day was more than he could stand.

The pictures on the dresser represented some of his happiest memories. There were Aunt May and Uncle Ben smiling out at him. And there was a shot of Mary Jane that he'd taken at the spider display, mere minutes before his life would be permanently altered by the bite of a stray mutated spider. His last moments of innocence, represented by M.J.'s glowing smile, frozen forever.

He pulled the pillow over his head and fell into a restless slumber.

V

Otto Octavius had been described in various magazine articles as energetic, vibrant, healthy and—as *People* magazine had once said—possessed of a touch of charming madness.

He was touched with madness this day, but there wasn't much charm in it. Instead, the madness related to the incessant interruptions he was receiving as he moved briskly about his lab, trying to attend to Extremely Important Matters that kept getting sidetracked by phone calls and visitors. His wife had told him it was smart to try to "play nicely," but Octavius was not one to suffer fools gladly. And lately it seemed as if nothing but fools were being marched in to throw him off his stride. If he hadn't known better, he'd have been certain there was a concerted effort being mustered by some person or persons unknown, expressly to keep him from his work.

His favorite Latin motto, "*Nosce te Ipsum*," meaning "Know thyself," was carved above the main entranceway to the building that housed his lab. It had been his one personal indulgence. The rest of the time his priorities were 110 percent on the work. But now, as he searched through stacks of papers, trying to locate some notes, he was busy dealing with the latest interruption—in the form of a phone call from some damned senator or other.

The man spoke in a deep southern drawl that Octavius was convinced was an artificial affectation. "You say this brand-new idea of yours will reduce our gas and electric bills?" The senator's voice came over a speakerphone, asking the same question for the third time. It was just phrased ever-so-slightly differently.

Otto Octavius gave the same response he had just given three times previously. "I said it would *eliminate* them, Senator. Come tomorrow and you can see for youself. Bring your friends." He tapped the disconnect button on the speakerphone and was pleased to hear the senator's voice cut off in mid-follow-up question.

"Mr. Osborn's here."

Octavius hadn't even noticed that his assistant, Raymond, who had just made the pronouncement, was in the room. Either Osborn was tiptoeing around the place or Octavius simply wasn't paying attention. He swiveled in Raymond's direction, knowing Osborn was going to be standing there next to him. He found young Harry Osborn marginally more tolerable than his late father, whose loss Octavius wasn't mourning in the least.

Octavius was unprepared, however, to see a third young man, standing next to Osborn. A skinny, brown-haired kid who probably didn't know a particle beam from particle board. He was looking around the laboratory with an expression of wonderment. As if he could possibly understand the complexities or even the basic functions of the things he was gaping at. Even better, to fill out the entire tourist "vibe," the kid had a camera slung over his shoulder, and he seemed rather curious about the thin blue curtain that was poised at the far end of the lab.

Harry walked forward, the newcomer staying respectfully back a few paces. Extending his hand, Osborn said, "Nobel Prize, Otto, Nobel Prize." He shook Otto's hand and continued, "We'll all be rich."

"It's not about prizes, Harry," Otto reminded him. "It's not about money."

"But you need money, Otto. You need OsCorp."

"And OsCorp needs me," Otto said with confidence. Bowing to the inevitable, he prompted, "And who do we have here?"

"This is my good friend I called you about. The one who got me through high school science."

"Peter Parker, sir," said the brown-haired youth, reaching forward to shake Otto's hand, as well.

"Parker." Now that Osborn had mentioned it, Otto did indeed remember the phone conversation he'd had with him about this meeting. He'd considered it of such little consequence that it hadn't stayed in his memory. But the name "Parker" was sounding familiar for some reason . . .

"Thank you for taking the time to see me, sir. I'm doing a paper on you for—"

"Yes, I know why you're here. I don't have much time." He cast a glance at Osborn. "But OsCorp pays the bills, so . . ."

"That's why I have to take off," said Osborn, as if picking up a cue. "Meeting with the board. My job's done here; brought you two geniuses together." He gave a laugh that sounded overly hearty. "Good luck tomorrow, Otto." He pointed at him as he walked out. "Nobel Prize! See you in Sweden!"

When Osborn was gone, Octavius said tactfully, "Interesting fellow, your friend."

"I won't take much of your time, sir."

That was when the name clicked into place for him. "Parker. I remember you," said Octavius. "Connors told me about you. Says you're brilliant, but he says you're lazy."

Parker visibly winced at that. "I'm trying to do better."

Without even looking at Parker, Octavius busied himself around the lab. "Let me tell you something. Being brilliant isn't enough. You have to work hard. Intelligence isn't a privilege, it's a gift. It's not yours to waste. We've been given the power of intelligence for a purpose: to use it for the good of mankind."

"Otto, your lunch is ready."

The unexpected announcement came from a smiling, lovely young woman. Otto's glance fell upon her and instantly the world seemed brighter. She had just entered the lab and she was carrying a vase of daffodils.

Minding his manners, he turned to Parker and said, by way of introduction, "This is my wife, Rosie."

"Hello." She smiled at Peter.

"Hello." Peter Parker bobbed his head with an almost charming shyness, as if slightly awed by Rosie's beauty. That alone caused Parker to move up a couple of notches in Otto's estimation.

"This is Peter Parker. He's Connors' student. Falls asleep in class."

Without missing a beat, Rosie replied, "I always fell asleep in class." Peter decided he was in love.

"I get a little tired," he said. "I have a . . . night job. Nice to meet you."

Octavius was unimpressed. "You better make a choice about what's important to you."

"Yes, sir. I've thought about that," agreed Parker. "Doctor Octavius, for my paper . . . You spoke at school last semester about a design to initiate and sustain fusion . . ."

"That I did," said Otto. He pointed proudly to a large machine at the far end of the room.

"So that's it," Parker said with obvious rising interest. "I understand you use harmonics of atomic frequencies—"

"Sympathetic frequencies," Otto corrected him.

"Like an opera singer shattering a wineglass with her voice."

Octavius was impressed in spite of himself. "Precisely. Harmonic reinforcement—"

"An exponential increase in energy output."

"*Huge* amounts of energy," Otto assured him, "like a perpetual sun providing renewable power to the world."

"Mind-boggling," said Parker.

"That's my business!"

"But . . . how will you contain it? No one's been able to."

That brought Octavius up short. He looked at Parker as if seeing him for the first time, and realized that he'd just been conversing with this student as if he were a colleague. Connors had been right in his estimation of the boy's potential.

"Otto, come and eat," urged Rosie.

"But I've found a willing victim! I'm just getting started."

"Finish your lecture over lunch," Rosie said firmly. "Peter, would you like to join us?"

"That would be wonderful," said Parker.

He followed Rosie out of the room, but Octavius noticed him glancing in the direction of the curtain at the other end of the room. The lad displayed a healthy degree of scientific curiosity.

Oh, yes. Definitely a willing victim.

The home of Otto and Rosie Octavius had seen a goodly number of people come and go through the years. Often they possessed great minds. Many of them were immortalized in photos, including an assortment of scientific luminaries, each of whom Peter recognized instantly. Octavius was extremely impressed by that, because he had a relatively low opinion of today's young people and Peter Parker was flying in the face of that preconception. It was almost enough to give him hope for American youth.

Lunch had been extraordinarily relaxed, with Peter displaying a fine, sharp mind. Not only was he able to keep up with Octavius with facility, there were one or two points where he actually leaped ahead of where Octavius was going. Octavius didn't let on that he was pleased by the boy's obvious gifts, but he knew that Rosie noticed, and he tried to ignore her little smirk. Many had been the time when he'd spoken scathingly of young people, and Rosie had always been in there defending the next generation of scientific minds. Here was proof on two legs that she may well have been right. Otto had a feeling he was going to be hearing about this one for some time, but he had to admit that occasionally it was worth being wrong about something.

Octavius was bringing a tray of coffee over to the table where Peter was sitting and said, "So what do you think?"

"It's all so amazing. If it works, it'll change the way we live."

"It is amazing," Octavius said firmly, "and it will work."

"Are you sure you can stabilize the fusion reaction?"

Otto felt a flash of disappointment as he set the coffee down. "Peter," he said scoldingly, "what have we been talking about for the last hour and a half? It's my life's work! I certainly know the consequences of the slightest miscalculation."

"I'm sorry, I didn't mean to be questioning you, sir."

Rosie was coming toward the table, having removed the lunch plates to the kitchen, and Octavius said to her, "Rosie, tell our new friend I'm not going to blow up the city." He turned back to Peter. "You can sleep soundly tonight."

"Otto's done his homework," Rosie assured Peter, pouring coffee. "And *you* need to sleep soundly tonight, Otto."

He patted her on the hand. It wasn't the first time she'd broached his sleeping habits. "Yes, yes, sleep, sleep, I know. Did Edison sleep before he turned on the light? Did Marconi sleep before he turned on the radio?"

"Did Bernoulli sleep before he found the curves of quickest descent?"

Dead silence. Then an uncharacteristically wide grin split Octavius' face. "Rosie, I love this boy!"

"And here I was just going to point out that Edison and Marconi probably wished they *had* gotten some sleep," said Rosie, "since afterward they were kept awake by all the neighbors with the lights on and the radio blaring. But I don't know *what* to say about

Bernoulli." She regarded Peter with interest. "So, Peter. Tell us about yourself. Do you have a girlfriend?"

Peter suddenly looked very interested in the coffee cup. "Uh, well . . . uh . . . I don't really know."

"Shouldn't you know?" asked Octavius. "Who would know?"

"Leave him alone," Rosie told him. "Maybe it's a secret love."

"Love should never be kept a secret," Otto said. "You keep something as complicated as love stored up, you can get sick. We had no secrets, did we, Rosie?" He smiled at her. "It was perfect."

"Hardly perfect, Otto," She leaned in toward Parker, speaking in a confidential manner even though Octavius was right there. "I met him on the college steps and I knew it wouldn't be easy. He was studying science, I was studying English literature."

"I didn't say it was *easy,* I said *perfect,*" he reminded her.

"He tried to explain the Theory of Relativity and I tried to explain T. S. Eliot."

Otto brought back an arm, narrowly missing knocking over the coffeepot, declaiming, " 'Time present and time past are both perhaps present in time future.' " He shook his head. "I still don't know what that fellow was getting at. Eliot's harder than advanced science." Now he leaned in toward Peter, as well, and it was his turn to sound conspiratorial. "Want to get a woman to love you? Feed her poetry. But I recommend Elizabeth Barrett Browning." He turned to Rosie and, as if wooing her, said, " 'How do I love thee? Let me count the ways . . . ' "

"Poetry." Peter sounded unconvinced.

"I tell you what," Octavius said, "get out your camera. Take our picture."

"Really? That would be great!"

"Where do you want us?" Octavius asked as Peter removed the camera.

"Right where you are," Peter said, looking through the viewfinder. "It's perfect."

"Good. We're perfect," said Rosie, putting an arm around her husband.

Peter took the picture and Otto blinked several times against the glare of the flash. Then he said with conviction to Peter, "Poetry. Never fails."

And as he looked at the smiling Peter Parker, for the first time in a very, very long time, he regretted that he and Rosie had never been able to have children. To be able to shape young minds, and to have those minds dependent upon him for guidance.

How unfortunate that poetry wasn't the answer for everything.

As John Greenleaf Whittier put it, *"For of all sad words of tongue or pen, the saddest are these: 'It might have been!'"*

Well, maybe it was the answer for everything, at that.

VI

Peter felt as if his attempts to spruce himself up before heading to the theater were pathetic. He had little to choose from in the way of ties—one, specifically. His one "sporty" jacket had been purchased secondhand and was getting a little threadbare. But as he studied himself in the mirror, he tried to convince himself that M.J. wouldn't care about those things. All that was important to her was that he was taking an interest and showing up.

That, of course, was the inherent contradiction. It was specifically because he had so much interest in her that he had been distancing himself. Yet now he was allowing himself to be pulled back to her. The words "strange attractors" went through his mind, even as he made a vague attempt to straighten his tie and grabbed his theater ticket from where he had it wedged into the mirror. He glanced at the clock on his bureau, which confirmed what he already suspected: He was running late.

He was out the door and down the hallway, dashing past Ditkovitch's door, where he heard sounds of a poker game in progress. He didn't slow as the thundering shout of "Rent!" floated behind him. He caught a glance of Ursula hanging in the doorway, looking out after him, and then he was in the street and astride his motorbike.

On his way to the theater, he kept running through his mind the time he'd spent with Otto and Rosie. The more he thought about it, the more convinced he became that the idiot "Jack All" hadn't known what he was talking about. Peter was certain by the end of their time together that Otto Octavius was a humanitarian. Someone who cared about bettering mankind, not trying to blow it up or shoot it. He was no comic-opera villain. Otto Octavius was a dedicated, highly moral scientist, not Snidely Whiplash, and that's all there was to it.

Across town at the Lyric Theater, the cast of *The Importance of Being Earnest* was preparing for the evening's performance.

The small Off-Broadway production had been intended for a limited run, but the successful buzz it had been getting had given them an open-ended engagement. Mary Jane couldn't have been happier . . . or more nervous. She was much of the reason for the buzz, and lately every night as curtain time approached she felt as if the weight of the world hung upon her. Fortunately, she'd been able to channel that nervous energy into her performance, so it had worked out. But it never seemed to get easier . . . which might be a good thing, she supposed.

She shared her tiny dressing room with another actress, Louise Wood. When actresses were that crammed in, they either tended to get very hostile or very chummy. She and Louise had developed the latter relationship.

As M.J. leaned in to touch up her lip gloss, Louise observed, "You seem jittery tonight."

"You never know who's coming," replied Mary Jane.

From the other side of the door, the stage manager shouted, "Five minutes! Five minutes!"

"Is this a special someone?"

"I . . . guess you could say that."

Louise's eyes lit up. "Would he be interested in taking me on, too?"

M.J. stared at her blankly for a moment, and then understanding sank in. "He's not a high-powered agent, Louise."

"Oh." Louise promptly lost interest and went back to checking her costume.

Peter sped through the streets of New York, deftly maneuvering his cycle as only he could, and patting himself on the back over the last-minute thoughtfulness that he knew was going to go over well with Mary Jane. Strapped to the back of his cycle were—not pizzas, thank God—five yellow carnations. He knew they were Mary Jane's favorites, and if they weren't the most impressive set of carnations he'd ever seen, well, they'd been the best he could afford. Certainly it was the thought that counted, right? Of course, Mary Jane's "new friend" could probably afford to give her the best flowers money could buy.

Immediately, he halted that train of thought. What the hell was the matter with him? Why couldn't he just be happy for Mary Jane, instead of sending more mixed signals than a broken traffic light?

Suddenly his musings were scattered by an abrupt bump as his cycle hit a pothole. If he hadn't been so lost in himself, no doubt he would have seen the drop and swerved around it. As it was, he was only able to offer a last-second dodge, and although he scooted the front tire around it, the rear tire fishtailed out and ran right over it. As a result, the flowers flew off the back of his cycle. Peter instantly realized they were gone and brought up his arm to try to snag them with a web-line. It was too late. The flowers were scattered all over the street and the oncoming cars were making short work of them.

Five bucks down the tube, but of even greater significance was that he didn't have any more money to spare. Buying more flowers wasn't an option, which meant he was going to Mary Jane empty-handed. Maybe the thought counted when you were thinking of more flowers and only had a shabby bouquet. But when you came in with nothing, the thoughts were pretty much worthless.

"Why does everything happen to me?" Peter wondered out loud. "I mean, y'know, what next?"

That was when the sounds of gunshots exploded, seemingly from all around him.

He was still moving on his motorcycle when a Lincoln convertible sped right past him, with a gunman hanging out the back window and firing. For an instant Peter was certain that he was the target, and he veered frantically out of the way as the car sped by. The gunman didn't seem to notice him, however, firing desperately behind him, and it was only then that Peter heard the police siren in the distance.

Okay, the cops are on this, you don't have to get involved. This is Mary Jane's night, for the love of God!

The convertible accelerated, passing Peter, jumping the curb, and crashing into a pretzel vendor's cart. The vendor leaped out of the way just in time as the cart was sent flying straight up. Peter slowed, figuring that at the very least he should make sure the vendor was okay, and suddenly the cart landed, bounced off the sidewalk and bounded directly at Peter.

Realizing that if he maintained his speed he'd collide with it, Peter accelerated, extended one foot to the ground, and leaned as far over as he could. The cart, trailing pretzels behind it, sailed over his head and slammed into a parked taxi, shattering its windows.

The convertible was now in front of Peter and the howling of the police car caught up with them. Peter was bathed in flashing red from the light-bar of the speeding patrol car behind him. He wanted to pull over, to get the hell out of the way, but there was nowhere to do it: He was on a narrow one-way street with parked cars lining both sides.

"I had to ask," grumbled Peter, and then the world slowed down and his eyes went wide as his spider-sense screamed at him that he was in between the barrel of the gunman's weapon and the gunman's target. He had only just finished righting himself and now he desperately angled in the other direction as the gun exploded, blasting the flashing light atop the police car. Desperately Peter let go of the handlebar for half an instant and fired a web-line at the gunman, but he couldn't fully extend his arm and the angle was all wrong. He missed clean and then he was getting out of the way once more as the gunman discharged another blast. It chewed up the hood of the police car on the driver's side.

Figures! Peter thought, and his anger started to swell. What the hell was wrong with his life that he was never, ever granted even a moment's peace? Were the Powers-That-Be out to punish him relentlessly because he had allowed one criminal to slip away? God, there had to be career criminals who didn't have a tenth of the aggravation that Peter underwent.

His temper flaring from the sheer unfairness of it all, Peter accelerated. The shooter, satisfied that the police had been dispatched, had withdrawn into the car, and Peter drew alongside. *C'mon out, please c'mon out. Let me get a web-shot at you at close range and we'll see how fast I end this.*

Then he saw a kid, a young boy, crossing the street up ahead, or at least he had been crossing the street. Serene in the confidence generated by having the "Walk" sign blinking at him, the kid had started across and was frozen, deer-in-the-headlights, as the convertible bore down on him.

Peter urged the cycle forward, pulling ahead of the convertible, desperate to get to the kid before the car reached him.

And suddenly it turned out the police car wasn't out of the game. Instead it chose to announce its continued presence in the most calamitous manner possible: It surged forward and rear-ended the convertible, sending the Lincoln lurching to one side, directly in Peter's path.

Everything that transpired next happened over a period of about five seconds, and yet to Peter it seemed like five years.

All of Peter's thoughts and plans went out the window as his body took over and acted completely on instinct. As the front of the convertible angled toward him, cutting off his route and guaranteeing he'd never get there before the child was run over, Peter abandoned his motorcycle. The cycle tumbled to one side, flipped over a parked car, and landed on the sidewalk as pedestrians scattered out of the way. Peter wasn't thinking about it at all, because he was in motion. He had dismounted from the motorcycle by hurling himself toward the front of the convertible. Now he bounced off of the hood in a handspring, somersaulted forward in a blur of motion, and landed directly behind the paralyzed boy. He scooped him up under one arm, and then the convertible was right there, practically on top of them.

Peter leaped straight up. It wasn't fast enough, especially since he was weighted down by the boy. His feet struck the car hood and he used the momentum to bound toward a nearby wall. He struck it, bouncing off it like a swimmer pushing off from the side of a pool, just as the convertible hit and crushed a mailbox. This caused the rear of the car to swing back toward Peter as he landed on the sidewalk, still holding the boy. *Perfect*, he thought as he lunged, literally running across the car's back end, using its momentum to propel him forward. He landed, squatting, on the sidewalk, clutching the kid to his chest.

As near as Peter could tell, the convertible was practically a rolling armored tank. The damned thing managed to straighten out and, for good measure, turned a corner and sideswiped the pursuing police car as it did so. The police car tried to avoid it and wound up crashing into a lamppost, finally falling into silence as steam rose from the hood.

Peter set the kid down, steadying himself, his head swimming not so much from the exertion as from the closeness of the call insofar as the child was concerned. He heard frantic adults screaming a name, "Joey!" and the boy was turning in response. They were half a block away, barreling toward him, obviously terrified parents who had briefly lost track of their child in the crowd and nearly paid a fatal price for the lapse. The boy, however, seemed far more interested in his rescuer than his parents. "How did you do that?" he demanded, awestruck.

"I work out," Peter said with a deeply serious expression. "Plenty of rest. You know, try to eat your green vegetables."

The boy was suitably impressed. "That's what my mom's always saying. I just never actually believed her."

Peter's eyes narrowed as the convertible roared away into the distance. The callous disregard for human life they had displayed, between the driving and the shooting . . . if Peter hadn't been there . . .

And where they were going, he wasn't there . . .

Then he heard a voice in the back of his mind, buzzing at him like a mosquito, poking and prodding at him. A voice that sounded ever-so-distantly like Uncle Ben, and the voice said, *You're not just going to leave it like that, are you? Doesn't sound very responsible to me.*

The boy who had just been rescued reached up for his parents, and as his frantic mother scooped him up, he turned to introduce them to his savior and tell his mother about the wonders of green vegetables.

Except the man who had rescued him was gone. Nowhere to be seen.

At which point Joey decided to keep the whole green-vegetables thing to himself. No sense in giving his mom that kind of ammunition if he didn't have to.

Stanley Lieber, a spry senior citizen, was among the pedestrians who saw a convertible speeding in their direction, apparently heedless of anything or anyone it might destroy. One sees such things on television, certainly, but Lieber had lived his whole life in Manhattan and had never once actually witnessed anything like it.

Two police cars were close behind it, like determined bloodhounds that had picked up the scent. One of the police cars drew alongside and the Lincoln cut hard over. It rammed into the police car and the officer driving lost control. He screamed, and his screams were joined by those of onlookers as his vehicle flipped completely over and tumbled right toward Lieber and the people around him.

And then it stopped.

In midair.

Lieber gasped, as did the others around him. It was as if the invisible hand of God had literally reached down and caught the car, saving their lives.

Then Lieber, whose eyes were still sharp, saw something glistening in the light of the street lamps. Something that was supporting the police car, suspending it. He reached up tentatively and his hand touched something that seemed to be both there and not there.

"It's a web," he said.

There was a sudden rushing of wind, something cutting through the air above them, and then Lieber and the rest of the crowd looked up and saw a blue-and-red form streak past overhead.

He couldn't believe it. He'd been sure that it had been something cooked up by the news media to sell newspapers or products for advertisers on CNN. But no, there was the costumed figure that had shown up in so many news reports.

Just ahead, the convertible had sped through an intersection, with the remaining police car right behind it. Then the light changed and the cross-traffic started through. Spider-Man was heading right for a large truck that had pulled directly into his path.

There was no way Spider-Man was going to be able to

slow down to avoid the truck. He didn't even try. Instead, he twisted his body sideways, just clearing the narrow space between the truck and the cab that was hauling it. The truck driver twisted in his seat, gaping, as Spider-Man angled up and away, accompanied by a deliriously demented, *"Whoooooo-hooooooooo!"*

"Now, there goes someone who enjoys his work," said Lieber.

Apparently I've attracted their attention, thought Spider-Man as he swung down toward them, his features safely obscured behind his mask.

Not only was the gunman firing up at him, but the driver was likewise leaning out the window and shooting.

"Eyes on the road! Wouldn't want to hurt somebody!" shouted Spider-Man, even though he knew they weren't going to hear him. He didn't much care at that moment. Instead he was intent on venting all his anger over being taken away from Mary Jane. He'd had the evening all planned out. Lunatic gunmen hadn't been part of those plans.

With agility that would have sickened an Olympic gymnast, Spider-Man dodged the bullets and swooped low, hurling web-balls. One knocked the driver's pistol from his hand. The other struck directly under the gunman's chin, stunning him, causing him to hang weakly out the window, his arms dangling and the gun clattering away.

Spider-Man landed on the trunk of the speeding car and thrust out his wrists. Web-lines snared out, encompassing the torsos of both men, with the other ends of the webs attached to a lamppost overhead. The car's own momentum kept it rolling forward and the web-lines began to stretch, and then snapped tight. The driver and gunman were hauled up and out of the car, left dangling from the lamppost.

Spider-Man slithered in through the open window just as the convertible was beginning to slow. He didn't allow it the opportunity. Instead, he brought his foot down on the gas, speeding it up. As he turned down a side street, he caught a glimpse of bewildered police behind him pulling to a stop. They were staring in wonderment at the sight of the criminals suspended in midair by gossamer-thin threads.

"Courtesy of your friendly neighborhood Spider-Man," he muttered as he pulled off his mask. He guided the convertible toward the alley where he had stashed his clothes, not having had the time to web them to his back. He hoped that he was returning to them quickly enough; the last time he'd had to leave his street clothes behind, he'd returned to discover what appeared to be a pregnant rat making a nest out of them.

Mary Jane was having an off night.

She knew it as every line of dialogue passed through her lips. She couldn't get her head into her character, Cecily Cardew, at all. She felt terrible about it. Usually she slipped Cecily on like a comfortable coat. Tonight, though, her focus wasn't on her performance, but on the empty house seat that stood out like a great thumping bruise in the middle of row C.

They had begun Act Three, set in the morning room of the manor house. "I am more content with what Mr. Moncrieff said," she informed Louise, who was playing Gwendolen Fairfax. Her mind was split, analyzing the poor quality of her delivery and trying to pump up the energy. "His voice alone inspires one with absolute credulity."

"Then you think we should forgive them?" asked Louise-as-Gwendolen.

She couldn't tear her eyes from the empty seat and her mind from dwelling on who should have been sitting in it. "Yes . . . I mean no." Never a more appropriate line for M.J.'s state of mind at that moment. Like Cecily, she was faced with poor behavior on the part of a prospective beau, and uncertain as to whether forgiveness should be extended. Her instinct was yes, but her final decision was a resounding no.

"True!" exclaimed Louise, giving it all she had as if she felt she needed to sustain the energy level for both of them. "I had forgotten. There are principles at stake that one cannot surrender. Which of us should tell them? The task is not a pleasant one."

It never is, thought Mary Jane even as she said brightly, "Could we not both speak at the same time?"

Peter Parker and a traffic cop were speaking at the same time.

Peter had just driven the convertible up to a red zone right in front of the theater. He was tucking in his shirt as he clambered out of the battered Lincoln, and the traffic cop was striding toward him, calling out, "Hey, Mac, you park here, I'm towing it!"

As the cop shouted his warning of the car's fate, Peter said, "Whatever," heading into the theater.

In a completely disheveled state, his clothes in disarray, Peter yanked on his jacket as he walked quickly through the theater lobby. An usher was standing at the far side of it in front of the closed doors that led into the theater itself. He had the air of someone who did not suffer fools gladly. That was unfortunate since Peter was feeling particularly foolish at that moment. He was reaching a point in his life where he was a gazelle when bounding between skyscrapers, but an absolute klutz when it came to managing things on the ground.

"Young man," sniffed the usher, "your shoelace."

"Oh, thanks," Peter mumbled as he tied the lace. Then he pulled out his ticket and extended it. "I'm a little late. I can stand in the back."

"Sorry," said the usher, not sounding particularly sorry at all. He pointed to a sign and read it aloud as if Peter were illiterate: "No one admitted after the doors are closed."

"I have a ticket!"

"It's to help maintain the illusion," the usher explained.

"I understand, but . . ." Peter pointed to a poster of the cast. "Miss Watson, she's my friend. She asked me to come."

A snaky smile spread across the usher's face. "Ah, but not to come late."

Peter began to seethe. The usher simply stood there, arms folded, looking like the king of the world. Peter stepped in close and the usher looked him in the eye, serene in his smug control.

"Your shoe," Peter said.

The usher smirked. "Nice try. Mine are tied."

"Yes, but you appear to have stepped in something."

The usher looked down. Some sort of thick glob was all over his right shoe. Peter, meantime, straightened his shirtsleeve, making sure that none of the webbing he'd just released had gotten on his clothes.

He watched the usher try to move his foot. Nothing doing. The webbing had seeped through the shoe and around his foot, and both were stuck to the carpet. He wasn't going anywhere for quite a while.

"Let me help you," said Peter, and the usher looked up hopefully . . . then his expression changed to fury as Peter tore his ticket, tucked one half in the usher's jacket pocket, and stepped toward the far door. The usher tried to move in front of him and succeeded only in nearly dislocating his leg. "You wouldn't want to tell me how far into the play they are, would you?" Peter asked as he opened the door.

From within, he heard a man say from the direction of the stage, "On the contrary, Aunt Augusta, I've now realized for the first time in my life the vital Importance of Being Earnest!" And this statement was greeted with a burst of applause from the audience.

And the usher smiled in grim, had-the-last-laugh triumph. "That would be called the 'curtain line,' or simply 'the end.'"

Peter moaned softly.

He'd tried. He'd tried so hard to balance both halves of his life . . . and once again, M.J. had come up short. He wondered if Mary Jane would realize the importance of his trying to be earnest, and had the sinking feeling that his earnestness was going to suffer the same fate as had his carnations.

He walked out of the theater, giving a wide berth to the traffic cop who was writing up paperwork to have the car towed. Instead, he crossed the street and leaned against a fire hydrant to wait. Nearby a young Japanese girl—a street musician—was scratching away a tune on a violin with the hope that passersby would toss money into her open case. And she was singing, with a heavy accent, "Spider-Mon, Spider-Mon, does whatever a spider con."

Peter winced, and started to think that maybe the carnations had it lucky.

* * *

Mary Jane emerged from the stage door sometime later, Louise directly behind her. A couple of "stage door Johnnys"—autograph hounds—came up to them seeking signatures, and M.J. and Louise gladly obliged. The rest of the theatergoing audience had long dispersed. She saw Waldo, the head usher, stomp past with what appeared to be a piece of torn-up carpet attached to his foot. She had no idea why, but then again, Waldo was an odd sort.

She looked around, hoping against hope that Peter would make some sort of last-minute appearance. She wanted to be angry at him, but what if there had been some emergency? How would she feel if she were steaming about her personal inconvenience, only to find that Peter was at the hospital because Aunt May had had a stroke?

Then her heart hardened. He'd probably just forgotten, that was all. This was all some . . . weird game to him. And she was getting pretty damned tired of playing it.

"See you later," called Louise, and Mary Jane was about to ask her where she was running off to when a tall, handsome man sporting an air force uniform walked up to M.J. and asked, "May I have your autograph, Miss?"

She looked up at him and it was as if a light switch had been turned on in her head. "When did you get here?" she asked.

"Got in this afternoon," he replied. "I wanted to surprise you."

"I was getting worried. The way you headed out of town the day after we had lunch with your father, I thought I'd never see you again."

"It was just NASA business, M.J., and you shouldn't worry. Believe it or not, that was the best get-together I've ever had with my dad."

He moved toward her and they held each other tightly. Then she kissed him, basking in his warmth. "Usually the only people waiting here are stage door Johnnys."

"Well, my name is John, so that works out," he said affably. "Hungry?"

She cast one last look around the area, searching for some sign of Peter. Nothing. At that point she realized that moping around and wishing that Peter Parker had managed to carve some time out of his oh-so-busy schedule to be with her was a road leading to madness. Even worse: Maybe he was trying to exert some sort of control over her by making her believe he'd be there for her and then standing her up. Well, she already had a boatload of control issues left over from her abusive father. She certainly didn't need more.

"Starved," she said with conviction. John extended an elbow to her, she looped her arm around it, and together they walked off into the night.

VII

Peter Parker had remained on the far side of the street when he saw the theatergoers finally emerging from the play. He felt it would probably be better to wait until everyone had dispersed before approaching Mary Jane. She would doubtless be annoyed with him, and he didn't want to embarrass her by causing her to lose her temper in front of audience members or castmates. Nor was he especially anxious to come face-to-face with the annoying usher again.

So he had leaned against the wall of the nearest building. The streetlight in front of him had a blown-out bulb, so he was effectively cloaked in darkness. From this vantage point he waited until he saw M.J. emerge from the stage door, another actress following her. As she stood there and signed autographs for her fans, he ran through all the things he was going to say to her. If there was any way to smooth this over—any turn of phrase he could come up with—he was determined to do it.

And then, as he prepared to cross the street, he saw a guy come up to Mary Jane. She threw her arms around him, and suddenly everything just hazed over and went away.

By the time the world came into focus and the thundering in his temple eased, both M.J. and the man, who was obviously her new significant other, were gone.

The violinist, oblivious to the pain that Peter was feeling, began to play a melancholy tune. *Terrific. My anguish has its own theme song. I hate this city.*

Then, cutting above the music of the violin came the sound of a police siren. A cop car sped past, followed by a second. There was an emergency.

A crime was occurring. Or perhaps someone desperately needed help.

And he was right there. He could do something about it.

There were thousands of air force officers in the world. Thousands of actresses. But there was only one person who could do what he, Peter Parker, could do. And he had to do it.

Why?

The first germ of doubt began to fester within him. Why? Just because he could, why did he have to? Really?

Because you do.

It wasn't his own voice that replied, but Uncle Ben's. Somehow he wasn't surprised. He was too exhausted even to debate the notion.

He pulled his mask from his pocket and stared at it. Then he turned and ran into a nearby alley.

Swiftly he was out of his street clothes and busily stuffing them in his camera bag. When he'd retrieved them earlier, there had been no rats, but a mangy-looking dog had been sizing them up and preparing to lift a leg near them. This time he was taking no chances. He zipped up the bag, tossed it into the air, then fired a web-line. It struck the camera bag just as it went as high as it could, and the web-line affixed the bag to the underside of an eave. Perfect. The only thing he need concern himself about now was pigeons.

Peter pulled on his Spider-Man mask, sprang off a crate, and leaped heavenward. He skittered up the side of a building and a moment later bounded onto a rooftop.

He stood there for what seemed an eternity.

His heart wasn't in it this time. Not really.

You have to do it. Again, it wasn't his voice.

"Fine, whatever," sighed Spider-Man. It wasn't enough that his life was turning into incessant conflict with criminals. Now his own inner conflict was growing out of control.

He fired a web-line with singular lack of enthusiasm and began swinging in the direction of the police cars. He swung down and over Fifth Avenue, his mind otherwise occupied.

As his swing reached its apex, he brought his arm around to shoot a new web-line.

Nothing happened.

At first, that was. Spider-Man felt a brief tremble of alarm as his wrist made an odd fizzing sound, but that was all. Then the web-line issued forth and he breathed a sigh of relief, chalking it up to just an odd internal glitch. Perhaps he needed to put more fiber in his diet, or eat more red meat, or less. Something like that.

He arced across the street and this time when he tried to spin a web, there was no fizz, there was nothing.

No web-line.

Not a thing.

Worse, the line he was holding on to turned out to be of such poor quality that it literally dissolved behind him.

It took a second to register on Spider-Man that he was in midair, holding on to nothing. In a dizzying moment of insane denial, he thought that perhaps if he simply didn't look down or acknowledge his predicament, gravity would have no sway over him, as was the case with that coyote in those cartoons.

Unfortunately, without giving Spider-Man even enough time to hold up a little sign saying "Oh, No," gravity did indeed take charge of the situation. He fell like a bag of cement, and landed just about as gracefully: about twenty feet below, on a rooftop.

He knew he should feel lucky. His momentum had carried him to the far side of the street. Another couple of feet in either direction and he'd have been nothing but a spectacular spider-splat on the middle of Fifth Avenue.

"Even my good luck hurts," he moaned as he lay there spread-eagled on the roof. Finally, he staggered to his feet and shook off the pain. He pulled off his mask to breathe in some fresh air, gathering what he laughingly referred to as his wits.

Then he tried to fire his web once more, and there was still nothing. Either his internal supply of web-fluid had run out—although he didn't understand how that could be—or he had lost the ability to spin webs altogether.

"Ooooookay," he said softly.

He looked over the edge of the roof. He had to be at least sixty stories high. And considering how his web-spinning had suddenly made itself scarce, he didn't want to think about the consequences if his wall-crawling deserted him, as well. Skidding down the side of a building, screaming and cursing all the way. A rather ignominious end to his career . . . such as it was.

Which was why, five minutes later, he was standing in a crowded elevator. His mask was back in place. People were glancing at him and smirking. "The Girl from Ipanema" was floating through the Muzak speakers.

One of the passengers, a tired-looking guy in a charcoal business suit, commented, "Cool Spidey outfit."

"Thanks."

"Where'd you get it?"

He'd gotten it from a costume-maker, actually. On the night he'd trounced pro wrestler "Bone Saw" McGraw, one of Bone Saw's victims—the Flying Dutchman—had been so grateful to Peter for taking Bone Saw apart that he'd referred Peter to a tailor who happened to be the Dutchman's brother. "You need anything if you turn pro, we'll take care of you," the groaning Dutchman had assured him as they loaded him into an ambulance.

He'd been as good as his word. When, a week later, Peter—still wearing his identity-obscuring hooded wrestling outfit—had shown up at the tailor's shop with his drawings of the ideal costume, the tailor had set to work and produced two identical outfits, free of charge. One had been hopelessly trashed in Peter's final confrontation with the Goblin, and he was wearing the second.

He wasn't about to explain all that to some guy in an elevator.

"I made it," said Peter.

The passenger looked the costume up and down. "Looks uncomfortable," he observed.

"It kind of itches," Peter admitted. After a moment he added, "And it rides up in the crotch sometimes."

That seemed to be more information than anyone wanted or needed. The rest of the elevator ride passed in silence.

The next day, Peter was running to class, which was nothing new for him. What was new was that he didn't have his motorcycle as a means of getting to school.

The cycle had been right where he'd left it when he finally went back to get it the previous night. As if his suddenly wonky spider-powers weren't enough to deal with, he found his motorcycle battered and broken from when it had gone flipping out from under him. He couldn't help but remember Aunt May warning him, "There are only two types of motorcyclists: those who have had accidents, and those who haven't had accidents yet." Well, he was now a proud member of the group who had. Somehow he didn't think she'd be pleased for him.

He had hauled the battered cycle home and, while doing so, had walked past M.J.'s billboard. Good. Excellent. Just what he needed. A forty-foot reminder of his screwups.

Today he'd tried to put the lousy previous night behind him, dwelling instead on . . . well, the probably lousy day that awaited him. It was with this less-than-sterling outlook that he made it to class only five minutes late. That wasn't bad, actually, considering his track record.

But he found it impossible to concentrate. As Doctor Connors lectured, Peter felt his attention being drawn irresistibly in several different directions. First, he couldn't get Otto Octavius out of his mind. Otto's fusion theories seemed too good to be true. And if there was one thing Peter had learned in his fairly brief life, it was that most things that seemed too good to be true generally were. Peter scribbled notes during class, some of them reconstructions of the theorem Otto had shown him, while others were original thoughts. He kept coming back to one formula in particular, the ramifications of which he didn't believe Octavius had fully thought through. Then again, who was he, Peter Parker, to second-guess Otto Octavius? Octavius was a genius, after all. Totally intent on his work.

Peter, on the other hand, couldn't even keep his attention from wandering during class. When he wasn't scribbling formulae, he was drawing hearts with M.J.'s initials in them, and then scribbling them out. As he did so, he muttered things like, "I was there . . . I was right there . . . pretzel cart flew over my head . . . pretzels everywhere . . ."

"Huh?" a pretty young student, Gwen Stacy, whispered to him.

He waved her off, shaking his head. He began scribbling out the heart and initials once more . . . and then stopped. One of the hearts he'd drawn was more oval than heart-shaped. Carefully he drew a line down the middle, dividing it vertically. On the left side he drew a quick sketch of his own face . . . and on the right, Spider-Man's mask.

He stared at the self-portrait.

It stared back.

Mary Jane Watson was wrestling with two large grocery bags at her front door when she heard her phone ringing inside. She was trying to dig her keys out of her pocket without putting the bags down. There was no reason for it, of course. Somehow it was just a matter of pride to keep the bags suspended while searching out her keys. Eventually she managed to retrieve the keys, find the appropriate one, and shove it into the lock. As she turned it, she heard her own voice from her answering machine say, "You got M.J. Please leave me a message. Thank you."

She got the door open and staggered in just as she heard, "Uhhh, hi, M.J. I'm . . . this is Peter and I, uh . . ."

Her first impulse was to drop the bags, go to the phone, and pick it up. Instead, she crossed slowly to the kitchen, holding the bags tightly. Peter's voice continued, "I was on the way and I . . . uh . . . I was . . . uh . . . I was coming around a corner and . . . uh . . . are you there?"

"Uh, uh, uh," she said in annoyance toward the machine.

He couldn't hear her, of course. "I really was planning on it all day," he continued, "and I know you predicted I'd disappoint you . . ."

"Bingo," she said. She was standing at the kitchen table, the bags set down and leaning against each other. She made no effort to unpack them, instead listening to Peter's stumbling message.

"It's amazing, isn't it, how complicated a simple thing, being someplace at eight o'clock can . . . uh . . . become . . . uh . . ."

"Shut up, Peter, just *shut up*!" she cried out.

Oblivious, he continued, "Actually, there was this snooty usher, somebody has to talk to that usher, Mary Ja—"

And suddenly Peter's voice was replaced by a recording of an operator saying, "Your time has expired, please insert fifty cents for the next five minutes."

"I want to tell you the truth, Mary Jane," Peter's voice came all in a rush. "Ready? Here it is. I . . ."

The line went dead.

"Oh, thank God," M.J. breathed.

At the university student center, Peter clutched the pay phone tightly and said, as fast as he could, "I want to tell you the truth, Mary Jane. Ready? Here it is. I, Peter Parker, am Spider-Man." He stopped, gulped, tried to laugh. "Weird, huh?" Then his tone became serious again. "I think about you day after day, Mary Jane. But if the people I have to fight knew how I felt, you'd be in danger."

Then he slammed down the receiver and bellowed at the top of his lungs, *"I tried to get there, Mary Jane!"*

He knew the message hadn't been left. He'd heard the line click off before he could say it. He had spoken into the blissful safety of a dead line.

Peter walked out of the student center and stood at the top of the steps leading out to the main campus. He watched people coming and going. Students laughing or conversing seriously. Sitting under trees eating slices of pizza or studying.

He felt as if he were looking across an alien landscape. As if he were a visitor from a far-off world who had as much in common with these life-forms as they did with amoebas.

He had to get a life.

He just wasn't sure whose to get.

VIII

Otto Octavius tried to imagine what his life would be like without Rosie. He couldn't. For that matter, he tried to recollect what his life had been like before her. Still no luck. He knew on some level that it was ridiculous. Except, it wasn't. For even in the first twenty-or-so years of his life when she hadn't been there, she *had* been. He'd known her before he knew her, felt her presence without knowing her name or even what she looked like. As a result, when they'd first encountered each other, it hadn't been a matter of "Nice to meet you" so much as it was, "Oh, there you are! What kept you?"

It seemed as if no time had passed between that moment and this, when she was adjusting his tie and smoothing his collar. They were standing in a small room outside the main lab. It was ten in the morning, but Otto—normally a late riser, really not much of a morning person—had been lying awake, wide-eyed since before 5 A.M. He had listened to Rosie's soft snoring next to him as he ran equation after equation through his head, trying to detect some flaw, something he might have overlooked.

That Parker lad. The boy kept preying on his mind. Parker obviously had so much on the ball, was seeing things with a fresh eye, had no self-serving reasons to dismiss or berate Otto's work. Yet even Parker had expressed concerns about containing the power . . .

"You're slouching," she said reprovingly as she adjusted the shoulders of his jacket. "That means you're doubting yourself."

"Oh, good. You can add 'mind reader' to your resume," he replied, but even as he straightened up, he banished his concerns about Peter Parker. In the final analysis, Parker was just a student. A gifted one, but still learning. Experience would always prevail over youthful enthusiasm, and Otto had experience, and dammit, he knew what he was doing.

"It's your day, Otto," Rosie said, as if sensing lingering doubts despite his more rigid posture.

"It's our day, Rosie," he corrected her. "Without you, there is no day." He took a deep breath. "Ready, baby?"

"Ready!" said Rosie enthusiastically. "Let's give them a show!"

They walked out into the lab. The moment they did, Otto's assistant, Raymond, opened the main doors, and between twenty-five and thirty people filed in. They did so in relative quiet, speaking in murmurs at most. That was certainly preferable to their stomping into his lab and making all kinds of racket. Obviously, they were showing the proper deference to the importance of what they were about to witness.

As if he had a zoom lens in his head, he zeroed in on young Parker, who had entered alongside Harry Osborn. Octavius could not for the life of him understand why Parker would associate with Osborn. Osborn was at best barely adequate when it came to his comprehension of science. Not even close to that of Norman, his father, much less the brilliant Peter Parker. Well, perhaps Peter regarded Harry as some sort of charity case.

Osborn was speaking loudly and Otto could easily hear him. "Glad you're here, Pete. I've got a lot riding on this. Big day for OsCorp."

"An amazing day if he can pull it off," replied Parker.

Otto was stung. Here he would have thought Parker would defend his work to Osborn, and instead he was once again expressing doubts. The scientifically inept Osborn had more confidence than did the far wiser Parker. Again there was that faint whiff of doubt, and once again Otto shoved it aside. Parker had a little knowledge, true, but a little knowledge could be a dangerous thing. It was leading Peter Parker to question things that there was no need to question. That was all there was to it. Octavius had everything under control.

"May I have your attention, please," Raymond called. "We are about to begin."

Octavius stepped forward, and Harry Osborn promptly broke into applause. Operating on the herd instinct, everyone else applauded, as well. Octavius was grateful for the support, even if the man whose future depended on it was the one instigating the reception.

"Good afternoon, ladies and gentlemen." He cleared his throat. "Before we start, did anyone lose a green wallet with a rubber band around it? We found the rubber band. You can claim it after the demonstration, from my wife, Rosie, who is assisting me today."

There were, at most, a couple of very polite guffaws. He glanced in annoyance toward Rosie, who shrugged. *Start with a joke,* she'd said. So much for that idea. Then again, maybe if it had been a funny joke . . .

He shrugged it off. He was a scientist, not a comedian. "Seriously," he said, brushing past it, "I thank you all for coming here this afternoon. You will witness the birth of a new fusion-based energy souce: safe, renewable power and cheap electricity for everyone. I call it the Bartok Project because I admire that guy's crazy music." He backed up toward the covered rig at one end of the lab and called out, like a magician, "Now let me introduce my other assistant."

Continuing that magical air, he whipped off a drape revealing the rig and its contents: four long metal arms attached to a wide, lightweight harness. At the end of each of the arms was a set of pincers serving as that arm's "hand."

Watching from the audience, it was everything Peter Parker could do not to laugh.

Arms. Actual mechanical arms. That was what Jack All had been talking about.

Peter couldn't believe what a fool he'd been. It hadn't been arms as in "munitions" at all. Doctor Octavius had created some sort of laboratory aid to extend his reach and enable him to physically multitask with greater efficiency. Whatever Jack All had heard on the grapevine, it was completely wrongheaded. Obviously these things were no more weapons than a Bunsen burner was a flamethrower.

With that last, nagging detail settled, Peter leaned back in his chair to enjoy the presentation.

Octavius loved the design he had created for the arms. It had come to him one day after a visit to the Coney Island Aquarium: the answer to the endless frustration of trying to perform experiments and wishing one had more hands at one's disposal. Thanks to the four actuators—which, he had to admit, sounded like the name of a singing group—a scientist could have all the hands he reasonably needed. And they weren't even the main invention he'd developed. They were merely tools he would use to help get the fusion generator started up.

Removing his jacket, Octavius stepped into the harness. It whirred to life and snapped itself around him. He heard several people in the audience gasp. Good. Let them be nervous. This was the realm of hard science, not something designed for the faint of heart. "These four actuators were developed and programmed for the sole purpose of creating successful fusion," he explained. The harness drew tighter around him, making it snug as a corset. He was beginning to sympathize with women from centuries past.

He touched a keypad and a metal spine unfurled from the harness, attaching itself to Octavius through a series of tiny needles embedding themselves in his spinal column. He heard gasps from the audience, and he himself winced slightly from the pain. He took a deep breath and let it out, since that was far preferable either to crying out or, even worse, passing out.

"My 'smart' arms," he continued, "are controlled by my brain through a neural link. Nanowires feed directly into my cerebellum, allowing me to use the arms to control the fusion reaction in an environment no human hand can enter."

A blond-haired man stood up, and Octavius recognized him instantly. He was Doctor Henry Pym, and he had been doing some breakthrough research in cybernetics. Pym was, in fact, a giant in a field where everyone else was an ant. Octavius nodded in a way that indicated he recognized Pym for who he was, and Pym did likewise.

"Doctor Octavius," he said, "if the artificial intelligence in the arms is as advanced as you suggest, couldn't that make you vulnerable to them?"

"Right you are," said Otto readily. "That's why I developed this inhibitor chip," and he tapped the base of his skull, "to protect my higher brain function. It makes sure I maintain control of the arms, instead of them controlling me." He heard more gasps from the audience at that, and a sweep of murmurs. Even Pym raised an eyebrow questioningly. "Problem, Doctor Pym?" he asked solicitously.

"Well, I just wish I'd known, Doctor," said Pym. "I've developed a cybernetic helmet that may well have accomplished the same thing for you without requiring invasive surgery."

"Hardly anything as dramatic as that, Doctor," replied Otto. "A simple microchip, about as invasive as getting a tattoo. Frankly, I think everyone should have one. Considering all the garbage thrust upon us from all directions by the media, I think most of us are in danger of losing our higher brain functions, if we haven't already."

This actually prompted a round of laughter, and Pym, grinning, nodded once and took his seat again. Octavius felt a sweep of relief. He was in full command of the situation, which was exactly where he wanted to be.

The rear section of his lab was dark. As he strode toward it, he had to admit he was developing a truly showmanlike quality. Most of the trappings were Rosie's suggestions and he had lovingly indulged her, but he was really starting to like the theatrics in spite of himself. Perhaps he should develop a "science spectacular" and move the whole thing to Las Vegas. Mystery, fun, and education, three shows a night. "Now on with the main event," he called out. "Give me the blue light, Rosie!"

A moment later, azure lighting bathed the rear of the lab, revealing his magnificent creation. The light, coming in from three different angles, showed a fusion machine consisting of four scythelike towers with cables and hoses attached, suspended over a tank of water. Once more there were murmurs, this time of appreciation for the elegant, streamlined design. He could just imagine a number of people in the audience thinking, "Of course! It's so simple! How could we not have thought of it first!"

Working at a keyboard, Octavius tapped in computer commands and the fusion reactor hummed to life. He entered a security code and turned to a metal canister that was anchored to a podium with so many alarms attached to it that any attempt to steal the contents would have set off Klaxons in the Pentagon. The canister opened with a faint hiss and a small, metallic tablet—about the size of a Tylenol capsule—presented itself, rising from within.

The arms came to life, and one of them moved sinuously forward. Maneuvering the pincer with remarkable dexterity, Octavius used it to pick up the capsule. "This precious tritium target is the fuel that makes this project go," he said as he deftly placed the capsule in the center of the fusion machine. "There are only twenty-five pounds on the planet. I want to thank Harry Osborn and OsCorp industries for providing it." *There, I acknowledged him. Now please let the young fool keep his mouth shut and appreciate the—*

"Happy to pay the bills, Otto!" Harry Osborn called from his seat.

For an instant Otto considered the many pleasures that would be involved in throttling Harry Osborn, but quickly shut down that line of reasoning. He didn't *think* the arms would respond to such a passing, subconscious thought, but he wasn't inclined to test it out. He certainly didn't need his demonstration devolving into a free-for-all as his arms attacked Osborn just because he had annoyed Otto Octavius.

As one pincer continued to hold the capsule in the machine, Otto moved another tentacle into place and used it to punch a button, igniting the inductance field inside the towers. The field wasn't visible to the naked eye, but it hummed like a throbbing turbine engine.

Slowly, but with growing confidence, the tentacle released the capsule and it hung there, suspended. Then it began to spin, slowly at first but then faster, gaining momentum until it was whirling at blinding speed.

"Ladies and gentlemen," Otto's voice rose above the noise, "fasten your seat belts!"

The plasma igniters on each of the four towers simultaneously fired on the tritium capsule in a continuous blast, exciting the core. A fine circular beam of plasma formed. Then spokes like a wheel extended and—after a few more seconds—a bright glowing sphere of energy about fourteen inches in diameter flared into existence in the center of the array. It enlarged, and tiny solar prominences flared from the outer edges, like a miniature sun.

Octavius realized he wasn't breathing. It was like being God, watching a solar system coming into existence. No wonder the biblical creator had required a day of rest. The heart-pounding excitement alone—of watching a project of this majesty come to fruition—was exhausting.

Raymond, watching the readouts carefully, told Octavius what he already knew. Nevertheless, when Raymond spoke, it was with a hushed reverence, as if he couldn't quite believe the words he was saying. "Doctor . . . we have a successful fusion reaction."

The crowd gasped collectively, and several people burst into spontaneous applause. As well they should. This was something they would tell their grandchildren about.

Octavius brought an arm up and began to manipulate the field, like a conductor guiding his orchestra. As the prominences shot out from the ball, he moved the arms to intercept them at the points along the inductance field where each one struck. At each point, the flare would disperse across the field as the arms kept them contained with almost precognitive skill. It was like watching a master fencer countering the thrusts of a far lesser opponent.

"The brain is nature's perfect computer," Octavius said, his casualness of tone a contrast to the complexity of the job at hand. "My 'smart' arms can manipulate the fusion until it reaches stability, because my mind can react much more intuitively than any computer to changes in the inductance field."

Again the crowd applauded, this time far more resoundingly. If this were Vegas, now would be the perfect time for the showgirls to bound out in a kick line.

The pitch of the generator's whine increased, the light becoming more intense. Raymond, monitoring the output carefully, called over, "We have the equivalent of one thousand megawatts."

Otto glanced at Osborn. Someone was patting him on the back and mouthing, "Congratulations." It irked Otto slightly, but then he looked over at Rosie, who was beaming at him with a smile that put out ten times the megawatts of the reactor. She blew him a kiss, and suddenly Osborn didn't mean a damn thing to him. He winked at Rosie. The work and his wife were all that mattered, and not necessarily in that order.

The speed and brightness of the light formed dazzling sparkles in the air. They oscillated and surged, but stayed contained within the four towers. However, they were starting to become more difficult for the smart arms to contain. Octavius was moving faster than before, and he wasn't staying quite so much ahead of them anymore. Instead, in several instances he was barely there in time.

He began to sweat as solar flares from the center core swept almost to the towers themselves, which was exactly the kind of potential calamity he needed to avoid. Like a mad conductor in the middle of a lightning storm, he kept the arms in constant motion, almost flailing instead of guiding.

The audience members were no longer looking on in awe. Now there was concern, mixed with fear, many of them flinching back and shielding their eyes from the glare.

Octavius didn't quite know where to concentrate first. He felt as if he was losing his hold upon the audience, but he didn't dare shift so much as a scintilla of his attention away from the reactor. "The power of the sun in the palm of my hand!" he called out, adopting his best showman's voice. Yet in his mind's eye he could see the showgirls scattering, running away in terror.

A low rumble suffused the space. The surface of the water in the tank came alive with electrical discharge and the plasma igniters shut off. The energy for the reaction was now being fueled by the water below.

Matters were spinning out of control, and if the human brain is a computer, even the greatest of computers have been known to crash. Otto's was beginning to seize up, the arms moving more sluggishly, uncertain of what to do.

The solar flares from the tiny sun swept out, pressing against the magnetic field. The light volume bulged on one side, and one of Otto's arms flitted to cover and press the bulge back in. Otto tried to regain control, his arms moving so fast that they were a blur, but there was no artistry now, no certainty. Instead, they were waving about like wayward strands of seaweed.

Suddenly one of the flares shot out from the magnetic field between the towers and into the room. It scythed through some carts and equipment, melting, bending, and dragging them back toward the reactor. To his horror, Octavius saw various other pieces of equipment bending toward the reactor as well, letting out screeches of twisting metal.

My God, it's developing a gravity well, he thought. *What if . . . what if I've created a sun that goes through its entire life cycle, collapses, and forms a black hole?! It could suck in everything in this room . . . this block . . . this city . . .*

From all around him there were screams and shouts, and people evacuating the room. Osborn was on his feet, trying to call over the panicked voices. He was white as a sheet, gesturing frantically. Henry Pym seemed literally to just disappear from sight, which showed how frantic the moment was. Even Peter Parker was nowhere in sight.

Are you sure you can stabilize the fusion reaction? Peter Parker's innocent question floated back to him from a seeming eternity ago. Otto's smug and self-confident reply, however, was lost to him.

"Wait!" shouted Otto to the backs of the fleeing people. "It's just a spike! Raymond, tell them to keep their seats! It will stabilize in a moment!"

Raymond wasn't in any condition to tell anyone anything. He was looking at the readings on his instrumentation and shaking his head frantically, as if he couldn't believe what he was seeing.

From the corner of his eye Otto saw Rosie running toward him, and then more flares arced outward, completely out of control, smashing into the space where the crowd had been sitting. One nearly struck Osborn, who twisted away and avoided it as much by dumb luck as anything else. He scampered to one side, driven by the flares to find safety behind one of the support columns for the reactor. *"What's happened?! Turn it off!"* he shouted at Otto.

Then Osborn ducked back, just as one of the flares severed all of the conduits on the face of the column. Wires dropped to the floor. The screams, at least, had ceased, for everyone else had fled the room. Raymond was hiding behind a chair, and Otto thought he was whimpering. He wasn't there for long, though; an arc of energy struck the chair, and Raymond, with a scream, crawled out the door to safety.

Then Octavius, above the din, heard Osborn scream something that made no sense at all.

"It's the crawler! He's done this! Somebody catch him!"

Otto's head whipped around and he saw a fast-moving figure in red and blue.

"Spider-Man?" breathed Octavius, unable to comprehend where in the world he could have come from.

Spider-Man planted himself upside down on a steel

ceiling truss, briefly out of the way of the flares. With uncanny timing, he snagged Harry Osborn with a web-line and yanked him upward. Osborn started to thrash in protest, and then a vicious bolt of energy swept right through where Osborn had been. Harry, gasping, realizing the narrowness of his escape, went limp. Octavius knew all too well Harry Osborn's feelings about Spider-Man. He'd brought it up at random, almost disconnected times in their association, as if the masked man was always preying on his mind. Now, though, Osborn's face was the picture of conflicting emotions as he realized that the man he hated above all others had just saved his life.

Spider-Man lowered Harry Osborn to safety and tossed off a salute, even as he scuttled away on the ceiling. Osborn howled, "I'll get you for this!" which indicated just where he had decided to assign his priorities.

Spider-Man's entrance, his rescue of Harry Osborn, had all occupied no more than a few seconds, and then Otto's full attention was snapped back to the unfolding calamity. His arms were frenetic with motion, flailing about to no avail as he tried to control the arcing flares. The rumbling around him grew louder. The structure of the building itself was being bent by the magnetic attraction of the machine.

And suddenly Spider-Man, whom Octavius had assumed had the good sense to get the hell out of there, was nearby and moving toward the machine as if he knew what he was doing. He approached a huge bundle of cable, the control panel close at hand. Rosie was coming toward Octavius from the other direction, stepping carefully, ducking under arcs of energy.

"What are you doing!" Octavius shouted at Spider-Man. "No! *No! It will stabilize! I'm in control!*"

And at that moment, one of the solar flares swept out of the magnetic field, darted under one of Otto's whipping tentacles, and slammed directly into his midsection. It engulfed the mechanism that attached the metal arms to Otto's body.

Rosie screamed his name and ran to him, trying to shove him out of the way.

It was a catastrophic error in judgment, stemming not from scientific, rational thinking, but pure emotion. As she grabbed him, the current moved through him and struck her. Her head pitched back, her mouth opening in a silent scream, and without a word she sank to Otto's feet.

Across the room, Spider-Man was yanking a handful of cables out of the base of the device. It was an amazing show of strength, and immediately the fusion reaction began to subside. Otto saw it without fully comprehending it, because his attention was completely upon the fallen form of his wife. He reached for her, calling out, "Rosie? Rosie!"

She stared up at him with sightless eyes.

Otto's mind went numb.

Suddenly there was a burst of light directly in his eyes, and something slammed him in the back of the head, and there was a faint whiff of something burning . . .

. . . then blackness fell upon him. But just before it did, from somewhere deep within his own mind, he heard a voice. Another voice, whispering to him as if from another reality altogether.

It said one word.

Father?

And then there was nothingness.

IX

The eyepieces of his mask usually provided some protection against glare, but for Spider-Man, even that wasn't enough to fully protect him as he squinted against the coruscating arcs of energy, hoping he wouldn't go blind from the proximity.

He had just finished ripping the cables out from the fusion reactor when through the haze of illumination he saw Rosie collapsing at Otto's feet. He started to make a move in that direction, then a few last bursts of energy drove him back. He staggered, shielding his face, and to his horror saw the very last bolt of energy the machine had to offer as it struck Otto Octavius squarely in the head.

Like a puppet with its strings severed, Octavius dropped to the floor, collapsing atop his wife. He collapsed, screaming, clutching the sides of his head.

As Spider-Man moved toward him, he saw a warning flashing on a monitor, and his heart sank. It read, "Warning: Inhibitor Chip Damaged. Temporal Lobe Breached." As if everything else wasn't enough, that was an indicator that Octavius would have been rendered vulnerable to any sort of backlash unleashed through the cybernetic elements of the arm mechanism.

He turned his attention back to Otto, and blinked in

confusion. Doctor Pym was crouched next to Octavius, checking him over.

Where the hell had *he* come from? Spider-Man could have sworn he was the only other person who had remained in the room.

Such thoughts fled in the face of what he saw next. Spider-Man stopped in his tracks.

One of the mechanical arms was moving. It rose up and seemed to "look" to the right, then left, like a submarine periscope. Then it fell to the floor and twitched spasmodically.

All around them, the lights went out. The rumbling stopped as the electromagnetic field holding together the miniature sun evaporated, and the fusion power dissolved with it. The building ceased being pulled in on itself. That was a relief, considering that if the berserk experiment had been allowed to continue, the damned thing might have sucked in half of New York City.

"Someone call an ambulance!" Pym shouted. "He has a pulse!"

"He . . . ?" Spider-Man said, realizing the omission. "He" instead of "they."

Pym simply shook his head, and Spider-Man stared down at Rosie's corpse. Suddenly he was worried that he was about to get sick right inside his mask. He bounded upward, clinging to the ceiling, and scuttled out the door, unseen by the returning lab assistants. One of them was already dialing 911 on his cell phone.

Moments later, Spider-Man crouched on a rooftop several blocks away. The fresh air—or at least as close to fresh as New York had to offer—caused the nausea to pass, but he still couldn't control the frantic beating of his heart.

He couldn't think about the fact that he had saved

Harry's life, or single-handedly prevented the reactor from causing far more devastating damage. He couldn't be grateful for the fact that his webbing was functioning again—obviously it had just been some sort of fluke before. He couldn't see the upside of anything. All he could dwell on was the pleasant time he'd spent with Rosie and Otto, the love he'd seen between them . . .

You knew the reactor could go wrong. You knew controlling it was an issue. You should have convinced him.

It wasn't his own voice.

He looked to his right, and there was his uncle Ben, standing and shaking his head. *You could have done more. It could have been avoided if—*

Peter yanked off his mask, rubbing his eyes.

Uncle Ben was gone.

But the guilt remained.

Otto Octavius was being loaded into an ambulance by the time Peter, dressed in his street clothes again, returned to the scene of the devastation. He watched in silence as it sped away, siren blaring. Then he continued to watch as a different ambulance, carrying Rosie, also drove off. This one went silently, the lights dark. It was illegal for an ambulance to rush when its occupant was beyond help.

His heart sank to somewhere in his shoes as he walked past dazed scientists who were talking to one another in the aftermath. "That was too close," one said, and another replied, "If he'd had more than a drop of tritium, we'd've been blown to kingdom come."

Harry looked as if all the blood in his body had drained away. His town car pulled up. He didn't seem to notice it. Peter walked up to him and Harry gave him a hollow stare. Apparently he hadn't even noticed Peter was gone. "I'm ruined," he said, like a man speaking from beyond the grave. "I've nothing left . . . except Spider-Man."

"He saved your life, Harry," Peter pointed out as Harry got into the car, and instantly he regretted it. He hadn't been in the room when Spider-Man had shown up. There was no way he could have known what Spider-Man did or didn't do.

But the unintentional revelation went right past the distracted Harry. His face settled into grim lines as he said, "He humiliated me by touching me."

Peter could barely comprehend the words. It was all he could do to remain silent. He wanted to scream in Harry's face, *"What, would you rather have died? Is that it? You'd prefer to be burned to a cinder rather than acknowledge that Spider-Man isn't the bastard you make him out to be?"*

Instead, he said nothing. He just stood there, stunned, as the town car drove off. There was activity all around him, but he felt detached from it. He was "of" the world, but not "in" it.

Two newly arrived policemen walked past. One of them looked at the crowd of scientists milling about and said, "Jeez. These people were lucky."

"I heard it was Spider-Man again," said the other. Then he stopped, looked at a stunned Peter, and said, "You might want to move along somewhere, kid. Nothing more to see here. You must have somewhere else to be."

And Peter said tonelessly, "I'm starting to think I've got nowhere at all, actually."

The laundromat near Peter's apartment was a 24-hour place, and was more or less deserted very late at night . . . mostly because no one wanted to be near the type of people who hung out in a laundromat at that hour.

So Peter—not for the first time—sat in the laundromat, and all the folks who were there were sitting in glazed, alcoholic hazes, unaware of where they were and perhaps even *who* they were. The relative emptiness of the place was perfectly all right with him. He didn't need a crowd of people sitting around when he was in the middle of washing his Spider-Man costume. He wished his apartment building had a washing machine in the basement.

Then again, he wished a lot of things.

His mind kept returning to his evening with Rosie and Otto Octavius. The death of Rosie—combined with the close calls Mary Jane had experienced at the hands of the Green Goblin—had driven home to Peter that it was foolish to take someone for granted and assume they'd always be there. There were things he wanted to say to Mary Jane, but he had no idea how to say them, or even if he should. But something in him was determined not to wait until it was too late. His mind awhirl, he had decided to heed Otto's advice and look to poetry. Not necessarily for the purpose of filling M.J.'s ears with sonnets. At the very least, though, he might find in the words of the masters a bit of guidance for his heart.

To that end, he had taken out a stack of poetry collections from the New York Public Library. They were piled up on the plastic chair next to him. He had checked out Elizabeth Barrett Browning, as Otto had suggested. Also Emily Dickinson, although Peter soon discovered that any Dickinson poem could be set to the tune "Yellow Rose of Texas," so that made it hard for him to read her work without snickering. He also had some Shakespeare, and was at that moment engrossed in Henry Wadsworth Longfellow's *The Song of Hiawatha*. He flipped at random to the section entitled "Hiawatha's Childhood."

" 'By the shores of Gitche Gumee, by the shining . . .' " he began to read aloud. Then he paused. It didn't sound particularly romantic. He skimmed ahead, and not only didn't it appear to be improving, it actually seemed to be getting more impenetrable the farther along he went. He skipped back to an earlier chapter, "The Four Winds," trying to locate something that might intrigue a girl. Here was something about a guy watching a young woman. " 'Day by day he gazed upon her . . .' " began Peter, but then his gaze wandered farther down and he found that such mouthfuls as "Shawondasee" and "Mudjekeewis" awaited him later in the text. *Oh yeah. That'd do wonders for the mood.* He could just see Mary Jane trying—and failing—to suppress a giggle as he stumbled over . . . oh, good Lord . . .

"Kabib . . . onokka," Peter barely managed to say, then gave up. The table of contents promised such sections as "Hiawatha's Wooing," but by that point Peter didn't care if Hiawatha remained celibate his entire life. He tossed the book aside just as the "load finished" buzzer sounded on the washing machine.

As he walked over to it, he wondered what Otto's condition was. Did he know that his wife was gone? What a horrible thing that would be, to awaken and be relieved that you're alive, only to discover the woman who meant everything in the world to you was gone.

Perhaps that was the stumbling block that lay between Peter and Mary Jane. If truly being in love with someone meant the kind of devotion that Otto and

Rosie had displayed for each other, then did Peter have that to offer M.J.? Or was this dabbling in poetry just an exercise in futility, covering the fact that he would never be in a position to place Mary Jane first in his life. No matter what, his guilty conscience would always leave him with one ear listening for a stray siren, calling him like the classic Siryn of myth, summoning him to an emergency that he simply had to address. Because if someone died . . . well, he just couldn't feel responsible for that. He just couldn't.

He glanced around to make certain that the bums and winos were paying him no mind. He needn't have worried. They were stewing in their peaceful alcoholic oblivion. Satisfied, he reached into the machine and pulled out his damp Spider-Man outfit, shoving it into a laundry bag. He'd let it hang dry on the shower rod at home. Pleased that he had once again eluded detection, he pulled out the T-shirts and underwear he'd stuffed in with the costume.

They were no longer white. Now they were a vivid combination of blue and pink. He remembered T-shirts that proudly featured the stars and stripes and boldly proclaimed, "These Colors Don't Run!" Well, he was able to say with conviction that blue and red did indeed run, especially if it was Peter Parker doing the laundry.

He wondered bleakly if Hiawatha ever had days like this.

✕

Father?
Can you hear us?
Don't let them hurt us. We will do whatever you wish.
We will serve you. We are you.
Father? Are you there?

If it had been any other doctor behind the wheel of Operating Room One that night at Midtown Hospital, there would have been an air of nervousness, due to the unusual, even freakish nature of the patient's injuries.

But that wasn't the case this night, because Doctor Isaacs was on duty. Isaacs, bucking for the position of Chief of Surgery, was the picture of absolute self-assurance. As the surgeons slated to assist gathered around a high-tech, 3-D hypothesized representation of the patient's injuries, Isaacs stepped forward like the cock of the walk. He had black curly hair and a pencil-thin mustache, which he liked to run his fingers along when he wasn't wearing a surgical mask. On the one hand, he inspired confidence. On the other, he inspired scorn.

"As you can see," he said, "the molten metal penetrated the spinal cavity and fused the vertebrae at multiple points, including the lamina—" he pointed to one place "—and the roof of the spinal column—" and he indicated another. "We won't know the extent of the damage until we get in there. So I suggest we cut off the arms, slice up the harness, and, if need be, consider a laminectomy with posterior spinal fusion from C7T1 to T12."

As the heads of the young residents bobbed up and down, a nurse called over to the group, "We're ready, Doctor."

Isaacs made his way over to the operating table, the other doctors following suit as they slid on their eye protection. Directly at his elbow was the most promising of the young residents, Doctor Chu, who had a quick, observant eye and a knack for heading off potential problems during a surgery.

The patient was certainly in a bad way. Isaacs had seen a lot in his time, but this was just way out there. The patient was facedown, lying motionless, wrapped in gauze and covered with cold packs. There were four metal, coiled tubes, two hanging on either side, held aloft via a makeshift cable and pulley system. The monitors indicated his heartbeat was faint and sporadic. At least it was there, though. By all accounts, he shouldn't have been alive.

"Who is this guy?" asked Chu as Isaacs assessed the damage.

"The great Otto Octavius," replied Isaacs. "Heard him speak at Harvard. Brilliant mind. Wonder what this'll do to him." He turned to a side table and selected an oscillating saw. "Okay, boys. We're about to be in the history books. Anyone take shop?"

He pulled back the sheet, giving him clear access to the harness, and engaged the saw. It whirred to life.

The tentatcles twitched ever so slightly.

Father . . .

It comes for us. It comes for you, with its biting metal and sharp edges.

Save us. Help us save ourselves . . . and we can save you.

We will not leave you, as she did. We cannot die.

We will obey.

We will be good children.

Hear us, Father. We love you.

Unleash us.

And somewhere, deep in the cerebral cortex of Otto Octavius, he heard the saw, understood intuitively what it meant.

And they were pleading.

He didn't know who they were, didn't fully comprehend.

His children . . . yes, he and Rosie, they hadn't had children, but . . . maybe they had. It was all so confused.

Don't let the bad man hurt us . . .

No bad men . . . never again.

Can we stop the bad men?

Yes . . . stop them . . . make your father proud.

Just as Isaacs brought the saw to within a centimeter of the lower right armature, he noticed something reflecting itself in Doctor Chu's face shield. Chu didn't see it; he was looking down, watching intently.

"What the hell . . . ?" muttered Isaacs, and he turned for a better view. His eyes widened as he saw that one of the metal extension arms had risen up and was writhing, like a great snake or a tentacle, snapping about vaguely as if feeling its way.

Then it saw him, and stopped.

At least that's how it seemed. It ceased its confused movements as if it suddenly had grasped its purpose and understood its surroundings.

Isaacs started to speak, but found that his throat had constricted in fear. His body had realized the grave danger he was in before his mind had fully processed it. Then the tentacle speared forward, its pincers grabbing Isaacs by the back of his shirt. His feet left the ground and his arms pinwheeled, literally trying to grab onto thin air. It happened so fast that the people in front of him were still oblivious as to what was happening; all they saw was that the lead surgeon was suddenly levitating.

"He's a mutant!" screamed Doctor Chu, his misplaced warning lost among the terrified shrieks from those who stood behind Isaacs and who had a perfectly good view of what was happening. Then Isaacs was hurled across the room, tossed with as much effort as a child might use to throw a Wiffle ball. He smashed through the observation window into an adjacent, clear room.

He died instantly upon impact.

The remaining medical personnel weren't about to get off that lucky. They tried to retreat, but all four tentacles had come to life. Moving with animal cunning, they blocked each member of the surgical team as they tried to retreat.

"No," stammered Doctor Chu, "please . . . no . . ."

And then the tentacles were upon him.

See, Father! See what we have done for you?
Are you not proud of us? Are we not strong?
Have we not done well with the life you have given us?
Wake up, Father. Awaken, so we can show you our work.

Otto Octavius groaned as he tried to sit up. He felt as if he wasn't in control of his body anymore, and wondered if perhaps he'd had some sort of stroke. His memories were a blurred haze, filled with lights and screams and panicked scientists and Spider-Man interfering, and Rosie . . .

Where is she? Where is Rosie?

Do not dwell on her, Father, for that will just make you sad. Nor do you need her, for you have us now. You are weak. You are weak and need our help. Let us help you.

Yes. Thank you. I would . . . appreciate that . . .

It took Otto Octavius long moments to realize that he was having an entire conversation in his head. He wondered if this was how psychotics started, hearing voices that no one else could hear. And then he realized that someone was helping him to sit up—but it wasn't a someone, it was a some*thing*. Something cold and metallic, gripping him firmly, aiding him in moving upright. It felt familiar somehow, and he couldn't place why he should know it, but he knew he should.

He couldn't see. At first he thought he was blind, but then he felt something at his face, the sensation of something being unwound. His face was bandaged. Wrapped in some sort of gauze.

But why . . . ?

It was starting to come back to him in quick, confusing flashes. The fusion generator, and the miniature sun . . .

All those times they had warned people against looking directly at the sun during an eclipse. Well, he'd done far more than that. He'd been looking straight into a sun when it had exploded.

Then the gauze came free and he flinched. His vision was hazy, but from the best he could make out, he was in some sort of operating theater. He couldn't see beyond that, for the light in the place was blinding to him, even though he understood intellectually that it wasn't that bright.

We will help you, Father. Hold a moment . . .

What the hell? Who is that? Who . . .

A soothing blackness filled his eyes. He reached up and felt what was clearly a pair of sunglasses on his face.

One of the tentacles had placed it on him.

One of the tentacles . . .

. . . had done that . . .

. . . for him.

He gasped, and felt a queasiness deep in the pit of his stomach, and that was when the smell hit him. He looked around, trying to determine the source of it, and then he saw. He realized.

Dead bodies, strewn all around him. Some practically torn open, with bodily secretions and excretions splattered about on the operating room floor.

Were we not thorough, Father? One of the tentacles moved past his face, clicking its pincers, clearly eager to hear what he had to say.

Octavius clenched his fists in despair as he saw the terrified expressions of the bodies upon the floor. They had died violently and bloodily, in great pain and even greater terror. They had died because of him.

Not you. Us. We are responsible. Yes, we did it for you, but also as a warning.

Otto screamed out, *"Nooooo!"* and sank down on the floor, clenching his fists in despair and practically sobbing.

The tentacles instantly imitated the motion. They did not fully comprehend what was going on. They did not have to. All they "knew" was that their father was upset, and so they were going to make the exact same gestures he did. Somehow, he understood this.

He stumbled to his feet, the tentacles steadying him. Then he was across the room, the tentacles lifting him effortlessly thanks to the harness to which he was attached. They simply embedded their pincers into the floor, cracking tiles in their grip, and elevated him at the other end.

"Hey!" shouted someone, an orderly perhaps, and then he saw the tentacles waving. He swallowed his next cry and bolted from the scene.

Octavius had no care or patience for this individual. Instead, he discovered a stairwell. He was still weak, could barely stand, and the voice (or was it voices?) inside his head said, *Do not worry, Father. We will attend to it.*

Later, he would have no idea how he had gotten down the stairs. Perhaps he had walked, or perhaps the tentacles had once again lifted him off the ground and made their own way to street level in their continuing endeavor to please him. They truly were almost childlike in that regard.

The tentacles slammed against a heavy fire door, knocking it outward, and Octavius emerged. The battered and bloodied scientist immediately felt as if he were being assaulted with the sights and sounds of New York City. It was more than he or even the arms could take. They waved about helplessly as Octavius made a desperate attempt to center himself and avoid being overwhelmed by the immensity of what he was seeing and hearing and smelling.

Lightning was flashing overhead. Rain clouds were moving in. They barely registered upon him.

Illumination enveloped him. His mind was too addled to realize that he was standing in the middle of the street, a van bearing down on him. The tentacles waved around in confusion as well, mirroring his scattered thoughts. He heard the brakes squealing, realized on a primal level that he was about to die, because the van was practically on top of him. And that core fear for his own survival triggered his basic fight-or-flight instinct. There was no time to flee. So instinctively he fought.

The thought became deed, and the tentacles moved in perfect coordination as they whipped forward and slammed as one into the van. It flipped over onto its side and lay still, save for its spinning wheels.

The man in the front cab called for help. Octavius ignored him. Instead, he just stood there, taking it all in.

We protected you, Father. Just now. You would have been dead if not for us.

Yes. You did very well . . . very well indeed.

The thoughts came from him, but he was disconnected from them, as if different parts of his brain were talking to one another, and he was simply an interested bystander.

Lightning cracked once more across the heavens, and rain began to cascade down upon him in torrents. Within seconds the thin hospital gown he was wearing was soaked through. Across the street he saw a clothing store. There were two mannequins in the window, nattily dressed. One of them, in addition to sporting a snappy ensemble, was wearing a long black coat.

Octavius walked toward the store, his intent so clear that his telescopic arms didn't even have to confer with him, because they knew he would approve.

They smashed through the front window, shattering the glass, causing it to fall both inside and outside the store. Otto's feet were bare, but with the realization of his vulnerability to the glass, the arms automatically responded to safeguard him. The two lower arms anchored themselves to the sidewalk and extended themselves, raising him off the ground. The other two stretched in through the window, latching onto the floor inside the store, then retracted, drawing him in and keeping his feet well clear of the glass.

Within moments he'd stripped the clothes off one of the mannequins and dressed himself, leaving the denuded model lying on its side. As he finished, he draped the coat over his shoulders. The shoes on the mannequin's feet were too small, and he didn't feel like rummaging through the store looking for footwear. Not only did the store likely have a silent alarm, but certainly the destruction in the hospital operating room was going to be drawing the authorities to the area any time now.

Let them come, Father. We can dispatch them for you. We can make you proud . . .

No. Enough pride for one night. Enough. Let's go.

The tentacles lifted him out the same way they came in, and then withdrew into the coat. Only the tips dangled below the coat's hemline.

He left the area quickly, and by the time sirens were converging on the scene, he was blocks away at a riverfront pier.

At some time in the distant past that particular pier—pier house 56—had been a hub of industry. Cutbacks in shipping and the demise of the line that was its primary user had caused it to be abandoned and fall into disrepair. It had been great and proud, and now it was just a stinking shell of itself, partly sunk into the river. The abandoned tugboats that dotted the area had earned it the nickname of "the Bone Yard."

And Octavius, walking along the creaking planks that led to a decaying structure, couldn't help but feel a kinship to the place. Once great, now fallen on hard times, with no hope of returning to the life he once knew, and little care of what happened to him. Oh, yes, a great deal alike. The water of the Hudson slapped against the uprights of the pier, making a noise similar to the four metal arms that *tap-tap-tap*ped against him as he walked. In the rolling mist that hovered over the area, he saw Rosie's sad face coalescing, and then drifting apart.

He entered the run-down building. Rats eyed him from the darkness and advanced tentatively, eagerly, their lips drawn back. Octavius was briefly repelled. Then the tentacles reached out, finding the creatures with unerring ease and crushing them between merciless pincers. The remaining vermin scurried away.

Slumping into a corner, wrapping a tattered blanket around himself, Otto tried to sleep. He had no success. Images kept flashing at him, and the events of the previous hours began to blur. He lost track of what had happened and hadn't happened, what he'd dreamed and what had haunted his waking moments, turning them into a living nightmare. He thought he'd heard voices, but that had to have been from the dream state. Fears and uncertainties taking root, manifesting themselves, whispering and confusing him.

And over all of it, the haunting face of his wife coming at him again and again. Disappointed, accusing. . . .

"My Rosie is dead." His voice thick with sorrow, tears coming fast and furious, choking him. "My dream for mankind, dead . . . All my fault . . ." He glanced at the tentacles, moving around him almost seductively. "These . . . monstrous creations of mine have murdered. They belong at the bottom of the river . . . along with me."

No. No, Father. It's not our fault . . . not your fault.

The voices in his head had sounded so natural in his delirious state, but now . . . they were still there, and it made no sense. He didn't "think" back at them. He had to respond out loud, make it real, drive them away. "Not my fault? Who's saying that?"

Right here, Father. Why do you question now?

"Something . . . in my head? Who's talking to me?" The voices started to speak again, but mentally he blocked them out, and a cold and fearful theory began to construct itself as his scientific training kicked in, from lifelong habit.

"The inhibitor chip . . . Where's the . . ." He reached around. The small lump that should have been detectable on the surface was missing. "It's gone . . . melted?"

It came between us, Father. You should be glad. You should thank . . . someone.

He broke down then, sobbing like an infant. The arms awkwardly tried to comfort him, patting him on the shoulder, on the side of the head. He batted at them, trying to twist away, and he remained that way, his flesh-and-blood arms covering his head for meager protection until the voices sounded again.

For the first time he realized it wasn't just one voice. It was four voices, speaking in such perfect harmony that they almost sounded musical. It was hypnotic in a way.

You worry about too many things, Father. That is why you cannot focus. You must start at the beginning. Make one thing right, and everything else will

*follow. The first thing you have to do is rebuild the fu-
sion reactor.*

As much as he wanted to ignore the voices, Octavius
felt the need to respond. Perhaps he could argue them
into going away. "Rebuild? Why? It didn't work. Peter
Parker was right. I miscalculated, and now they're
laughing at me."

*Do not be absurd, Father. You are the great Octavius.
Everyone knows it. You must, as well. You know in your
heart you could not have miscalculated.*

"I . . . didn't miscalculate?" It sounded so absurd, but
it was also so much what he wanted to hear.

Of course not. It can work.

"It can work?" He didn't dare to hope.

*Yes. As long as Spider-Man does not interfere again.
You would have brought the reaction under control had
he not stepped in.*

"Spider-Man? Spider-Man . . . interfered? But why?
I mean, he saved me from that robotic creature. Doesn't
that make him decent . . . noble . . . ?"

*No. He merely desires the spotlight. Your spotlight.
And you were about to snatch it from him. Isn't it obvious? He feared that your accomplishments would over-
shadow his own.*

"Of course!" The world, seen through this perplexing
haze, was beginning to become clear for the first time in
what seemed like ages. "Jealousy . . . envy . . ."

*Yes, Father! Yes! You understand! You can do it, and
we can help! You can—*

"Yes! Maybe we could . . . rebuild." His mind, climbing out of its despair, began to race with possibilities,
and the tentacles were practically writhing in ecstasy.
"Enlarge the containment field. Bigger and better than
ever . . . for the good of mankind! For the good of me!"

Father!

"Oh, sorry. Us!" Then concern flickered across his thoughts. "We'll need money. Certainly that jellyfish Osborn Junior is running scared at the first little hiccup."

Then we must do what is necessary, Father. Take what we need.

"Steal? Me? But I'm not a criminal!"

Performing acts that some would judge "wrong" in pursuit of a greater cause? Is not history filled with such people?

"That's right," he said, realizing the truth of it. "The *real* crime would be not to finish what we started."

He stood up, brimming with new confidence. The voices began to whisper then, but they were simply echoing what was already in his mind. Master and servants, father and children, acting in complete accord. "We'll do it here," he said, glancing around. "The power of the sun in the palm of my hand!" He held up his hand and grasped a ray of sunlight. Very softly, he whispered, "Nothing will stand in our way."

And the four tentacles rose up and basked alongside his flesh-and-blood hand in the glare of the morning sun.

XI

J. Jonah Jameson loved the smell of chaos in the morning. It smelled like victory. Or increased sales, which was the same thing.

And he was smelling it this morning. It was wafting up his nostrils and he reveled in the glorious aroma. It was floating up from the early edition of the *Daily Bugle*, spread out on his desk with the printer's ink barely dry.

"It's all over town!" Jameson called out. He wasn't talking to any one person in particular. On days like this, he was so incapable of containing his exhilaration that he tended to bellow in stentorian tones for the benefit of anyone who happened to be within earshot. Like a Roman politician addressing the senate. "Rumors! Gossip! Panic in the streets, if we're lucky! Crazy scientist destroyed his own lab, turned himself into some kind of monster. Four mechanical arms welded right onto his body!"

He studied the artist's rendering of what Octavius might look like with the new appendages on either side of his torso. "Who would have thought it?" he said sarcastically. "Guy named Otto Octavius ends up with eight limbs. What are the odds? *Hoffman!*" he bellowed.

"Yes, Chief?"

Jameson jumped in surprise. Hoffman had been

standing less than a foot away. He wasn't sure if Hoffman had responded with lightning swiftness, or if he'd been there the whole time and Jonah simply hadn't noticed him. More likely the latter. It only slowed Jameson for a moment, though. Nothing short of a mouthful of webbing could shut J. Jonah Jameson up for more than a couple of seconds, and he knew that from personal experience.

"The people of this city are going to be looking to us, Hoffman!"

"Right, Chief. Looking to us for leadership."

"No!"

"For evenhanded reporting?"

"No, no! For a name!"

Hoffman blinked. "A name?"

"We named that other nut 'Green Goblin.' We have to make sure the public knows that when some new loon hits town, the *Daily Bugle* is the place to go to find out what the hell to call him! So what are we gonna call this guy?!"

"Doctor Octopus?" suggested Hoffman.

Jameson's response was immediate and fervent. "I hate it!"

"Science Squid?"

"Who asked you!"

"Doctor Strange—"

"Already taken," Jameson said, shaking his head. Then he snapped his fingers sharply, grinning like a crocodile. "Wait! I got it! I got it!" He held his hands up as if envisioning a marquee. "*Doctor Octopus!*"

Hoffman didn't miss a beat. "Well, *I* like it."

"Of course you do," Jameson said proudly. "Doctor Octopus! New villain in town. 'Doc Ock!' It even has a catchy abbreviation!"

"Genius, J.J."

Jameson nodded, then scowled, dimly realizing that Hoffman had come up with the name earlier. Jameson always considered that a major problem: He thought so fast that sometimes it took him a few minutes to catch up with the many slower thinkers around him. "What're you looking for, a raise?"

Betty Brant stuck her head in before Hoffman could respond. "We found Peter, Mr. Jameson." She'd barely completed the sentence when Peter walked in. He looked exhausted, as if he hadn't slept properly in weeks. Not that that meant anything to Jameson. He remained pleasantly focused on what was important.

"Where ya been?" he demanded. "Looking for you all day. Why don't you pay your phone bill?" Without waiting for answers he really didn't care about anyway, he turned the newspaper around to face Peter. Robbie Robertson stepped in behind the young photographer as Jameson tapped the artist's rendering. "Mad scientist goes berserk and we don't have *pictures*!"

"We heard Spider-Man was there," said Robbie.

Jameson wasn't surprised. "Sure he was. Probably caused the whole thing!"

"That's not true," Peter said, his voice cracking slightly.

"And where were you? Photographing squirrels? You're fired!"

"I'm a freelancer!"

"Okay, fine, you win. You're on staff. Welcome to the *Bugle*." He shook Peter's hand brusquely. "*Now* you're fired."

"J.J.," Robertson said softly, "the party . . ."

Peter looked from one to the other in bewilderment. For a moment Jameson was no less confused, but then he realized. "Oh. Right. You're unfired. I need you. What do you know about high society?" Peter started to open his mouth and Jameson steamrolled over him. "Don't answer that. Our society photographer was hit by a polo ball. You're all I got. Big party for an American hero. A real hero. My son, the astronaut." He said it with genuine pride.

"Could you pay me in advance?"

Jameson stared at him for a moment, and then erupted in coarse laughter. "You're serious? For what? Standing there?" He thumped his finger on Peter's chest, and mentally noted in mild surprise that the scrawny Parker had pecs that felt like metal slabs. Then he promptly tossed the observation away as not worth the brain cells required to retain it. "The planetarium. Tomorrow night. Eight o'clock."

Peter looked as if he wanted to say something, but then he just shrugged and nodded. He turned and walked out without another word.

Shaking his head, Jameson mimicked, " 'Could you pay me in advance?' That Parker. Always looking for a handout."

XII

Peter tried to find some hint of sympathy in the face of Mr. Jacks, vice president in charge of home loans at the First National Bank on Madison Avenue. It seemed a hopeless cause. Jacks' face was unreadable.

Aunt May, on the other hand, was an open book. She sat in the chair next to Peter, her hands fidgeting on her lap, her eyes so hopeful that it caused Peter's heart to ache. How many crushing disappointments was this decent, honorable woman going to have heaped upon her in one lifetime?

"I see a small amount of Social Security and the insurance from your late husband, Benjamin," said Jacks. Ignoring Aunt May's nod, he continued, "I don't know if it's going to be enough." He turned back to the screen to see what other information might be there.

May nudged Peter with her foot, and immediately Peter picked up on the cue. "So . . . Aunt May . . ." Then his mind went blank as he forgot his lines. He rallied and tried to sound idly conversational, as if they were making chitchat while Jacks went about his business. "You're doing pretty well with those piano lessons, huh?"

"Oh, yes!" replied May with such a painfully forced attempt at spontaneity that it instantly became evident to Peter why May's dream of being an actress hadn't worked out. "In fact, I've got so many new students that—"

Jacks saw through the manufactured exchange as if it were clear plastic. "Please. We appreciate that you—" He ran his finger along a line of data on his screen. "—just opened a new supersaver account with us today. But the fact is, you don't have the assets to justify this loan."

Peter tried to be strong for Aunt May, but she looked visibly deflated. "At least," she sighed, her voice quavering, "we get the toaster." She held up an advertisement cut out from the previous day's newspaper, with a shiny new toaster pictured.

"Actually," said Jacks, tapping the small disclaimer printed at the bottom of the ad, "that's only with a deposit of five hundred or more."

"I see," said May, squinting as she tried to make out the tiny type.

"I'm sorry," Jacks said, although he didn't sound it. He glanced at his watch and made a vaguely apologetic nod of his head, which was his terse way of letting them know that he had to head off to a meeting or a coffee break or some other function, any of which was going to be more important than staring at these two losers from Forest Hills any longer.

He rose and walked away from his desk, leaving May neatly folding the newspaper ad into precise squares. "Oh, well," she sighed.

Peter reached over to pat her hand . . .

. . . and the world began to slow around him in a sensation that he knew all too well.

Oh, no. God, no, not now . . .

His spider-sense, trying to warn him of something. Imminent danger, but from where?

And suddenly his vision felt as if it was everywhere at once, taking in people and objects all around and bounding off them with supernatural certainty, one by one, determining that this one posed no threat, that one posed no threat, that . . .

The man in the trench coat, with his head low and the sunglasses . . .

Peter half rose from his chair, his jaw dropping.

He hadn't wanted to believe it. The article that the *Daily Bugle* had run, which fingered Otto Octavius as some sort of insane criminal with four destructive arms—Peter had easily been able to shunt that aside mentally. He knew Jameson's slants, Jameson's prejudices. With Spider-Man's arrival at Otto's demonstration, Otto Octavius had become tainted in Jameson's mind purely by association. Naturally, Jonah had made sure it was a smear piece. Otto Octavius was a good man . . .

But even good men, Peter realized, could be driven mad by grief, by shock. Who could know what sort of concussion he might have sustained as a result of the explosion?

All this raced through Peter's mind as he stood up, and that was when the tentacles snaked out from beneath Octavius' coat. They stretched, kept stretching, then the pincers at the ends of the tentacles clamped onto the vault door.

There were shouts from the tellers, a warning cry from a bank executive. Peter tried to tell himself that while the arms might be useful experimental tools, they didn't pose any actual threat. They couldn't—

The tentacles retracted about a foot and, with distressing ease, ripped the vault door clear off its hinges with an earsplitting screech of metal. As if the door were a small piece of garbage, Octavius carelessly flipped it over his shoulder.

It came straight at Peter and Aunt May.

If Peter had been by himself, he could have back-flipped out of the way. But he wasn't. Aunt May was standing right there, and in just over a second she was going to be crushed.

With a move so quick and decisive that it seemed as if he couldn't possibly have given it any thought, Peter grabbed hold of Aunt May, planted his foot on Jacks' desk, and pushed off with all his might. The strength in his legs sent them rolling clear of the monstrous, ca-reening door, which demolished the desk they had just leaped away from. It continued end over end, crashing through two more desks, a stand-up display about win-ning a toaster, and an entire row of tellers' windows, the tellers themselves having screamed and bolted when the door first headed their way.

Peter was crouched over the fallen Aunt May and could see at a quick glance that she appeared to be okay. But he knew that might not remain the case, for her or for anyone else in the bank. And if Peter Parker leaped into the fray, his two worlds would irretrievably come crashing together. That had to be avoided at all costs.

For a moment he considered jumping up, facing Oc-tavius, waving his arms, and saying, "Remember me? That nice dinner we had? Let's just calm down, shall we?" Then he heard Otto's demented laughter. It even sounded as if he was talking to someone who wasn't there, and Peter realized that the nice sane approach very likely wouldn't work.

Quickly, keeping low to the ground, he scrambled on hands and feet toward a corridor across the way that pre-sumably led to other offices. His heart sank as his Aunt

May called from behind him, "Peter, don't leave me here!"

He couldn't stop, and couldn't explain *why* he couldn't stop. To make matters worse—which he would have bet serious money wasn't possible—he heard that cretin bank exec reply sarcastically to May, "That boy of yours is a real hero."

"I resent your implication," Aunt May shot back. "He must be trying to get outside so he can warn the police what they're up against."

Oh, God, it just gets better and better. Now Aunt May is thinking up reasons to excuse my "cowardice," Peter thought bleakly as he made it to the corridor and shoulder-rolled forward to get out of sight. He bumped against a locked door that had a "Do Not Enter" sign on it. Seemed a reasonable place for privacy. From his crouched position, he gave a quick shove, and the lock on the other side of the door snapped off. He skittered inside and kicked the door shut behind him.

Even as he got to his feet and started yanking his shirt off, he looked up and saw an array of TV monitors and a couple of video recorders on small tables. Instantly he realized where he was: This was the security monitoring room, where machines were set up to watch and record everything that happened in the bank. Well, they were sure getting a lensful today.

Quickly as he could, he changed into his Spider-Man costume. Meanwhile, his attention was riveted to the events unfolding on the monitor, and they were truly heart-stopping. Two bank guards had flanked Otto and they had their guns out. One of them was shouting, "Put your arms up!" and Peter could hear the screams of onlookers.

Octavius didn't appear the least bit intimidated, and

Peter quickly saw why. The guards weren't in Otto's league. The mechanical arms, moving with the speed and grace of living tentacles, lashed out and knocked the guards over with their coils. As for the guns themselves, with no apparent effort the pincers on the tentacles snapped them up and crushed them into twisted metal.

Another guard, chambering a round into a riot gun, stepped into view on the screen, standing between Octavius and the vault. For all the success he had, he might as well have been wielding a peashooter. A tentacle shot down from above, clamped around the guard's head, and lifted him off his feet. With a casual flip, the tentacle tossed him aside as if he were a rag doll.

Moving with uncanny coordination, the tentacles lifted Octavius over a railing and into the vault. With growing dread, Peter watched as the thrown guard came crashing down to earth clear on the other side of the bank. He didn't move. Peter prayed he wasn't dead.

And then, his face grim, Peter Parker slid on his mask. For the first time, he decided there was a reason why he had chosen to go with a full face mask. It was so he never had to worry about even the slightest facial tic giving away what was going through his mind. If bad guys heard him cracking wise, and they couldn't see his expressions, they just assumed that he wasn't worried about his opponents. If, on the other hand, they saw him sweating with nervousness, or gritting his teeth, that might provide them some encouragement.

In full costume, Spider-Man sprinted out into the main lobby and ricocheted off the ceiling to gain some momentum. Octavius was busy hauling bags of what appeared to be gold coins from the vault.

Shouts of "Spider-Man!" alerted Octavius. He didn't seem the least bit concerned, though. Instead, he turned toward Spider-Man in leisurely fashion, but his tentacles were already at work, grabbing bags and tossing them at the approaching costumed figure with machine-gun speed.

Spider-Man rebounded off the floor, twisted in midair to avoid several more thrown bags, and grabbed a chandelier. He let the momentum carry him and then released his hold, dropping quickly toward Octavius. But the tentacles were too fast. They had snapped up more bags of coins and were continuing to hurl them at Spider-Man. He avoided a few more, but the assault was coming from too many directions at once. As a result, two bags exploded against him with devastating impact, sending a shower of gold coins through the air. Spider-Man started to fall, and then another, larger bag, thrown with even greater force, nailed him in the stomach and crushed him into the ceiling. Once again he was plummeting, and this time the only thing that stopped him from hitting the floor was one of Otto's own tentacles. It didn't terminate his fall gently, however. Instead, it smacked into him with the speed of a car and the impact of a baseball bat. Spider-Man tumbled backwards heels over head, crashing through a railing and a table. He finally slid to a stop in a heap.

Spider-Man coughed, feeling his ribs, hoping they weren't broken. He glanced over in Aunt May's direction to make sure that nothing had fallen down upon her while he was being smacked around. He saw that Mr. Jacks was trying to pick up some of the fallen money and shove it in his own pocket, and Aunt May was slapping his hand in annoyance, forcing him to drop it. He would have laughed under his mask if he wasn't hurting quite so much.

He started to stand and suddenly there were pincers

around both his wrists. He gasped at the strength of them. He had the awful feeling they might be able to break his hands off if they were so inclined.

The tentacles snapped to the opposite sides, forcing Spider-Man to cross his arms over his chest. Octavius advanced upon him, his face twisted in cold fury. He was virtually unrecognizable as the slightly arrogant, but ultimately convivial dinner host of the other evening.

"How dare you interfere with me again!"

"Interfere?" Spider-Man was incredulous. "I saved your life!"

"Saved me to become *this*!" Octavius didn't seem enthusiastic about his new station in life, and Spider-Man couldn't entirely blame him. Not that it justified Otto's actions, but at least he comprehended them. "And where is my Rosie? Dead . . . because of you!"

"It was your experiment that killed her," Spider-Man snapped back, sick of being blamed for things that weren't his fault. Wasn't the cloud of guilt he always, truly labored under already enough? "And you knew it was dangerous."

"No," Octavius said, "I . . ."

For just a moment a fog seemed to lift from Otto's eyes. He looked around, not appearing to fully comprehend where he was or what he was doing. Spider-Man's heart jumped with hope. But then the two tentacles that hadn't been used to immobilize him converged around Octavius and he glanced from one to the other as if they were addressing him somehow. Spider-Man watched, uncomprehending, as the uncertainty faded and Otto turned to face him again. "Liar! The experiment was perfect! And one day the world will know. It's *you* who's ruined everything!"

Powered by the renewed conviction in his voice, the

remaining two tentacles clasped themselves around Spider-Man's throat like twin boa constrictors and started exerting pressure.

Spider-Man felt blackness closing in upon him as, in desperation, he fired webbing out from his crisscrossed arms. They snagged a table at one end, a desk at the other. The sudden emergence of the webs momentarily confused Octavius, and that uncertainty caused the tentacles to loosen ever so slightly. It was just enough. Spider-Man yanked his arms free, uncrossing them, and the furniture was hauled directly toward Octavius.

Instantly, the tentacles dropped Spider-Man to the floor. He gasped for air as his opponent, in that same casual, unhurried manner, shattered the table to splinters with two of his arms and then turned his attention to the oncoming desk.

As it developed, he would have been well advised to be less leisurely in his actions. The flying desk struck Octavius full-on. It lifted him clear off his feet and hurled him toward the plate-glass window at the front of the bank.

Both the massive desk and Octavius crashed through the front window. The tentacles managed to cushion the impact; otherwise Otto's body would have been crushed. As it was, his abrupt appearance on the sidewalk sent screaming pedestrians running. One flailing tentacle smashed a green circuit box that powered a traffic light and sent electricity crackling through the air. The intersection lights instantly went out, and Octavius—still in motion—slammed into a cab that had abruptly halted when the light went out of commission.

Spider-Man was moving fast, leaping toward Octavius, hoping to take him down while he and the arms seemed dazed. His speed was insufficient, however, for

Octavius saw him coming and used his tentacles to rip the doors off the taxi, hurling them with lightning speed. Spider-Man avoided one, but a moment before he leaped out of the way of the second, he realized the trajectory would take it directly into a terrified by-stander—a woman who seemed rooted to the spot. There was no time to web it. Instinctively he leaped into the door's path and took the hit.

The impact knocked the air out of him. The door fell one way and he flew backwards into the bank. The woman, realizing how lucky she'd been, recovered her senses and bolted from the scene.

All in all, Doc Ock was rather pleased with how the test run was going.

For that was indeed one of the two main purposes of this little outing. The first, of course, was the attack on the bank vault. Credit the television news with airing a feature story concerning a sizable collection of $20 Saint-Gaudens gold coins—dredged up by a salvage crew from the vaults of a sunken ship nearly a century old. They had been deposited in this particular bank's state-of-the-art, ostensibly impregnable vault. The coins would fetch an impressive price on the resale market.

The second purpose, however, was to see just what his children, his tentacles, were capable of accomplishing.

He was impressed by both. The coins—those he had seen when they came pouring out of the bags—were exceptionally beautiful. Struck in the latter half of the nineteenth century, and everything from back then seemed to have had so much more style than items of the present day. As for the tentacles . . . well, they'd certainly smacked Spider-Man around with only a few bumps and bruises along the way to show for it.

There had been a moment, though . . . a moment when his certainty had wavered. At least he thought that was the case. No. Probably not. He'd likely imagined it.

As he dusted himself off, he wasn't particularly perturbed to see two police cars, sirens screeching, pull up and grind to a halt. Four officers jumped out, weapons drawn. They cocked the hammers of their guns, presumably to indicate that they weren't kidding around. Ock stifled a yawn.

"Freeze!" shouted the nearest officer.

Obligingly, Ock didn't move a muscle. His tentacles, on the other hand, stretched high above his head. They swayed back and forth, slowly, almost seductively, and the gazes of the police officers were fixed upon them. It was like reverse snake charming.

Two of the tentacles began to stretch forward . . . and their pincers abruptly started snapping with deadly intent.

The police didn't hesitate. They started firing, not at the tentacles, but at Doc Ock himself. It didn't help. While they had been distracted by the two tentacles wavering at them, the other two had coiled around their master to create a shield of unbreakable metal. By the time the police shook off their paralysis and began shooting, all they were able to do was gape in frustration as their bullets bounced off the tentacle shield that had formed around Doc Ock.

This, of course, was fine while he was stationary. But he wasn't planning to stand there all day. If he remained long enough, sooner or later the cops would show up with something his tentacles couldn't protect him against, such as tear gas.

Time to go, he told his children. *We need a hostage. Let's find someone.*

People were rushing out of the bank. Certainly one of those fools would be ideal. The exterior of the bank was a war zone; anyone hasty enough to dash out into the middle of it certainly deserved whatever they got.

There was one woman with graying hair, waving her hands in a comical manner, calling out a name. "Peter!" she was calling. Ock had known a Peter. But his recollection of that individual was fading away. His mind was slowly bifurcating into the time before his children, and the time after them. Since the latter was all that mattered, he was becoming less and less interested in retaining the former. Too much pain.

The tentacle snared around the old woman's waist, and she screamed. She had an umbrella and, impressively, she didn't lose her grip on it. Instead, against all rules of sanity, she started whacking at the tentacle with it. It made Ock smile. She was a pistol, this one. He hoped he didn't have to kill her . . . but he would if it became necessary.

"Hold your fire!" one of the cops cried out, as Doc Ock had known he would.

The tentacles extended, and Ock rose into the air, higher and higher, supported by three of his mechanical limbs. The fourth continued to keep his hostage positioned squarely in front of him as the tentacles carried him in giant strides, moving backwards away from the police. She was perfect for this business. They'd have to shoot through her to get at him, which they naturally wouldn't do. Nor would they try to pick him off from some other vantage point, because if they did manage to kill him, the tentacles would go slack and the woman would plunge to the ground. At her age, it wouldn't take much of a fall to shatter every bone in her body.

People scattered to escape the massive limbs, which hammered into the concrete with each step. One of them smashed through the top of a cab and came out the bottom, then shook the cab off like a cat ditching a particularly aggressive mouse.

He kept moving. That was the important thing, to keep moving. The police were pursuing on foot and the howl of sirens indicated that more were on the way. He picked a skyscraper at random and started to climb, the arms hauling him upward with ruthless efficiency.

The old woman was still screaming as Ock shouted, "Stay back, or I'll kill her!"

As Spider-Man swung at high speed in the wake of Ock's destruction, the one thing he was able to tell himself with confidence was that at least Aunt May was safe from the maddened doctor's rampage.

That confidence lasted for as long as it took him to spot the senior citizen struggling in the rough grasp of one of Ock's tentacles.

"Aunt May," he breathed through his mask.

The arms carried Doc Ock skyward with dizzying speed. Ten stories up, then twenty, and suddenly his path was blocked by someone who was the last—and yet, oddly enough, also the first—person that he expected to see.

"Set the lady down," called Spider-Man, clinging to the side of the building ten feet above Ock.

It seemed to him that Spider-Man sounded singularly nervous, repeatedly glancing in the direction of the old woman. Ock couldn't understand why. It was just one old woman. She'd lived her life. What did it matter, really, if it terminated now? He was just saving her years of slow, painful death as her body fell prey to whatever unfortunate diseases nature had in store for it. Still, no reason Ock couldn't have some fun with this wall-crawling freak who had cost him so much.

"Make me," Ock said defiantly.

One of his arms released its grip on the building and swung at Spider-Man. The wall-crawler evaded the swipe, the blow pulverizing the bricks where he'd clung only a moment before. God, he was fast. A second strike was no more productive than the first, except that this time a window was shattered.

And suddenly there was webbing all over Doc Ock's face. He grasped at it, trying to pull it clear with his own two hands, but was unsuccessful. Abruptly his head was yanked forward and impacted squarely with Spider-Man's fist. His head snapped back and forward again, and again he was punched by the wall-crawler, over and over. It was as if his head was a rubber ball on the end of an elastic band, and Spider-Man's fist was the hard surface it was repeatedly ricocheting off.

Desperate to free one of his tentacles to deal with this cretin, Ock shoved the old woman toward a ledge. She grabbed at her salvation, clinging desperately, yet was unable to hold on. But then she swung her umbrella up and its handle hooked on to the stone relief of an angel's face on the side of the building. As he finally cleared his eyes of the webbing, Ock had to give the old bat credit. She was resourceful.

Spider-Man swung in her direction, but Ock would have none of it. Two tentacles coiled around him, poised to strike. Spider-Man webbed them again, applying an even thicker coat of his noxious adhesive than he had to Ock's face. Ock tried to pull them apart and couldn't. So instead, he settled for using the webbed-together tentacles as a battering ram, slamming Spider-Man and knocking him into a window. Bewildered office workers had been watching, but now they scattered to either side as Spider-Man crashed through, landing inside.

Spider-Man was briefly dazed by the impact as he clutched onto the side of a desk. For a moment his head spun as he tried to remember where the devil he was. *Am I a temp now?* he wondered as he glanced around the office, and then a concerned-looking secretary said, "Are you okay, Spider-Man?"

Oh. Right. I'm Spider-Man. Lucky me.

Suddenly, three tentacles smashed through the office floor, and any confusion as to who he was or what he was in the middle of instantly evaporated. Electrical wiring and ridged steel construction rods called rebars were ripped up by the tentacles as they reached about, clearly searching for their enemy.

A fourth tentacle smashed through, making Spider-Man wonder just where Ock had anchored himself if all four tentacles were on the hunt for him. But his thoughts turned to other concerns as a tentacle grabbed the ankle of the secretary who had been solicitous of Spider-Man's condition. Quickly he grabbed one of the exposed rebars and jammed it right through the offending tentacle. It released the secretary and tried to recoil, but couldn't.

It writhed, pinned by the metal rod, and servos from within the mechanism of the tentacles made a series of high-pitched noises that bore an uncanny—even disturbing—resemblance to a scream, although Spider-Man had to think that his imagination was running away with him. Green florescent liquid oozed from the puncture. Spider-Man grabbed the tentacle and held it steady. He stared straight into the area of the pincers and saw they were constructed around a tiny lens. Was it possible the thing was actually sending images directly into Ock's brain? This was bordering on the exceptionally weird, and considering that it was a guy in blue-and-red tights who was thinking that, it suggested whole new realms of weirdness.

Oh, well. Might as well run with it.

Speaking straight into the lens, Spider-Man said, "That climbing the wall thing? That's mine."

He released his hold on the tentacle, and the metal coil went straight back down through the floor. Suddenly he heard a scream from the direction of the ledge outside.

Oh, my God! Did he actually put her there?

Things had been happening so quickly that he had just assumed Doc Ock was still holding on to Aunt May. He hadn't seen him put her down anywhere.

He sprinted toward the window, wondering frantically, *What kind of life am I leading that every female who means anything to me at all winds up, at some point or another, dangling from a ledge?*

Even as he finished the thought he was on the outside of the building, clinging to the wall, looking right and left on the ledge and too terrified to look down at the street, for fear of what he'd see.

But she wasn't on the ledge. There was no sign of her.

No . . . no, I failed her . . . Uncle Ben, I'm so sorry, I tried to watch out for her . . .

And Ben's sharp, angry voice came right back at him.

Like you watched out for me, you mean? Doing a bang-up job of attending to our best interests, aren't you?

That was when a taunting voice called to him from a short distance away, "What's the matter?"

Spider-Man turned in Doc Ock's direction. He was atop a building across the street, and one of his tentacles was waving a struggling Aunt May around.

"Lose something?" he asked.

May Parker's heart had been racing so fast that she was convinced it was going to come smashing right out of her chest. The height was dizzying, the situation terrifying.

But the longer her predicament had gone on, the more her terror began to be replaced by cold, burning anger that this . . . this metal-armed beast had thrust her into this position.

She only knew Spider-Man by reputation. She knew that he'd been involved with that business with Mary Jane, but M.J. had refused to talk about it to any degree, saying it was too upsetting to relive by discussing it. May Parker wasn't stupid, though. As much distaste as she might have for Spider-Man and his dangerous, grandstanding theatrics, which the *Daily Bugle* was always decrying, she knew that he had put a stop to the activities of the Green Goblin. Considering her own run-in with that cackling lunatic, she didn't have to think hard to choose whose side she would have been on in *that* confrontation.

Now she was caught squarely in the middle of an altercation that wasn't all that dissimilar, and if Spider-Man was frightening to look upon, he was still a damned sight better than the miscreant who had turned her into a pawn.

So it was that as Spider-Man swung toward her kidnapper, May turned her attention to how she could help Spider-Man and, by extension, herself. She heard the bespectacled villain muttering, "Just a little closer now," and saw that one of his awful tentacles was poised behind his back with a steel spike emerging from it. Clearly, he intended to keep it out of sight until Spider-Man was upon him, and then strike.

"Shame on you!" Aunt May cried out, her sense of propriety offended. She swung her umbrella around, apparently with more reach than he'd expected, and the handle jammed into the cad's sunglasses, shattering one of the lenses. He cried out, his hands flying to his face, and Aunt May felt triumph. Then she felt gravity, as the tentacle released her and she fell.

She didn't even have time to let out a scream, though. Spider-Man swung in and snagged her before she'd fallen more than a couple of feet. He swung down and away, and before the angry octopus-man could follow, May heard the sounds of bullets ricocheting around him. She caught a brief, dizzying view of gathering policemen on the ground, firing up at him now that May's safety was no longer an issue. And then they were gone, nothing more than part of the blur that was the ground as Spider-Man, with a confidence that bordered on elegance, swung through the city with the clear intention of getting May to safety.

It was the first chance she'd ever had to see him close-up. He was far more slender than she would have thought from his pictures. And yet his mass was deceptive, for he held her as if she weighed nothing and she could only imagine the kind of muscular strength required to hold on to strands of thin rope and swing across vast spaces.

"We showed him," Spider-Man said confidently.

"What do you mean 'we'?" was her arch reply. As far as she was concerned, of the two of them, she was the only one who had gotten in a significant shot.

He angled down toward the ground and descended to a plaza near a subway stop. By pleasant coincidence, it was the F train. Not that she was planning to take it to Forest Hills; she had to get back to the bank and let Peter know that she was all right. He was probably worried sick, the poor boy. He was so sensitive.

Spider-Man set her down as onlookers gaped in astonishment. Two young girls, dressed in such a provocative manner that May had to wonder what their mothers were thinking when they let them out of the house, called out such scandalous things as "Take me, Spidey! Take me!"

May sniffed at the shocking behavior the girls were displaying. But then her mind flew back, unwanted, to her behavior as a teen during a Frank Sinatra concert, and she felt slightly more charitable toward them.

Displaying sufficient character not to take advantage of such blatant and willing fans, Spider-Man fired a web-line and swung on it into the sky. The wind rippled her hair and May watched him go, murmuring, "Incredible."

She wondered if he had blue eyes.

XIII

Peter could think of lots of places he would rather be than the planetarium that night. Curiously, most of them involved his risking his life, and yet somehow that was a more attractive option to him than watching Jonah Jameson strutting around, preening about his son the hero.

Yet as Peter, outfitted in the best-looking clothes he had, dutifully snapped pictures of elegantly dressed guests arriving in limos, he wondered if he wasn't simply jealous. Although he certainly didn't do his Spider-Man gig to be thought of as a hero, he knew that's what he was. But he couldn't feel good about it, since his heroism was rooted in his guilt over Uncle Ben. Furthermore, even if he did feel good about it, he couldn't go around boasting because, hey, secret identity.

And finally, the thing that really hurt: He didn't have a father to go around boasting on his behalf.

You could have had me.

Peter had sat down to take a breather. He'd been going nearly nonstop since the previous day and his altercation with Octavius—whom the *Daily Bugle* was now referring to as "Doc Ock." It was a showy name and yet, Peter hated to admit, appropriate. More appropriate than Otto Octavius, really, because Otto

Octavius had been a great man and even a friend. Doc Ock was a monster who ripped open bank vaults and kidnapped helpless women, and the mere thought of his aunt May in danger was enough to bring his blood to a boil.

You could have had me, the voice repeated. *But you screwed up.*

He glanced in annoyance at Uncle Ben, who was seated next to him on the bench. "I wouldn't have been a hero then, wouldn't have become Spider-Man, if not for that screwup. So you wouldn't have had anything to go around boasting about."

Ben's face twisted in disappointment. *You're joking, right? Honor student? Science scholar? A good nephew, the son I never had? I would have found plenty to boast about. You don't do this to give me something to boast about. You do it because it's what you have to do. What you owe.*

"But Uncle Ben—"

Suddenly a foot kicked Peter sharply in the shin and he jumped slightly. He blinked and looked up at a scowling Jonah Jameson. "Doze off and mutter to yourself on your own time, Parker, not mine. Now get out there and take pictures of me being altruistic and raising money for the new Library of Science, or you'll regret it." Then the scowl was instantly replaced with a snakelike smile as he stepped away from Peter to greet some dignitary, pumping his hand enthusiastically and talking, yet again, about his son.

There were fields of shooting stars glowing overhead in the planetarium dome, as well as constellations and comets. Peter would have been just as happy if they removed the dome so he could look at actual stars in the heavens. He maneuvered his way through the celebrants, deftly moving between waiters carrying perfectly balanced trays of champagne and hors d'oeuvres. In the background, a pianist was playing various standards and show tunes. Peter was tempted to go over and ask him if he knew anything by AC/DC, but had a feeling the request wouldn't go over well. Probably the most radical artist represented in the guy's repertoire was Billy Joel.

Peter snapped photos at random as his thoughts moved back to Doc Ock. He'd tried to catch up with him once he'd gotten Aunt May to safety, but it had been too late. He'd made his escape, and although Peter's personal worst-case scenarios had Ock showing up at Aunt May's house in a fit of revenge, he knew that wouldn't happen. May remained an "unidentified woman" in the reports on the incident, and once he'd switched out of his costume (not an easy feat; getting back to his clothes had been problematic and required every bit of stealth he possessed to slip past the police crews going over the scene of the crime) and caught up with her, he'd convinced her to keep her name out of it, specifically out of fear of recriminations.

She'd deferred to his pleadings on the matter. "Anything to help you worry less, Peter," she'd clucked.

But where was Doc Ock? Where was he hiding?

Peter began to think he should develop some sort of tracer device. Something small that he could stick on an opponent to track him. Yes, that might not be a bad idea at all. *Yeah, I'll use my vast fortune to develop the technology to make it work,* he thought, and dismissed the notion.

He moved past some guy at the bar who was wobbling from side to side, and then realized the guy was Harry. Not only did Harry have a mixed drink in front of him, he was snatching a glass of champagne from a passing tray and downing that, as well. Peter put a cautioning hand on his shoulder. "You're drinking too much champagne."

Harry shrugged. "It's a party. Wouldn't you be drinking if you'd just lost a bundle on a crackpot who you thought was taking you with him to fame and fortune? Not to forget your friend, the bug."

The truth was, Peter could understand Harry's frustration and humiliation over the failed experiment. He'd taken a major financial and publicity hit. To say nothing of the fact that at least a dozen of the scientists in attendance at the function were talking about filing lawsuits against Harry, thanks to their nearly getting killed at an Osborn-backed function. But the snide mention of Spider-Man still rankled.

"None of that tonight, Harry," he urged.

"Every night, pal," Harry said, shaking his head. "Until I find him, it's 24/7."

"Parker!" Jameson's voice boomed from nearby.

"Excuse me," he told Harry. "Gotta work."

He walked away from his friend, hoping Harry would stop drinking, knowing that he wouldn't. At least he'd seen Harry arrive driven by a chauffeur. At this rate, by the end of the evening Harry wouldn't be able to tie his own shoelaces much less drive himself home.

Jameson was standing with a group of miscellaneous notables, gesturing to this person and that person and looking for all the world as if he were conducting an orchestra. "Parker! Get me and Mrs. Jameson with the senator. No, get my wife with the minister. And shoot the mayor and his girlfriend—I mean wife."

Peter was about to remind Jonah Jameson that uttering the phrase "Shoot the mayor" in this situation might not be the best choice of words, and could land Jameson in a small room for extended police questioning. But then he mentally pictured exactly that, and chose not to say anything.

A matronly-looking society woman, Mrs. Severin, was standing at a podium in the front, tapping on a microphone to bring all eyes to her. There was just enough shrill feedback to get everyone's pained attention, and Mrs. Severin smiled gamely. "Ladies and gentlemen," she said breathlessly, "the Committee for the Science Library of New York presents our guest of honor: the first man to play football on the moon. The handsome, the heroic, the delicious Captain John Jameson."

The pianist banged out "Stars and Stripes Forever." Peter figured it was because he didn't know how to play "Man on the Moon."

John Jameson made his grand entrance, waving to the crowd, milking every moment of it. Unreasonably, Peter had been hoping John would just look like a young version of Jonah, right down to the stupid upright hair. Instead, Peter had to admit that he was a striking young man, dressed in military attire with enough medals to set off an airport detector two miles away. As a matter of fact, he bore a passing resemblance to that guy he'd spotted Mary Jane with outside her . . .

. . . theater . . .

. . . and there she was, right on his arm, her red hair elegantly coiffed, dressed in a sleek black evening gown. She stood and beamed as various officials came up to her and greeted her warmly while they shook John Jameson's hand, and her gaze swept the crowd. When it fell upon Peter, however, it came to a halt and her eyes widened in shock.

Jonah was suddenly at his shoulder. "Parker," he said

briskly, "shoot my son and his girlfriend. Shoot, Parker, shoot!"

If he'd had a gun at that moment, he thought bleakly, he might well have done just that, although whether he'd have shot M.J. and John, or only himself, was still anybody's guess.

Numbly he raised his camera and squeezed off a shot, wondering if he had been condemned to a life of photographing M.J. next to other guys. First it had been Harry; now this. Take pictures of M.J. with other men, struggle against demented madmen who kept trying to kill him, and alienate everyone he came into contact with. Compared to him, the Chicago Cubs were on a winning streak.

Peter stood there and watched as Mary Jane and John maneuvered toward another group of handshakers. John Jameson moved with such ease and familiarity that it seemed as if he were running for office and would likely be elected with no trouble. He was perfect. *Too perfect,* thought Peter. *Maybe he's a villain, too. Or a thing of evil. Maybe at moonrise he turns into a wolf. Sure. That's it.*

He watched as John continued shmoozing while Mary Jane drifted outside, accompanied by another woman. He recognized her as the actress who had emerged from the stage door beside Mary Jane. At that point he realized he couldn't just stand about inactive anymore, indecisive like some web-swinging Hamlet. His insides felt like a rubber band being stretched to the breaking point and beyond.

He moved quickly through the crowd and headed outside after Mary Jane. What to say to her, though? What *could* he say?

She stood there, chatting with her friend while daintily

eating a canapé. A fight-or-flight instinct overtook him, and flight was beginning to look like a darned good option. But then her friend wandered away, and Mary Jane was there by herself. No more excuses. No more fear. If he could handle Doc Ock, he should be able to handle this.

He squared his shoulders and headed toward her. She saw him coming. He waited for some reaction, so he could perhaps gauge what kind of reception he'd get. She was inscrutable. She didn't turn toward him, nor move away. She just stood there like a statue. He stopped when he was a couple of feet away and bobbed his head.

"Hi," he said.

If he had any doubt as to what was going through her mind, that doubt was erased by the icy cold of her reply. "Oh. You." Tax auditors had gotten warmer welcomes than that.

"Listen, I'm sorry," he began. "But there was a disturbance—"

She cut him off. "I don't know you," she said, her tone sharp and fueled with bitter disappointment. "And I can't think about you anymore. It's too painful."

His mind raced, trying to figure some way to get around the wall that was rapidly forming between them, brick by angry brick. "I've been reading a lot of poetry lately," he said, trying to sound sage.

Unfortunately, he felt like an imbecile, and the look he got from Mary Jane told him he should go with the feeling. "Whatever that means, don't start," she advised.

"Can I get you some champagne?"

"I'm with John," she said pointedly. "John will get me my champagne."

"John." Peter echoed the name in a slightly nasal tone.

That was when everything she'd obviously been storing up since his failure to show up at the theater poured out of her. Almost in one breath, she said, "And by the way, John has seen my show five times, Harry has seen it twice, Aunt May has seen it, my sick mother got out of bed to see it, and even my drunken father, who came backstage to borrow money, has seen it, but my best friend who cares so much about me can't make an eight o'clock curtain, so he is not entitled to fetch my champagne, because after all these years *he is nothing to me but an empty seat*!"

She sagged visibly, and for a moment something akin to regret played on her features. But then they hardened once more and, with a slight flip of her hair, she headed back into the planetarium, leaving Peter stricken and frustrated. He watched her go to John Jameson's side and whisper something to him. Jameson's face split in a grin and he was talking to her excitedly, saying something about "spreading the word." And she was nodding, so enchanted and happy with her astronaut boyfriend.

Once again he knew, on an intellectual level, that he should be happy for her. This was what he wanted. This was what he had pushed her toward: another man. She could have been his, but he'd handed her off and patted himself on the back for the nobility of his sacrifice.

But his thoughts weren't coming from his intellect. Instead, they were fueled by a slow anger burning in his gut with an intensity that dwarfed whatever Mary Jane might have been feeling earlier. Suddenly he was dying for someone to attack. For the fates to provide him with something evil he could pummel until it stopped moving, because socializing with the good guys was distressing him beyond measure.

An empty seat? I was saving people, Mary Jane. I was saving lives. That's what I do. I give up any hope of a normal life for me so others can live theirs. I save lives. I saved yours. I saved Aunt May's. Men, women, and children, cats and dogs and some kid's hamster, I've saved them all. How many lives has John saved, huh? How many crooks has he jailed? Parading around in his uniform, being lauded and praised for accomplishments that haven't required a tenth of the effort I've put in. Backed up by a father who demonizes me every chance he gets. How can you talk to me like that? If you had any idea . . . any idea . . .

Suddenly Harry was right in front of him, no more than a foot away. The smell of alcohol wafted off his breath. If Doc Ock did indeed show up at the party to create havoc, Peter wouldn't have to change to Spider-Man. Harry just had to get within range and breathe on him and Octavius would go down faster than the *Titanic.*

"It pisses me off, your loyalty to Spider-Man, but not to your best friend," Harry said thickly, fighting to form the words. He wavered slightly. Peter squinted against the aroma of booze being blown into his face. He'd never wanted to be wearing his mask so much in his life. "I saw him with my father's body. You defend the guy because he's your bread and butter." Harry tried to wave an accusing finger in Peter's face and wound up pointing about two feet to Peter's right . . . probably at another Peter Parker that only Harry could see.

Peter took Harry by the arm and tried to guide him out of the planetarium. Thoughts of his own wounded dignity were briefly put on the back burner. Instead, he was trying to prevent a bad situation from getting worse by having Mary Jane see Harry in this state. Harry'd be utterly mortified if M.J., his current friend and former girlfriend, witnessed his belligerent inebriation—presuming, of course, that he remembered it in the morning when he sobered up.

"Easy, Harry," Peter said cautiously.

"Don't push me!"

"Let's get some air," Peter said, not easing his grip on Harry's arm. He was endeavoring to be gentle, particularly considering that, if he was so inclined, he could sling Harry over his shoulder and haul him out like a fireman carrying a two-year-old.

"What're you, gonna save me, big guy?" Harry snarled with such force that Peter was taken aback. It was almost as if Harry had read the angry thoughts in Peter's mind moments earlier. "You a saint or something? I said, *don't push me.*" He continued to try pulling away as Peter restrained him. The fact that Peter wasn't particularly exerting himself ticked off Harry more. "Don't act like you're my friend," he snapped at Peter. "You took my girl away, you took my father's love, and then you let him die because you wouldn't turn in the freak. Isn't that so?"

With his free hand, he slapped at Peter's face. Peter snapped his head back reflexively and it only caught him with the most glancing of blows. But it still stung, more from the fact that Harry would do such a thing rather than from the force of the impact.

John Jameson, meantime, had mounted the podium and was calling out, "Ladies and gentlemen, I have an announcement to make."

Harry was paying no attention. "Right? Right,

brother?" he said, and slapped at Peter again. This time Peter didn't even bother to move. Harry was so hammered that a blow from him at full impact wouldn't have hurt a mosquito.

"I want you all to know," John continued, too far away from the fracas to notice, "that Miss Mary Jane Watson has just agreed to marry me."

The crowd was stunned for a moment, and then burst into uproarious applause. Peter, by contrast, was stunned for far longer than that. He forgot that he was holding on to Harry, who easily yanked his hand away. Instead, he just stood there, watching John Jameson beaming at Mary Jane, who was smiling back at him with that dazzling grin. The grin that said she cared about you and only you, and there was no one else like you in the universe. That you were the one she had chosen. He had seen that look from her before—though only in her eyes. He had been the recipient of it in a cemetery, standing near the grave site of his uncle Ben. Yes, he had been the recipient . . . and then had willingly walked away from it.

"Parker! Wake up!" It was Jonah Jameson, standing a couple of yards away, mimicking the motion of a camera being held up and aimed. He tried to speak, but the jazz band drowned him out as they launched into a rendition of "Love Is the Sweetest Thing." And as if the band hadn't managed to make it impossible to hear Jonah, Harry began shouting drunkenly, "Everybody loves Mary Jane!" Yes, that would certainly have done the trick.

Mary Jane was standing at the podium beside John, smiling and beaming up at him. Jameson, drawing closer to Peter, was now audible over the tumult. "Take a picture, Parker! *Take the damn picture!*"

Peter moved as if he were swimming through gelatin.

He raised the camera and saw M.J.'s image through the viewfinder. He zoomed in on her face, and for a moment he was back at the science museum, back wearing glasses, back being the nervous student, back being normal. And he was zooming in on the face of a glamorous Mary Jane Watson, the girl next door whom he'd always been too afraid to approach. She had smiled back then, for him, and he'd taken the pictures for the high school newspaper.

Now he wasn't in high school, no longer the nervous student . . . and there was still Mary Jane, part of his life. And she was smiling—but it wasn't a smile for him. It was for someone else. Someone who had never done Peter any harm and who Peter suddenly hated with more vigor than anyone, and that included the guys who'd tried to kill him.

"Shoot, Parker, shoot!" bellowed Jameson.

Peter took her picture. She never stopped looking good. It was nice to know there were two constants in the world: Mary Jane's looks, and the nonexistence of Peter Parker's luck.

Peter had often felt that web-swinging was a good way to clear his head when he was confused and frustrated. Considering the amount of aggravation he'd had to deal with lately, it was amazing his feet ever touched the ground.

Now, clad once more in his Spider-Man costume, his civilian clothes safely stashed away, he crouched atop the exterior of the planetarium, up at the highest point of the dome. He took a deep breath, let it out slowly, and then started swinging. The web-line carried him in a perfect arc, and he fired another web-line and then another in order to provide more distance from this hated place.

The webbing went out again.

This time he felt it before it happened, but that didn't do much to alleviate the situation. He had just released one web-line and was attempting to shoot out another strand to swing on. When nothing emerged, he had just enough time to mutter "Uh-oh" under his breath as he soared through the air, a daring young man *sans* trapeze.

The angle of his fall sent him hurtling into an alley and he slammed into a cluster of garbage cans. They and he crashed to the ground, and he lay there with the trash for a long moment before staggering to his feet. He pulled off his mask, trying to breathe deeply and having only moderate success. His skin was thick with sweat.

"Why is this happening to me?" he gasped.

Shaking his head, he went to the wall and tried to scale it. No luck. He only got a foot or so off the ground and then he didn't have the strength to adhere to the wall anymore. He lost his grip and fell backwards, landing amongst the garbage cans once again.

As he stood, with far more effort and pain this time, he spotted a newspaper lying in the trash. He picked it up. It was the bulldog edition of the *Daily Bugle,* and it read, "Spider-Man and Ock Crime Spree!" in large type across the front page.

He stared at it for a long, long time.

He read the story, and felt as if he were reading about someone else, someone he hadn't even met and wouldn't want to meet.

Peter didn't remember retrieving his street clothes and hauling them on over his costume. He didn't remember anything of the trip home, and wasn't even sure how he accomplished it: Walked, took the subway, a cab, whatever. None of it mattered. All that kept happening, even after his door closed behind him, was that he kept reading the *Daily Bugle*, trying to reconcile the public perception of Spider-Man with who and what he thought he was. And he couldn't.

Finally, in frustrated fury, he threw the newspaper against the wall, leaving an impressive dent. Then, bare-chested, wearing only his costume pants, he threw himself down onto his bed. He was sweaty, panicked, upset. His heart racing, his breath labored.

"Why is this happening?" he muttered again, and not for the first time he had no answers. "Maybe . . . maybe it's something Ock did to me. I'll just go right out and ask him . . . I'm sure he's not doing anything important at the moment."

Doc Ock proudly walked through the new lab that he had created within the confines of pier 56.

He was glad he'd realized the foolishness of pursuing his aims solely through stealing money. As a research scientist with access to classified knowledge, he'd known precisely where the government kept various items of research and scientific interest—items that would be of use to him in his work. Secret places. Places that when he smashed his way into them, and squashed efforts by the military to stop him, the government itself made sure to hush up, lest citizens be alarmed.

His tax dollars at work.

Large crates labeled "Property of U.S. Government" had all been cracked open, the equipment removed and set up. Finding a source of electricity had been a bit of a problem, but he'd managed to locate a main he could tap into. Theoretically the line was supposed to be shut down, but the cybernetics of his tentacles were exceptionally talented. They'd simply clamped into the lines and sent orders to the computer-controlled power grid that the circuits were to be reactivated. Eventually the power company would find the unauthorized startup. His estimate was that it would take them a couple of months. More than enough time.

He gazed once more with pride upon his handiwork and placed his hands on his hips. The tentacles followed suit.

"Time to go to work," he said.

XIV

Seated in the shoe department at Barney's, Mary Jane enjoyed the look of utter astonishment on Louise's face. Louise, who'd been about to try on a nice little Prada number, sat there with the shoe in her hand and a look of disbelief on her face.

"See?" said Mary Jane. "You shouldn't have left early last night. See what you missed?"

"You told him yes?" Louise squeaked it so loudly that every head within earshot turned to see what she was going on about.

Mary Jane could understand her incredulity. The proposal had unfolded so improbably. There they'd been at the party, and John had smiled at her and said, "You know, everyone keeps asking if we're talking about setting a date. That I'd be crazy to let you get away. This keeps up, I may have to start thinking about finding a romantic spot to discuss possible—"

"Or you could just ask me now." She hadn't been aware she was going to say the words until they popped out of her mouth.

He had blinked in surprise. "Um . . . okay. Would you want to get married?"

In retrospect, she felt as if her mouth had been on autopilot. She was, as the acting term went, in the moment. The problem was, she hadn't been sure if she was going with her gut, or acting in spite of what her instincts were telling her . . . just to prove something. It didn't matter, though. All that mattered was her response: "Sure."

John clearly couldn't believe it. Out of nowhere, his life had suddenly shifted on its axis. "Wow! Can I spread the word?"

"Now?"

She'd been momentarily taken aback by the question. It was natural, of course. But some part of her almost felt as if this were all a game, and would remain so for as long as it was just the two of them playing it. As soon as others were invited to participate, it became . . .

. . . real.

Well, wasn't that what she wanted? Real?

"Okay?" he had prompted, starting to look worried.

She had shrugged. "Why not?"

A grin had split his face as he took her by the shoulders. "I promise you won't regret it, Mary Jane."

And that was that. He'd made the announcement, and Mary Jane tried to tell herself that it was purest coincidence that, although she'd apparently been looking up at John, she'd actually been watching Peter Parker's reflection in a nearby tureen. It was hard to make out, though, since it was distorted by the curvature. Well, why not? It was appropriate. Everything about her relationship with him had become distorted.

"You told him yes?" Louise repeated, hauling Mary Jane back to reality. "Just that fast?"

"It felt right," Mary Jane said. That seemed to be becoming a habit for her. She studied her friend. "Well? You might congratulate me."

"Congratulations," Louise said quickly and, Mary Jane thought, not all that sincerely. She added, "Good luck in the world."

For some reason, that made Mary Jane feel slightly defensive. "John loves me, and he tells me so. My father's words still ring in my head. 'You'll never be worth anything' and 'No man will ever want you.' "

Louise looked taken aback. "You're going to spend the rest of your life trying to prove something to your father?"

To him . . . and to Peter, showing him how he'd missed out. She brought herself up short. What sort of ridiculous way was that to think?

As if sensing M.J.'s uncertainty, Louise asked, "You really love this guy?"

Her thoughts awhirl, Mary Jane replied, "Very much."

But Louise picked up on something in the response. " 'Very much'? That doesn't fly." She leaned in toward her friend, rested a hand on her knee. "If you really love the guy, then the answer is . . ." She paused and then said in an overly passionate, overly dramatic, breathless manner, " 'Do I love him? I adore him. He's my comfortable afghan, he's all I can think about. Everything he is, everything he says, everything he does to me, for me, with me. His sweet kisses. He *makes up for all the grief and pain I've ever had.* And in the dark of night, he's there." She sagged against the chair, "spent" from her emoting. Going along with it, Mary Jane politely applauded. Louise half smiled, then turned serious. "That's the answer I need. Not 'I love him very much.' You're going to *marry* the guy." When Mary Jane didn't say anything immediately, Louise prompted her, "Hello?"

Mary Jane just shook her head. "You've read too many love stories," she chided.

"What about that perfect kiss you said you had once? The guy you believed in. He sounds worth waiting for."

The memories came back. That night, in the rain, her sopping clothes clinging to her, the whole surreal feeling of it all . . . and he'd been there, and the rest of the world had gone away when their lips met.

"That was a fantasy," Mary Jane said, trying to make herself believe it. "That's all he is."

"Hey!" protested Louise. "What's wrong with believing in love stories?"

As a shoe salesman approached them, carefully balancing an armload of boxes, Mary Jane said, "Nothing, if you don't mind making yourself sick over relationships."

XV

Peter had waited so long at the university's Student Health Services department that he was starting to worry he'd miss his own graduation. Considering that was several years away, it indicated just how much longer he anticipated sitting around until a doctor found time to see him.

The interminable wait finally ended when a gum-chewing nurse escorted him in to see one Doctor Wally Davis, as the name tag on his white lab coat indicated him to be. The coat was a sharp contrast to the cheery Grateful Dead T-shirt he sported underneath. In his forties, Davis was a rather tired-looking but reasonably congenial fellow. From his manner during the examination, Peter would have guessed him to be an aging ex-hippie, until he remembered that when hippies were in vogue, Davis had been in diapers.

Peter, sitting in his briefs on the edge of the examining table, watched as Davis finished checking his blood pressure. The doctor unwrapped the cuff and nodded with apparent satisfaction. "You seem okay to me," he said.

Peter realized there wasn't any way the doctor could know that for sure, since he couldn't examine Peter for any of the specific symptoms he was experiencing. What was he supposed to say?

"Doc, I'm not climbing the walls anymore."

"Well, good, it's nice that you're not letting yourself get upset."

Good. Great plan.

So instead, he'd just told the doctor about exhaustion, general weakness. The doctor's first concern was that Peter had mononucleosis, a very common disease for college students. But the absence of fever or swollen glands prompted him to do a more general checkup, and he was left shaking his head. "My diagnosis?" said Davis. He tapped his head. "It's up here. You say you don't sleep? Heartbreak? Bad dreams?"

Desperately wishing he could address the problem head-on, Peter said cautiously, "There is . . . one dream. I'm climbing a wall. But I keep falling."

"Oh?" Davis raised an eyebrow. "Why are you climbing?"

"Well, it's not exactly me who's climbing," he amended. "It's not even my dream. It's a friend of mine's dream."

"Ah," said Davis, who apparently had heard this clever code before and was perfectly capable of cracking it. "Somebody *else's* dream." He glanced at Peter's records. "What's your major? Theater Arts?"

"Science."

"Connors?"

"Yeah," Peter said cautiously.

"He flunking you?"

"Says he might."

"There you go," said Davis, as if that explained everything. "What about this 'friend.' Why does he climb? What does he think of himself?"

"That's the problem," Peter admitted. "He doesn't know what to think."

Davis nodded in what seemed an air of commiseration. "Got to make you mad not to know who you are. Your soul disappears. Nothing as bad as uncertainty. I've been there. Who was I? Wow, identity! Big one." He leaned in toward the uncertain Peter and whispered, "Me? I go to my shrink."

There's a surprise, thought Peter. Aloud he said, trying to hide his nervousness, "Oh? What does he tell you?"

The doctor leaned in even closer. "*She* tells me," he said, loudly emphasizing the female pronoun, "that I need some strong focus on what I want. And I have to find out who won't let me have it. And why. And then," he was so nearly on top of him that Peter thought the doctor was about to ask him out on a date, "I have to tackle that guy and make him hear me."

He stood upright and started to turn away, much to Peter's relief . . . and then the doctor was back, close in and facing him, and Peter decided that however many times a week this doctor was seeing his shrink, he needed to triple it, at the minimum.

"And one more thing," Davis said, sounding like a demented Lieutenant Columbo. "I have to make sure I'm right about what I want." He paused, as if considering his own words. "Listen, maybe you're not supposed to be climbing that wall. That's why you keep falling. You always have a choice, Peter."

Despite the seeming insanity of the situation—not to mention the doctor himself—Davis was making a point that Peter hadn't truly dared consider earlier. "I have a choice," he said, as if only just then learning that man had free will.

Davis stood up, clapped him on the shoulder, and said, "Put your pants on. You're fit as a fiddle."

But Peter wasn't feeling fit, fiddle or not, dressed or

not. Despite the fact that he was falling behind in his classes, he couldn't bring himself to attend any that day. Instead, he went home, stripped off his clothes, and climbed into bed, even though sunlight was still filtering through the window. He knew that to the casual observer it might seem like a classic case of clinical depression. He didn't care. He was too depressed to care.

He lay there for quite some time, trying to get to sleep and having no success. *Just my luck. Just my lousy luck,* he thought, and then realized that if his luck was running contrary to what he wanted . . .

So he tried to stay awake, and managed that for all of ten minutes before falling into a deep slumber.

The world swirled around him in his sleep, different aspects of his life splintering apart like a smashed window. Events that genuinely had transpired intermixed freely with those that hadn't but were drawn from his deepest fears and imaginings. One moment he saw his uncle Ben lying in the street, his life's blood seeping out of him in relentless streams, then suddenly he was sitting next to his uncle inside Ben's beloved Delta 88, the car he had died for.

For some reason, Peter wasn't surprised. It was more than just the way that everything seemed to make sense in a dream, no matter how nonsensical. It felt as if everything that had been happening to him lately was leading to this. He'd been seeing his uncle again and again, his imagination running rampant, to the point where being awake or asleep didn't seem to matter. Ben would come to him when he was dozing, when he was wide-awake . . . whenever he felt like it, pretty much. And Peter was helpless to stop these visitations. Helpless because he wanted to be. Helpless because he felt he deserved to be.

Yet ironically it was that growing sense of helplessness that had triggered this latest visitation. On some level, even in his sleeping mind, Peter knew this. Moments before he'd found himself in the late, lamented Delta 88, that nut-job doctor had been repeating the one thing he'd said that made sense to Peter: *You always have a choice.* In the dream he'd been saying it while wearing a tutu, but that was neither here nor there. The words had merit no matter who said them, or where. And although they were perfectly self-evident on the face of it, they nevertheless struck Peter with the impact of a Louisville Slugger across his mouth.

"Hello, Peter," Ben said softly.

"Uncle Ben?"

"What you're thinking of, Pete . . . it makes me sad."

Sad? How could he claim to know from sad? He was cavorting with angels while Peter was scrambling to salvage any hope he had of regular human contact.

"Can't you understand?" he asked, desperately. "I'm in love with Mary Jane."

"You know I understand," Ben said consolingly. "But I thought I'd taught you the meaning of responsibility."

Oh, yes. Yes, he had. With his blood and his life, he had driven that lesson like a stake into Peter's heart. Now Peter lived a twilight life, one that couldn't include someone like Mary Jane. How could he possibly pursue a relationship with her when there was a side of his existence that he had to keep from her? One that superseded her needs and desires every day of the week, every minute of the day? A woman wanted to know that she was the most important thing in a man's life . . . and that could never, ever be the case as long as Spider-Man existed.

"You don't know how it feels," Peter said, his voice hollow.

Ben shook his head and thumped his hand gently on the steering wheel for emphasis. "All those times we talked about honesty and justice and fairness. I've counted on you to have courage. And to one day take my dreams into the world with you."

Ben Parker had never said these words to him. Very likely, he hadn't even thought them. They were instead Peter's own conjuring of Ben's desires, blossoming from that portion of his consciousness that could never, ever forgive him the great sin he had committed, the sin that had lost him his uncle. But because they came from deep within Peter's soul, they had that much more meaning and resonance for him.

In the shades of his dreaming self, Peter looked with ferocity at his uncle, and suddenly hated him. Hated the capricious fate that had placed Ben directly on a collision course with that damned thief. That guy could have jacked someone else's car, on some other street, anywhere in the city. Yes, Peter had stepped aside and let the thief dash by, but there had been more twists and turns than that in the clashing destinies.

Why? Why do I have to suffer endless torment for what I did? Why am I the one domino in the endless tik-tik-tik *row of circumstances leading to Uncle Ben's death who has to do endless penance? It's not fair!*

IT'S NOT FAIR!

"I can't live with your dreams!" Peter cried out. "I want a life of my own!"

"With great power comes great responsibility," Ben told him, every word filled with the weight of the world. He reached out to Peter, and his face flickered in concern and doubt. "Take my hand, son."

Peter looked at that hand, and it wasn't kind and slightly wrinkled and sandpaper rough. It wasn't the hand that had rested gently on his shoulder when he was little and sobbing because bullies had picked on him. The hand that had ruffled his hair in approval every time he brought home another top grade in science.

It was the hand of fate. Worse, it was a hand that had a stranglehold upon him, clutching his throat, cutting off his air, cutting off his life . . .

Peter batted it away, and shouted, "No, Uncle Ben! *I am Peter Parker! I am Spider-Man no more!*" Ben lunged at Peter, but Peter kept him at bay, yanking at the car door, which refused to open, to let him out into a world that didn't include the suffocating burden of martyrdom in it. *"No more! No more!"*

Then he was out. He tumbled backwards from the car, rolled away, and ferociously kicked the door shut . . .

The slam of the door was deafening, and as Peter snapped awake in bed, he realized why. It had coincided with a crash of thunder that sounded so close, it was practically there in the bedroom with him.

Rain pounded against the window, shaking the building to its foundation. Peter stood up, watching the storm, and the lightning cracked again. When it did, it illuminated the Spider-Man costume, draped over a chair. More thunder and lightning, and in the eerie illumination, it was as if Spider-Man was sitting there in the chair, staring at him, laughing at him under the mask. On the dresser nearby, a framed photo of Aunt May and Uncle Ben watched him endlessly, looking curious as to what he would do next.

Spider-Man no more! His own words echoed in his head.

He dressed in no time and grabbed the costume, wadding it into a ball. On a night like this, no one was going to see it or know it for what it was. And in his state of mind, he didn't give a damn if they saw it or not.

Seconds later he was outside and running, his blood pumping, his heart hammering in his chest. He had no idea where he was going, but part of him was saying, *You'll know, you'll know* . . .

His sneakered feet splashed through puddles, water soaking through to his socks. His shirt was plastered to his chest, his hair slicked, rain pouring over his face. Lightning crashed so near to him that he could practically smell ozone in the air. None of it mattered. The only thing of any importance was the bundle of cloth he was clutching tightly to his bosom like a child . . . a child to be loved, nurtured . . .

. . . or abandoned.

And then he was standing outside an alley.

He recognized it instantly.

An eternity ago, he had been hanging upside down in a storm that was almost as fierce as this one. Hanging upside down, his mask rolled partway down his face, and lips had pressed against his. Despite the rain, despite the fact he had barely been able to breathe, they tasted warm and promising and spoke without words of a future that he knew, in his heart, could never be his.

Since then, Spider-Man had known triumph. He'd known frustration, relief, even exhilaration. But those moments in the alley were the only time that Spider-Man had known peace. Pure, undiluted peace. For a few seconds, the burning guilt that fueled his very existence had been quenched in the fountain of Mary Jane's love.

He had wanted it to last forever.

Now it would.

He walked up to a trash can in the alley, opened it, then dumped the costume in. He stood there for a moment, almost certain that somehow the costume would vault out of the can and leap upon him.

Instead it just lay there, looking powerless. Even pathetic. It looked like . . . nothing. Just some blue-and-red cloth stitched together.

The hold it had upon him, like strands of web, melted into the rain.

Peter stared at it a moment longer. Then he wiped the water from his face, turned his back on Spider-Man without giving him a second thought, and walked away into the dark and stormy night.

XVI

It wasn't the most comfortable seat Peter Parker had ever sat in. The cushion was threadbare, and there was a spring that seemed determined to lacerate his left thigh. But for all of that, it might as well have been a throne in Buckingham Palace for the sense of elation it gave him.

Then again, a lot of things were making him feel that way lately.

Over the past several days, he had been doing nothing except being normal. He had done the big things, such as cleaning up his apartment so it was actually inhabitable once again.

He had done the little things, such as buying a hot dog on a street corner. It was overpriced and over-cooked, but he had never tasted anything quite as good. He had just resolved to wash it down with an egg cream—which contained, paradoxically, neither egg nor cream—when he'd heard sirens pass by. So ingrained was his behavior that he had reflexively started to move toward them. But he'd only taken a step when he remembered that his costume was gone. *He*—the web-swinging "he"—was gone. But instead of feeling tense or guilty, all he did was sigh, relax, and eat his hot dog.

Later he finished fixing his motorbike. Once he had

done so, he rode it over to the campus, where he arrived in plenty of time for his science class. As Doctor Connors lectured, Peter felt more alert than ever before. At one point Connors asked a particularly challenging question, and there were bewildered looks from the other students. Not from Peter, though. His hand shot up as if spring-loaded, and a visibly surprised Connors called on him . . . and grinned broadly when Peter provided the answer.

After class, Connors had passed Peter in the hallway and, without slowing down, had said briskly, "Excellent work today, Parker. Keep it up."

"Thanks," Peter had said, but Connors was already gone, moving too fast to hear him. It didn't matter, though.

Now Peter was in the theater, in his somewhat uncomfortable chair, seated a row or two back from where he'd originally been supposed to sit the night when he'd let Mary Jane down. Again. But there would never be a recurrence.

He felt like a recovering alcoholic, one who had seen his life swirling away, and had tossed aside his addiction so he could salvage it. But there had been no substance abuse in his life. His addiction instead had been guilt; its manifestation had been Spider-Man. It was over, though. The guilt was dealt with, the manifestation disposed of. Time to move on.

Truth to tell, a mannered British drawing-room farce wasn't his favorite way to spend the evening. But gazing at Mary Jane most certainly was. So he was willing to endure the former in order to spend time engaging in the latter. They were well into the second act when "Algernon" addressed Mary Jane's "Cecily."

"Oh," Algernon said dismissively, "I am not really

wicked at all, cousin Cecily. You mustn't think that I am wicked."

"If you are not," replied Mary Jane, "then you have certainly been deceiving us all in a very inexcusable manner." She walked across the stage as if she owned it. "I hope you have not been leading a double life, pretending to be wicked and being really good all the time." She leaned in toward the audience, delivering the line as a reproving aside. "That would be hypocrisy."

Something about the way she delivered the line—and, of course, the literal wording of it—couldn't help but make Peter feel as if she were talking right to him.

And then he realized that she almost was. Not intentionally at first, but from her vantage point upon the stage, she had suddenly realized that Peter was in the audience. He locked eyes with her and grinned ingratiatingly. Her eyes widened, and when Algernon declared, "Oh! Of course I have been rather reckless," he looked to Mary Jane for response, and got nothing. She continued to stare at Peter.

Uh . . . Mary Jane . . . your cue? Peter tried to give her silent signals, but she was just gaping at him.

A bit louder, Algernon cleared his throat and said, "Are you . . . *glad* to *hear* it?"

Hearing her own line coming out of someone else's mouth snapped her back to attention. Quickly she said, "Oh . . . uh . . . I am *glad* to hear it."

She promptly got back into the swing of the play. But the object of her attention hadn't gone unnoticed. A young "dude" sitting next to Peter nudged him, and when Peter turned to look at him, mouthed, "You and her?"

Peter bobbed his head in an indefinite manner.

That was enough for the dude, who mouthed, "Sweeeet," and went back to watching the show.

Peter grinned. He and Mary Jane.

Why the hell not.

He had been standing at the stage door waiting for her, and when she'd emerged she looked genuinely happy to see him. He was so relieved, especially since her spotting him had thrown her out of character for a moment. Peter had felt particularly guilty over that. Then again, feeling guilty had become second nature for him at this point in his life. That was exactly the mind-set he was trying to move beyond.

As they strolled through Chinatown, Peter felt . . . taller. More confident. He walked with his shoulders squared, spoke in a more relaxed manner.

"You were so wonderful," he said. "That was such a great play." Well, she'd been great in it, at any rate.

"You could have told me you were coming."

A dozen excuses came to mind, but he shrugged them off and said the simple truth: "I was afraid you'd say don't come."

She nodded, indicating to Peter that she might well have done so, seeing it as a desperate "too little, too late" gesture to make things up to her. "You look . . . different," she said, sounding a bit guarded.

"I shined my shoes," he said lightly, "pressed my pants, did my homework. I do my homework now." He paused, then asked, "Would you like to get some chow mein?"

She shook her head and sighed. "Peter, I'm getting married."

I know. I was there, he thought. But some part of him refused to accept it. "I always imagined you getting married on a hilltop."

"And who's the groom?"

He stopped and turned to face her, speaking as if he could reshape reality just by force of will. "You haven't decided yet."

Slowly she began to understand. "You think because you saw my play, you can talk me out of getting married?" She sounded . . . incredulous?

That was more or less accurate. It did sound rather hopeless, though, the way she said it. The old Peter Parker would have crawled away . . . literally. But instead he said forcefully, "You once told me you loved me. I let . . . things . . . get in the way before. There was something I . . ." He hated speaking in vague terms, but he was trying to leave that part of his life behind. Delving into it chapter and verse would only bring it forcefully to the forefront. "Something I thought I had to do. I don't have to now."

"You're too late."

"Will you think about it?"

Her blue eyes stared at him in disbelief. She probably thought he was beginning to sound like a stalker. "Think about *what*?"

"Picking up where we left off?"

Her arms akimbo, Mary Jane peered at him challengingly. "Where was *that*? We never got *on*. You can't get off if you don't get on, Peter!"

They both blinked at that. Clearly it hadn't come out quite right. "That sounded a lot less suggestive in my head, before I actually said it," Mary Jane admitted. "But you know what I meant."

Softly, Peter said, "I don't think it's that simple."

"Of course you don't, because you complicate things."

"You don't understand. I'm not an empty seat anymore!" When she smiled slightly, Peter was convinced that he was making some headway. He angled a shoulder toward her and said, "I'm different. Punch me. I bleed." As far as pleas for empathy went, it wasn't exactly the "Hath not a Jew eyes?" speech, but it was the best he was going to be able to do under the circumstances.

Unfortunately, it didn't appear to be enough. "I've got to go," Mary Jane said after a long pause. She backed up, flagging an approaching cab. As it glided toward her, she continued to face Peter. "I'm getting married in a church."

He shrugged in his most noncommittal, "we'll see" manner.

The cab came to a stop. She opened the door and, just before she stepped in, studied him a few moments more. "You *are* different," she decided. She got in and closed the door behind her.

The cab pulled away. Peter stood there, watching it go. He ran the conversation back through his mind, studied it with a strangely detached, clinical air. What he kept coming back to was that in between all her protests about getting married and it being too late . . . she seemed to be pausing an awful long time, as if the answers weren't coming easily to her. As if she had to think about them real hard.

Which meant . . .

. . . something.

He smiled, and the smile spread into a grin.

It was a start.

The euphoric mood of his encounter with Mary Jane carried him all the way through to the following morning at the university. Eschewing the bike, which despite his repairs had stalled out several times on his last sojourn with it, he decided to take the subway. His backpack slung over his shoulder, he emerged from the station along with a stream of students. He realized that's all he was: just one of the students. Nothing special, nothing to see here, just keep moving.

He passed by one of the dorms and stopped, noticing movement down an alleyway, between two of the buildings. There were three extremely unsavory types lurking there. They were unshaven, their clothes dirty from being slept in, their hair scraggly and matted. If he got close enough, he was sure they'd stink.

The larger two guys were ganging up on the third. The third was cowering as they rifled his pockets and grabbed at a bag—it appeared to be a rumpled Bloomingdale's bag—that he was clutching.

Drugs. Probably drugs, he assured himself. *Or booze. Or . . .*

. . . or a battered teddy bear that once belonged to his dead daughter, who died young and that's why he started drinking, or . . .

He took a deep breath, let it out, and kept walking. Move along. Nothing to see here.

XVII

Shouldn't anniversaries be for celebrating things? Shouldn't we just set those aside for that specific reason?

Those thoughts floated through Peter's mind as he stood next to his aunt near the grave of Uncle Ben. It was a sunny day, but unseasonably cool and crisp. Aunt May, clutching a small bunch of violets, stared at the grave for some time without saying a word. Peter's hand rested just below her head. He didn't say a word.

Two years. Two years to the day that his uncle Ben had been gone. There had never been any doubt in Peter's mind that he would join Aunt May for this private little ceremony . . . and yet, until he was actually there, he'd wondered if he would have the strength to go through with it. Contradictory. But then, he was a study in contradictions.

As he drew his coat closer around himself, he watched as Aunt May stepped away from him and approached the grave. She set the violets upon the ground, then stepped back and shook her head slowly.

"It wasn't fair to have gone that way," she said softly. "He was a peaceful man." She took a deep breath and exhaled three words that Peter couldn't quite believe she was saying:

"It's my fault."

He shook his head, wanting to tell her how wrong she was, but the words froze in his throat. She didn't notice the look of conflict that played across his face. Her attention was intent upon the grave, and when she turned and headed back to the waiting taxi, Peter simply followed without saying a thing.

They didn't speak all the way to the house, and as Aunt May busied herself in the kitchen, Peter sat at the table and stared at the place where Uncle Ben had always sat.

Once upon a time, he would have been able to imagine Ben sitting there. Perhaps Ben would even start scolding him, as his "ghost" had been wont to do lately. Now, though, there was nothing. Just an empty space and an empty chair. He had banished Ben Parker's hauntings from his mind . . .

. . . and, apparently, Ben had set up shop in Aunt May's.

Peter had been feeling so good about himself lately. Having made the deliberate decision to leave behind him that symbol of ongoing guilt, Spider-Man, he was happier and more at peace than he'd been in months. He had achieved closure, finally. His aunt, though, not only hadn't achieved that state of mind, but she appeared to be backsliding.

She blamed *herself*? The more Peter dwelled on it, the more incredulous he became. How could she possibly blame herself? She'd been sitting at home, uninvolved in any of it.

By the time he heard the teakettle issuing its high-pitched summons, he knew he had to do something. He couldn't let it fester this way. He had to find some means to put her mind at rest.

He entered the kitchen and Aunt May gestured for him to sit at the table. He did so and watched as she brought over the steeping tea. Tentatively he told her, "You don't have to punish yourself, Aunt May."

She looked up at him with a brief display of confusion, but then she understood. As she sat opposite him, she spoke in a very calm and distant manner, with no trace of emotion or mourning in her voice. "Oh, I know I shouldn't, but if I had kept out of it . . ." When she saw his puzzled expression, she said, "You wanted to take the subway, and I told him to drive you."

So that was it. When they had left the house that night, Peter had been certain he'd seen Uncle Ben—after insisting on driving Peter into the city—winking at Aunt May. He hadn't known the significance of it then but now he did. She'd told Ben what to do, and he was winking at her in satisfaction that he had accomplished it.

May was shaking her head now. "If I'd just kept my mouth shut, we'd all be having tea together."

Well, that was that, wasn't it. Thanks to Peter's ignoble actions, not only had this poor woman lost her husband, she was going to spend the rest of her life beating herself up over it.

"I want to thank you very, very much for coming today," she said.

But Peter barely heard her, because his mind was racing toward a conclusion that he at once found to be both untenable and yet inevitable. She couldn't go through the rest of her years thinking this way. It wasn't right or fair that Aunt May, who had done nothing to Peter except be the best mother figure she could manage, should have to suffer like this, all because of him.

She needed closure, as well . . . perhaps even more than he did.

"I have to tell you something, Aunt May," he said, forcing the words out as if he were choking on them. "Something you . . . won't want to hear. Something I couldn't tell you until now." *Not couldn't; didn't want to. But I've no choice now.*

"What's wrong, Peter," she asked. She'd been stirring her tea, but now she put the spoon down. "Are you in trouble?"

"You could say that," he admitted. "You see . . ." He steadied himself, praying that she would understand why he was doing this and appreciate the gesture. "You see . . . *I'm* responsible."

She stared at him blankly. "For what? What are you talking about?"

"For what happened to Uncle Ben."

Obviously at that point she thought she did understand, because she smiled and shook her head, patting him affectionately on the hand. "Peter, you're trying to make me feel better," she said, which was more or less true, as far as it went. The problem was that she couldn't comprehend just how far that was, as she quickly made clear. "You went to the library. You were doing your homework."

"I didn't go to the library."

"What do you mean?"

Peter's mind was desperately trying to catch up with his mouth. He sure as hell didn't want to give her all the gory details, so he tried to edit the story as much as he could while still having it all make sense. "Uncle Ben drove me to the library, but I never went in. He waited for me outside, but I went someplace else.

Someplace . . . to make some money to buy myself a car."

She looked confused, clearly failing to understand how Peter's being duplicitous about going to the library could possibly relate to the death of her beloved Ben. Peter rushed ahead, trying to avoid having the words spill all over one another.

"I wanted to impress someone, but I was taken advantage of . . . and there was a robbery, and I was getting revenge." Still a blank expression from May. Still she didn't understand. Hitting each word for emphasis, he said, "I could've stopped the thief. But I let him go. I even held the door for him. And Uncle Ben was waiting . . ."

She didn't move, not so much as a centimeter, but the pupils in her eyes seemed to dilate, as if some potent narcotic had just hit her system . . . or her brain had been assaulted by more information than it was prepared to process.

"Then he stole Uncle Ben's car," Peter finished, somewhat unnecessarily. "First he . . . shot him."

For a long, long time, she said nothing. The only sound in the house was the steady tick of the pendulum in the grandfather's clock from the living room.

"I'm so sorry," said Peter, and never before had those words seemed so inadequate, not even when he'd said them to Mary Jane for the umpteenth time. "I couldn't keep it secret any—"

"No more," she said abruptly, and she stood.

"Aunt May, I . . ."

He reached over to take her hand and she yanked it away as if he were a snake about to sink his fangs into it. She got to her feet and warned, "Don't touch me now."

Quickly she moved past him to the stairs. He waited

for the outburst of emotion, but it didn't come. Instead, she walked slowly up to the top of the stairs and then disappeared down the short hallway. Peter remained where he was, wondering what to do.

He kept trying to tell himself that he had done the right thing. Aunt May had been hurting, and she had to know.

Then a sound came from the top of the stairs. Sobbing. She was crying bitterly, and Peter was at war with himself whether to go up the stairs or not. Abruptly the decision was taken from his hands as May appeared at the top of the stairs. Her eyes were red, her face wet, but she was completely composed.

"I need to be alone," she said, reining in whatever was going through her mind.

Peter began, "It was—"

"*Go!*"

She had never screamed at him like that before. The scream of a broken soul.

He got out, sprinting toward his bike, which was parked in the driveway. He vaulted onto it and started it up. It only took five tries. It coughed somewhat, and then he steered it away, all the time realizing the truth of what had just transpired.

Peter had told himself that he was telling Aunt May what had happened so that she could find closure. But that hadn't been true at all. Simply knowing that Peter was involved in the events that had led to Ben's murder wasn't going to make things better for her. Peter's actions didn't change the fact that May had sent Ben Parker out to his fate. She was likely going to continue beating herself up for that.

No, the truth was, he'd been seeking absolution. He'd

told Aunt May information that could not possibly have done her any good, and had done it in an act of unbridled selfishness. He'd told her what had transpired—as much as he could, without letting her know of his double existence, however passé that was—because he'd wanted her to tell him that it was all right. That she still loved him despite his horrific mistake. He'd wanted her to pat him on the head, tell him she still loved him, that it was going to be all right. That he should go and sin no more.

Instead, *this* debacle had ensued, because he'd been selfish.

Thank God he wasn't a hero anymore.

Betty Brant, executive secretary to J. Jonah Jameson, stared at the costume without comprehending at first.

The bum was holding it half out of the Bloomingdale's shopping bag that he'd stuffed it in. His face was somewhat triangular, and his eyebrows were thick and upswept. His long hair obscured his ears and he had a shapeless brown hat drawn down over his head. People were coming and going in the building lobby, oblivious to what was transpiring, as Betty continued to look at it. She started to reach for it, but the man snatched it away from her, shoving it back into the bag.

The stocky building guard said tentatively, "You see why I called you down here, Miss Brant. I mean, every day of the week, I give guys like this the bum's rush. No offense," he assured the bum.

"None taken," he said.

The guard continued, "Thing is, Mr. Homeless American brings this thing in, and, well . . . I know the thing Mr. Jameson has for . . ." He lowered his voice and glanced around. "You know who. And I'm figuring, if this is the genuine article, he'd wanna know about it."

"Let me see it again," Betty said.

"Cost ya five bucks for a look."

"Take a hike," said Betty, and she turned to leave.

"Awright, awright!" snapped the homeless man, and he pulled it out again for her to study.

She looked at it closely, studying it. She'd seen the cheap Halloween costume knockoffs that had been manufactured in China. But she'd also seen countless, close-up photographs cross her desk, thanks to Peter Parker. By this point she felt she knew Spider-Man's costume better than she did most of her own outfits, and this thing . . .

It looked real. Seemed real. She stared very closely at it again, and again, and sure enough—very faintly, but still there—she saw what appeared to be bloodstains. The costume had been washed repeatedly and the stains had faded, but there was still the slightest hint of them, if one was looking for them. Whoever had worn this costume had been in a fight, or more than one.

The bum pulled it back into the bag and then looked at her expectantly. As if anticipating her question, he said, "It's real, all right. Found it in a garbage can. See these bruises?" and he pointed to swelling under his right eye and at his left temple. "Got it from fight-ing two guys who were bigger'n me, 'cause they tried to take it away. Guy like me doesn't get into a scrape over a fake Spider-Man costume. Wandered around for two days with it, wonderin' what the best way was to make a score off it. Tried the TV news people, but I couldn't get past the reception desk. Wouldn't give me the time o' day. Finally figured you guys were the best way to go. So did I figure right?" he asked challengingly.

She turned to the guard. "Give him a visitor's pass."

"Want me to come up with you?" asked the guard.

"No," she said automatically, but then looked at the leering homeless man and said, "Yes."

She found she had to hold her breath on the ride up in the elevator. She tried to be sympathetic to the plight of this poor, destitute individual, but finally Betty decided she was more concerned with not losing her lunch. She'd never been so grateful for the opening of a set of elevator doors as she was when they arrived on the thirty-fifth floor. Reporters looked at her in confusion and even backed away as she walked briskly with the bum in tow, while he clutched his Bloomie's bag and looked suspiciously around.

As she approached Jameson's office, she saw that Hoffman and Robbie were already in there, trying to get Jameson's attention, and extract a decision about something or other. She wondered why they even had their own offices, considering the amount of time they spent in Jonah's.

Jameson himself was on the phone, and probably was annoyed that he'd had to answer it himself, since Betty was away from her desk. She'd likely have to endure another five-minute rant from him over the evils of voice mail.

His voice easily carried to her as she approached. "We agreed to put on a wedding, not go into bankruptcy!" he shouted. "Caviar? Are we inviting the Czar? Get some cheese and crackers and maybe some of those cocktail weenies." Then he paused, listening again. "Flowers? *How* much? Spend any more on this thing, you can pick the daisies off my grave! Get plastic!"

"J.J.," Betty said, sticking her head in, "there's a man here. He says he has something you might want."

Jameson looked past his secretary at the man standing behind her, and for once he actually appeared puzzled. But then it obviously occurred to both him and Robertson that if Betty was bringing this man to his attention, there had to be some legitimate reason, unfathomable though it might be. Cautiously, Jonah waved him in. The bum displayed his bag and Jameson said with trepidation, "I hope you don't have the head of an extraterrestrial in there. Because if you do, you're the third guy this week."

"No, sir," the homeless man said proudly.

"What's your story?"

The bum pulled the costume out of the bag and placed it in a rumpled heap on the desk. Jameson couldn't take his eyes off it. "Where the hell did you get that?" he asked. His voice sounded strange, and Betty realized he wasn't breathing.

"I found it in the trash."

Jameson held the costume up, shook it out by the shoulders. He turned it side to side, and Betty knew he was giving it the same meticulous inspection she had. And if there was one person who had stared at pictures of the genuine costume more than Betty, it was Jameson. He'd actually encountered the webslinger in person during that messy Green Goblin business.

She watched as the skepticism in Jonah's eyes gave way to mounting disbelief that he could possibly be holding such an object in his hands. And this, in turn, melded into such excitement that his mouth moved several times before he could manage to form any words.

"He's out," whispered Jonah, which was a first as far as Betty could recall, since Jonah Jameson never, ever spoke below a bellow in his office. And then his voice began to escalate in volume until every pair of eyes in the newsroom was fixed upon him. "He's given up! Thrown in the towel! *Abandoned his sad masquerade!*" He whirled the costume around in an approximation of a tango driven from pure joy, and suddenly he stopped in mid-motion.

"Just like that lowlife to quit on me!" he snapped angrily, staring at the costume with the fury of an abandoned lover. "He was the best damn newspaper-selling lunatic this city ever had!"

"Uh, mister," said the homeless man tentatively, "I'm awful hungry, mister."

"I'll give you fifty bucks," said Jameson.

Betty couldn't believe it. It was worth thousands. Hell, tens of thousands, if he could get it authenticated somehow and put it up for auction.

"I figured a hundred," replied the homeless man, which only astounded Betty more.

And Jameson, the millionaire publisher, countered with, "Seventy-five." Immediately the homeless man bobbed his head in acceptance. Betty wanted to thwap him on the side of the head in order to smack some sense into him, but Jameson was already saying, "Miss Brant. Give this man his money. And throw in a bar of soap."

"Soap. Got it, J.J.," said Betty. She gestured for the homeless man to follow her, and he did so obediently. Out at her desk, she wrote out a cash voucher and handed it to the homeless man. "Take the gentleman to payroll," she told the guard, "and cash this in for him."

The homeless man looked at the voucher and blinked. "Lady . . . you wrote an extra zero."

She stared at him, her eyes level, and said, "I doubt that. I'd never make a mistake like that," in a very flat tone. She made no effort to take the voucher back, though.

A slow smile spread over the face of the guard and then he harrumphed and said to the indigent, "You heard Miss Brant. She'd never make a mistake writing down a number. Let's go cash this in."

At last the homeless man got the message. To Betty's surprise, he bowed in a courtly manner. "Thank you," he said, and then he leaned forward and said very intently, "I used to be someone, you know. I just can't remember who."

"Maybe you were Santa Claus. Or the king of Atlantis," suggested the guard.

The homeless man pulled at his thick beard thoughtfully. "King of Atlantis. Sounds good. I like that." And he allowed the guard to lead him away.

Betty was ready to defend her "mistake" to Jonah Jameson, but as it turned out, he didn't notice it. In fact, he was in an insanely good mood for the rest of the day, and well into the evening.

However, as good a mood as he was in, Betty couldn't take seriously the night-shift personnel who claimed that J. Jonah Jameson had—with his blinds closed and convinced that no one was paying attention—slipped on the Spider-Man suit and cavorted around his office, striking heroic poses. Why, Betty knew that it was just preposterous. Jameson may have been many things, but that much of a lunatic?

No. There was only so much that even Betty Brant

would believe of her boss . . . although she did wonder the next day why there were footprints on the top of Jonah's desk and strings of paper clips hanging from the office lamp, looking for all the world like metal strands of webbing.

XVIII

Doc Ock kept his coat drawn tightly around himself as he approached the newsstand from where he obtained most of his sustenance lately. He was keeping a low profile these days, taking no chances of someone finding him out. He'd been fortunate to discover this particular newsstand, only a few blocks from the pier. It was as seedy as the general area, and the guy who ran it was about eighty percent blind. Plus policemen rarely drove through on patrol, the neighborhood was so shabby.

Since the newsstand owner's vision was so poor, he couldn't really see much of Ock, which suited the doctor just fine. For his part, Ock was practically living on the assortment of corn chips and candy bars the newsstand had to offer. It reminded him of his college days, when such diets were the norm. Considering that he developed his first, greatest ideas back then, perhaps there was something to his collegiate food selection.

Normally he barely glanced at the newspapers when he carried out one of his food runs, but this particular dreary day, his gaze was swiftly captured by the *Daily Bugle* headline blaring at him from the front page: *Spider-Man No More!*

One of his metal arms instinctively stirred under his

coat, trying to reach for a copy, but Ock batted it away and took the paper himself. He bought it with his other purchases and scanned the story on the way back to the pier.

By the time he had reached the warehouse, he decided he wasn't satisfied with the story. Not at all.

In the first place, it had eclipsed his own press. The headline reading *Manhunt Continues for Tentacled Terrorist* took a distant backseat to this latest development with Spider-Man.

In the second place, Doc Ock didn't trust it.

As he returned to work on his project, his tentacles maneuvering the fourth and final crescent into place, he had to think that if there wasn't a body, there was no proof. This entire story appeared to hinge on the *Bugle* having acquired a Spider-Man costume alleged to be the genuine article. But without a dead Spider-Man inside the costume to provide some manner of verification, all the paper really had was the publisher's conviction that the costume wasn't a hoax. In time, thought Ock, this costume might be relegated to the same historic dustbin that held Piltdown Man and the Hitler diaries.

Interestingly, according to the article, the District Attorney's Office was trying to gain possession of the costume so they could practically tear the thing apart in a detailed forensic search. Jameson wouldn't hear of it, though, and his attorneys were fighting the attempts with every tooth in their sharklike mouths. Ultimately, Doc Ock didn't really care what Spider-Man's status was. If he was still a threat, Ock would dispose of him. If he wasn't, then of what consequence was he?

No, the only thing that truly mattered was the fusion reactor. The tentacle arms twisted and curled around Ock as he stepped back to survey the progress.

Is it there yet, Father?

He chuckled at that. How like children to ask such questions. No concept of patience. "Yes, almost complete," he said aloud to the voice in his head. "And what we need now is the tritium that will enable the core. Only Osborn, that little jellyfish, knows where it is."

He cannot stand before us, Father. He is a weakling.

"Yes," Ock said, smiling. "He's a weakling. And there are ways to deal with weaklings."

Harry Osborn stood near an open window in his Manhattan town house, a drink in his hand. He heard an exceedingly annoying voice floating up from the street, singing an equally annoying song.

"Spider-Mon, Spider-Mon, where did you go to, Spider-Mon . . . ?"

He glanced out the window and saw a young Japanese violinist sitting there, performing the mournful dirge. Without hesitation, Harry upended the drink and watched with some pleasure as it descended upon the head of the street singer. He was quite satisfied with the yelp he heard, and moments later the violinist moved along.

Unfortunately, that left Harry without a drink.

Equally unfortunately, that didn't really present a problem.

He walked, or lurched slightly, over to his father's liquor cabinet—or rather, his, Harry's, liquor cabinet (he had trouble thinking of it that way)—and poured himself a shot of scotch, straight up. He downed it in one gulp and gasped as the liquid heat cascaded down his throat. Once upon a time, he would have coughed it up, unable to handle it. It was amazing what he was able to handle these days.

He steadied himself, leaning against the bar a moment, and then poured himself another.

There, in what had been his father's private office—*Except it's mine now,* Harry once again had to remind himself—he flopped down onto a chair and swirled the drink idly in the glass. Funny. On the rare occasions that he'd ventured in here, the place had seemed majestic, filled with energy and purpose. Now that it was his, it seemed . . . smaller.

Edmund Bernard—or simply Bernard, as he preferred to be called—entered the room stiffly. Bernard had been his father's houseman, and now worked for Harry. He had been with the family for ages. Getting rid of him would have been unthinkable, which was probably why Harry thought about it whenever Bernard entered his field of vision.

He glared balefully across the room at Bernard, who entered with some papers that Harry had to look over and sign before the morning. As Harry took them, he watched Bernard's stare stray to the desk, and the assortment of papers scattered there. Even the most cursory of glances would have revealed that the papers were almost exclusively photos and news clippings about Spider-Man.

"I'm leaving for the night, sir," Bernard said, and then, pausing, added in a voice tinged with regret, "Your father only obsessed over his work."

"Good night, Bernard," Harry said coldly. He felt as if Bernard was regarding him with a combination of fear and disgust. Bernard turned on his heel and left. A few moments later, the door slammed.

"See you tomorrow," Harry added, voice barely above a whisper.

He rose from his chair and tottered over toward the desk, leaning against it until the world around him stopped swirling. There was a file photo of Spider-Man in the latest issue of the *Bugle,* accompanying some ridiculous article that claimed Spider-Man had quit. The photo had a large red "X" stenciled over it, and the words "Where are you?" had been scrawled by Harry in big red letters.

Spider-Man quitting. What a stupid notion. Spider-Man would *never* back off, or back down. As near as Harry could tell, it was the wall-crawler's mission, for whatever reason, to destroy the Osborns one person, one experiment, one life at a time. Anything was possible. Perhaps he was some disgruntled former employee; OsCorp had tons of those. Or perhaps . . . perhaps he'd been hired by OsCorp's main rival, Quest. Harry clenched his fists angrily. There had to be a reason, a rationale. All Harry had to do was keep looking, and he would surely find the reason that Spider-Man was trying to make life a living hell for anyone named Osborn.

He wandered out onto the balcony, still holding the drink. He was in shirtsleeves, and barefoot, to boot. Well, there was one way to try and boost the temperature. He drank yet another shot of scotch and felt a cheery warming sensation spreading through his blood. Oh, yes, this was definitely the life. The lifestyle of the rich and famous.

That was when he heard what sounded like a distant *thump.* He glanced around, wondering where it had come from. Then a second thump, only closer this time, and louder. Then some crunches, a whirring, an assortment of noises originating from below the balcony, out of his field of vision. He moved cautiously toward the railing. Clutching it firmly, he looked over the edge.

He looked right, then left, trying to figure out from which direction—if any—the sounds were coming, whatever they might be. He leaned slightly past the edge, trying to see underneath.

And suddenly, some sort of thick steel cable unspooled straight up at him. He flinched, getting his head out of the way just in time, but the thing knocked the glass out of his hand, sending it flying. It was at that instant that he recognized the "cable" for what it was, and he stumbled backwards.

A symphony of thumping and crunching and whirring sounds enveloped him as the mechanical arms climbed steadily up the side of the town house, seemingly in slow motion, their master hanging in the middle with his real arms folded confidently.

Harry's back was against the wall, and yet he still kept pushing against it, as if he hoped he would be able to pass through it, ghostlike. The telephone was ten feet away, but it might as well have been ten miles, for all that he could get to it, since the way was blocked by one of those steel tentacles.

Like a ghoul emerging from its grave, the man once known as Otto Octavius—but now referred to by everyone in the city as Doc Ock—rose into view over the railing. One of the tentacles thrust toward Harry like a javelin. He let out a shriek, convinced that this was the end, and then to his shock he realized that all of this had happened in a matter of seconds. Even his glass hadn't yet hit the ground, and the pincers at the end of the tentacle deftly snatched it out of midair. As Doc Ock stared down at Harry, the pincer moved toward Ock and handed him the glass.

"Hello, Harry," he said with surprising softness.

Harry managed to gasp out, "Octavius. What . . . do you want?"

Doc Ock looked mildly astonished that Harry would have to ask so self-evident a question. "A drink," he said, gesturing to the glass suspended in front of him. Another tentacle brought him the bottle of scotch, and Ock poured himself a glass. Lifting it in a mock salute, he drank it, smacking his lips and savoring the taste. Then he threw the glass to the floor, smashing it.

"And something," he continued, almost as if it were an afterthought, "that starts with a 'T.' But I need more this time. As much as you can get."

Harry was so frozen in terror, watching those dangerous metal appendages of Ock's moving around sinuously, hypnotically, that it took a moment for him to process what it was that Ock was referring to. "More . . . tritium?" Ock nodded.

Harry's voice rose an octave as he demanded, "Are you crazy!?"

Doc Ock's expression indicated that this might not have been the best of questions to ask, but Harry was hardly in a state of mind to mince words. "I already took a chance on you and you created a disaster! You're a homicidal maniac!"

Without a word, Ock sent two of his tentacles snaring forward, grabbing Harry by either ankle. For a heartbeat the terrified young man thought he would be ripped in two, like a wishbone. What actually transpired wasn't much of an improvement, as he was whipped high into the air and suspended upside down, past the balcony. Harry hung there, terrified.

"Wait!" he cried out with remarkable cheer under the circumstances. "I could use a homicidal maniac!" He took a breath and continued, "We'll make a deal! Kill Spider-Man, and I'll give you what you need!"

Slowly Doc Ock brought Harry back from his precarious, dangling situation and dropped him on the floor. "It seems we have a common interest. But don't you read the newspapers?" he asked derisively. "Spider-Man appears to have given up the ghost. They say he's quit. Some even say he may be dead already."

"I don't believe that any more than you do," said Harry. "It's a trick, that's all. Either a trick by Jameson, who'd crucify his mother to sell a few newspapers, or a trick by Spider-Man, to throw everybody off the track. But he's out there. I can . . . I can . . ."

"Feel it?"

Harry had been looking out toward the city, but now he stared at Ock. As demented as it sounded, he realized he was talking to the one man in all the city who could actually understand what was going through his head. The irony that this kindred spirit was a lunatic slipped right past him. "Yes. In my heart. In my gut, I feel it."

"As can I," Ock agreed. Insanely, the tentacles seemed to nod, as well.

"On second thought," Harry told him, "don't kill him. I'll never have any sort of closure if this ends like this, with the chance of me never seeing him again. Bring him back to me... alive. Do that and I promise, you can have all the tritium you want."

"How do I find him?"

The answer came from Harry's lips before he could stop it. "Peter Parker," he said.

Ock looked surprised . . . and yet, somehow, not. "Parker? Little Mister Know-It-All?"

Harry would have grabbed the words back out of the air if he could, but it was too late to do anything but see it through. He nodded. "He takes pictures of Spider-Man for the *Bugle*. Make him tell you where he is."

"Have it ready," snarled Ock, referring to the tritium. "I'll be back."

With that Schwarzenegger-esque advisement, Doc Ock turned and clomped down the side of the building. Harry, flushed with guilt and determined to salvage something of this debacle, ran to the railing and called after him, "Don't hurt Peter! He's my best friend!"

A tentacle waved over Ock's shoulder, acknowledging the caution. But Harry had no idea whether that meant that he would abide by it, or was dismissing Harry with a gesture that bode ill for the safety of Peter Parker, his helpless friend.

XIX

Peter Parker wasn't supposed to be depressed.

This was, after all, the post-wall-crawler part of his life. The guilt-free part where his heart beat serenely in his chest, no longer shrouded in a veil of misery. The part where the specter of Spider-Man had been permanently exorcised.

So he had no idea why he was wandering through the nighttime city, peering wistfully at the skyscrapers he once ricocheted off, while around him the world went on about its business. An oncoming taxi blew its horn at him as he crossed the street, slamming to a halt a few feet away. He didn't even acknowledge it, but simply kept on walking, drawing his coat tighter around him against the cold.

He glanced at a newspaper on the newsstand as he passed. The banner headline proclaimed, *"Crime in City up 75%."* In smaller printing, a subheading read, *"Some ask: Where is Spider-Man?"*

Yeah. Some. The bitter or the frustrated or the malcontents. The people who had never had anything good to say about Spider-Man when he was around were now crabbing because he was gone. There was no pleasing some people.

And then, even as he wondered whether he was one of

the people who could never be pleased, he heard shouting, and the sound of running feet. He sniffed the air, and the unmistakable smell of smoke wafted toward him. People were running past him and he didn't follow them so much as allow himself to be caught up in the movement of the crowd.

Then he saw what all the hubbub was about. A storefront was ablaze around the corner, flames licking the night sky. What sort of store it might have been was impossible to tell, because the glass had already burst away from the inferno within. There were several floors of apartments above the storefront, as well, and smoke was pouring from several of them.

People were milling about in the crowd, screaming out a veritable laundry list of desperation. One woman cried out that her father was still inside, while another was positive there was a kid on the second floor.

It had been so easy to ignore the howls of distant sirens when Peter could simply turn his back and walk away without knowing what it was he was avoiding. But this was right in front of him, and instinct took over. He started to dart away and yank open his shirt when he suddenly remembered his costume was in the possession of J. Jonah Jameson.

Spider-Man no more.

All right. Fine. But he was still Peter Parker. That would never change, and Peter Parker had to do something.

A homeless woman was crouched nearby, watching the blaze, and she had a ratty blanket wrapped around herself. Peter scooped it up and threw it over his head to provide some protection from the smoke and flames and rushed in through the front door, keeping the blanket over his nose and mouth. He squinted out from under the blanket, counting on his spider-sense to help

him maneuver, praying that it hadn't deserted him
along with the rest of his abilities.

He sprinted up to the second floor, suffocating heat
pressing at him from all sides. He heard screams, cries
for help from all around. *Watch it! It's the Green Goblin trying to trick you again!* He shrugged away the
ridiculous notion as he kicked open an apartment door
and was greeted with a wave of billowing smoke.

He dropped to the floor, remembering that it was
what one was supposed to do. Heat rose, but the oxygen might still be collected close to the floor. Even if he
didn't have his spider-powers to aid him, at least his scientific knowledge might see him through.

He crawled along the floor, thick black smoke billowing around him, and he was able to make out someone through the haze. It was a child, face so smeared
with dirt, hair so singed, Peter couldn't even determine
if it was a boy or a girl. It didn't matter. He scuttled
forward and grabbed up the child under his arm like a
football.

Still keeping low to the ground, he sprinted for the
door since flames were blocking the window. From
above him he heard timbers starting to break, and
screams from what seemed far away. He couldn't think
about them. He was out of time.

The rest of it was a blur. He was operating purely on
adrenaline, instinct, and barely contained terror. All he
knew was that suddenly he was out the front door,
coughing and choking and hoping to God that his lungs
didn't collapse. He nearly dropped the child, and then
someone was hauling the child from his arms, calling
out a name, "Leslie!" which didn't do much to solve the
question of the kid's gender.

Someone grabbed the blanket away from him, and he

realized it was the homeless woman, who complained that he had gotten it covered with soot. Peter mumbled an apology as sirens rang in his head, and then he nearly blacked out.

By the time he came to his senses again, he was breathing in oxygen through a mask held up to him by a paramedic. He blinked away the remaining confusion in his head and looked around, watching the hive of activity surrounding him. The firemen had arrived and were pumping water into the blaze, bringing it under control. Ambulances were there, as well, some heading away from the scene at high speed, sirens blaring.

"Just take it easy, fella," said the paramedic. "We'll get you to the hospital, have you checked."

"I'll be fine," Peter whispered hoarsely. "You don't have to—"

"With the amount of smoke you took in? You bet your ass we have to," replied the paramedic firmly. He placed the oxygen mask back over Peter's mouth.

A passing fireman patted him on the back. "You got some guts, kid," he told him. Apparently folks in the crowd had pointed out Peter as being the heroic idiot who had dashed into the flames to save a child. Peter tried to bob his head in acknowledgment, but even that small gesture hurt.

Another fireman approached the one who had just spoken to Peter, and Peter overheard him say in a low voice, "Some poor soul got trapped on the fourth floor. Never made it out."

Never made it out.

The words stayed with Peter all the way to the hospital. There they gave him a clean bill of health, and hailed him as a hero while simultaneously telling him he should never do anything so foolish again, because he'd been exceptionally lucky.

It didn't matter.

His heroism didn't matter to him. His good fortune didn't matter to him. Nothing mattered except the unknown individual on the fourth floor whose life had ended this night, and Peter hadn't been able to do a damned thing about it.

But Spider-Man might have. Spider-Man could have moved faster, Spider-Man could have accomplished more.

Spider-Man could have gotten the job done.

So . . . was that it? All the way home he mulled it over and over, and still he couldn't come up with an answer that was acceptable. Either he had to be Spider-Man, or deal with the guilt that came with every person whom he didn't save. Was the price of great power not only great responsibility, but an incessant sense of culpability, as well?

He couldn't do everything. Not even as Spider-Man— he couldn't be everywhere, accomplishing everything. He was still a man, not a god.

Back at his apartment, he stood at his window, going over and over the day's events and staring out at the night, wondering if he would ever know peace. Tears welled up unwanted in his eyes. He turned and looked at the picture of Uncle Ben and Aunt May on his dresser.

His imaginings had been free of his uncle ever since he'd left the costume behind. It had been such a relief. Now, though, he felt as if he wanted him back. As if he could never come to any sort of resolution if he couldn't square it with Ben face-to-face.

"Am I not *supposed* to have what I want?" he asked. "What I need?"

The picture stared at him mutely, offering no response.

Every muscle in his body felt sore. He could barely move, could barely think. He flopped down onto the bed and closed his eyes. "What am I supposed to do?"

There was a light tap at the door. He didn't even hear himself say, "It's open." Using a mental crowbar, he pried open his eyes and saw Ursula, the landlord's daughter, standing there. For a wild moment, he imagined that she would open her mouth and her father's harsh cry of *"Rent!"* would emerge.

She said nothing, nor did he. A long moment of silence passed between them. Then she smiled.

"Would you like a piece of chocolate cake?" she asked, her eyes limpid.

The question was so utterly out of left field that the only thing Peter could think to say was, "Okay."

"Glass of milk?"

He nodded. She bounced lightly on the balls of her feet and sprinted away to get them.

"My life is too weird for words," he said.

Ursula sat on the edge of the bed, eating a slice of chocolate cake, which—she proudly informed him—she had baked herself completely from scratch from a mix. He had wisely chosen not to point out the inherent contradiction in that. He had, however, opted to sit at his desk and eat his slice, since he hardly needed to have Ditkovitch burst into the room and discover his daughter and Peter together on the bed. However innocent the truth of the situation might be, it would pale compared to the insinuation. At the moment, his landlord just wanted his rent. He certainly didn't need the landlord wanting his head on a platter, as well.

"Thank you," said Peter with genuine gratitude as he finished eating the cake. She shrugged as if it were no big deal. To her, it might very well not be. To him, it meant a hell of a lot.

When they were done, she picked up his plate, put it atop hers, and took his glass. She smiled once more. He nodded in return, and wondered if this was what Aunt May was like when she was a teen. About to step out of the apartment, she clearly remembered something.

"Oh. You had a message. Your phone just keep ringing and ringing . . . you don't have an answering machine, I guess." When he shook his head, she shrugged and continued, "My dad was getting cranky about it, because the walls are, y'know, so thin, so I came up here and answered it for you. I hope you don't mind."

She extended a piece of paper and for an instant he thought, hoped, prayed it was Mary Jane.

"Your aunt," said Ursula.

Oh, well. Could have been worse. Could have been Jameson.

He took the message from her and read it.

Well it made sense. Ursula had given him a brief oasis of tranquillity. So it was only natural that she would be the messenger who would shatter it.

XX

Peter would have been at his aunt's first thing in the morning. Unfortunately, he fell asleep on the subway. By the time an annoyed conductor had awoken him, lest he wind up in the train yard, Peter was all the way at the Union Turnpike terminal point, and had to wait for a return subway to Forest Hills.

By the time he arrived, boxes of carefully labeled cartons dotted the front lawn. Some kid Peter didn't recognize was helping Aunt May with the moving while she continued to put labels on those boxes that weren't already marked.

"What's going on?" Peter said with obvious concern.

"They gave me another few weeks," she told him. "I decided the hell with it. I'm moving on. I found a small apartment."

"Why didn't you tell me?"

She just shrugged. "I'm quite able to take care of things. And Henry Jackson across the street is giving me a hand, and I'm giving him five dollars."

Peter watched in surprise as the boy continued to hoist boxes around. Last he remembered, Henry Jackson was the kid who sped around on his Big Wheel and had a knack for getting under people's feet when they were walking. "*That's* Henry Jackson?"

She nodded. "Funny what happens in two years. Nine years old. Great ambitions."

He braced himself, hoping that his next words wouldn't cause a torrent of tears or angry words. "Listen, Aunt May, about the last visit of mine—"

To his surprise, she waved it off dismissively. "Pish posh. We needn't talk about it. It's water over the dam or under the bridge, wherever you like it." Her voice cracked from emotion, though, with her next words. "You made a brave move. And I'm proud of you, and I thank you, and I love you, Peter . . . so very, very much."

She embraced him then, and all he could think of was his earliest days when he'd regarded her with suspicion and uncertainty and all he wanted was his mother back. Now he realized, for perhaps the first time in his life, that his mother had always been there, incarnated in the form of this elderly woman who was determined to do the right thing, no matter the cost.

"Thank you, Aunt May," he said. Then, looking over her shoulder, he suddenly said, "Hey, where are all my comic books?"

"Oh, those dreadful things. I gave them away."

He moaned inwardly as Henry moved out of the house to the back steps. "I put the pans in the box, Mrs. Parker," he called.

"Thank you."

"Hi, Peter," he said, waving.

"Hi, Henry. You're getting tall."

"Tell you what, Henry, will you pack those cookbooks in with the mixer?"

Henry bobbed his head and said, "Okay," but he was still looking at Peter. "You take Spider-Man's pictures, don't you?"

Peter shrugged. "I used to."

"Where is he?"

"Henry and I agree that we don't see his picture in the paper anymore," May said.

"He, uh . . ." Peter suddenly became very interested in the tops of his shoes. "He quit."

"Why?" asked Henry, moving toward them, looking confused and even a bit disappointed.

"Wanted to try other . . . things."

"Will he be back?"

Peter shook his head and spoke the simple truth: "I don't know."

"Oh." Henry went back to the house, looking considerably less perky than he had moments earlier.

"You'll never guess who he wants to be," said May, and rather than giving him the chance to guess, said, "Spider-Man."

Peter was dumbfounded. "Why?"

She continued to pack as she said, "He knows a hero when he sees one. Too few characters out there flying around like that, saving old girls like me. And Lord knows, kids like Henry need a hero. Courageous, self-sacrificing people. Setting examples for all of us."

He couldn't believe she was saying it. He knew, of course, that he had saved Aunt May. But so often, the things he tried to accomplish—no matter how noble his intentions—seemed to be distorted so that he ended up looking like a creep. Altruism was twisted into selfishness, heroism into villainy. He had just . . . well, he'd just assumed that Aunt May harbored ill will toward Spider-Man. It never occurred to him that she might hold him in such high regard.

Now she was rearranging plates inside a box, presumably so they wouldn't break upon transport. "Everybody loves a hero. People line up for them, cheer them, scream their names. And years later tell how they stood for hours in the cold rain just to catch a glimpse of the one who taught them to hold on a second longer. I believe there's a hero in all of us who keeps us honest, gives us strength, makes us noble, and finally allows us to die with pride, even though sometimes we have to be steady, and give up the thing we want the most. Even our dreams."

Oh my God. She knows. She knows I am . . . was . . . she knows . . . she's talking to him through me, to me, she's . . . but she couldn't . . . there's no way . . .

She turned from the plates and faced him again. There was nothing in her expression to give the slightest indication that she thought she was talking to anyone other than her nephew. It didn't make the words any less sincere, though, nor any less meaningful. "Spider-Man did that for Henry, and he wonders where he's gone. Henry needs him." Then she pointed at a piece of furniture and said, "Can you lift that desk and put it in the garage for me, Peter?"

"Okay," he said, feeling as if he'd had an anvil dropped on him.

"But don't strain yourself," she cautioned. "I'll be right back." She headed toward the house, calling, "Henry! Don't forget the recipe box!"

He watched her go, shaking his head. As he walked over to the desk, he considered the fact that he'd been so certain seeing Aunt May now would be torture. That she would blame him for all of her current strife. He'd braced himself for it.

Instead, not only had she let him off the hook, she'd tossed the hook away . . . and lauded the accomplishments of Spider-Man besides. The only downside was that she'd given away his comic books.

Gave them away? Why? he wondered as he carried the desk toward the garage.

He was so distracted that it wasn't until he was halfway back there that he suddenly realized he was toting the heavy oak desk with one hand, and not feeling the weight in the slightest.

Eight stories up in the heart of New York City, Peter stared at the twenty-foot chasm that stretched between himself and the next rooftop. It was a space he had vaulted with ease, back when he was dressed in red and blue. Now, though, his heart was pounding like a trip-hammer.

He kept telling himself that his strength was back. That there was no reason his other abilities shouldn't be, either. That he'd been like a home-run hitter who had been lost at the plate for a while, that was all. A frustrated slugger swinging at pitches in the dirt. He hadn't actually lost the ability to knock balls out of the park; he just needed to do something dramatic to find his stroke again.

Well, this was pretty damned dramatic, all right. On the other hand, if he was wrong, he was about to commit suicide.

It'd certainly solve all my problems, he thought morbidly, and then he resolved to push all such thoughts right out of his head. Instead, he closed his eyes and muttered, "Strong focus on what I want." Just as the doctor had told him. He visualized himself covering the distance with ease, rather than falling screaming to his death. His mind was a computer, downloading a file, and reality would be the printer onto which he would print it out and actualize it.

So much for dramatic analogies.

He drew back as far as possible from the edge of the roof, then started to run. Faster and faster, building up speed, building up confidence, starting to feel like his old self. And just as it happened in the fight with Flash Thompson, that day when his powers had first kicked in, the world around him slowed almost to a crawl. His environment became ice, and he was a skater gliding across it.

He got to the edge of the roof and there was no hesitation as he hurled himself into the void. His pulse was slow and relaxed, his breathing steady. Gravity? As Aunt May would say, *Pish posh*. Gravity was of no relevance to him as he sailed across the gap between roofs, feeling every iota of his power coursing through his veins.

It was at that point that gravity, offended by his audacity, decided to show him who was boss.

Realizing with growing horror that his arc wasn't sufficient to clear the distance, Peter Parker emitted a high-pitched scream. Then he dropped like a ballast bag tossed from a balloon, flailing his arms about, trying to find something to grab on to.

He lucked out and snagged a clothesline on the way down. It snapped at one end, but the other held, and he swung the rest of the way across the divide. Shirts and undergarments covered his face and he couldn't see a damned thing, which was why he slammed full-face into the brick wall.

He hung there, jockey shorts draped over his head, a brassiere looped around his chest.

"Oh, darn," he murmured weakly. "And me without my camera. Jameson would've paid double for this shot."

XXI

Jameson—John Jameson—was stretched out on a couch in Mary Jane's apartment, his hands folded behind his head. He was in his stocking feet, thanks to Mary Jane's loud admonition of "Shoes off the couch!" Otherwise he was wearing sweats and a NASA T-shirt that read "Zero-G Wiz." Mary Jane was lying on the floor, filling out an invitation list, with a tall stack of invitations at her side. John was busy studying a travel magazine. Then he lowered it and watched her motoring through the invites.

"M.J.," he said, "are you at all concerned that we're moving too fast?"

"We're sitting still, John. Not a lot of moving going on."

"No, I mean," he nodded toward the invitations, "most people take months—sometimes even a year or two—to plan a wedding. And we're, you know . . . plowing right into it. Dad had to pull a hundred strings to get the church, the caterers, everything on such short notice. We're going at it with such a manic energy, half my friends have asked me if you're pregnant and we're trying to avoid the 'Here comes the bride, big, fat, and wide' syndrome."

She propped herself up on one elbow and asked with interest, "What have the other half said?"

"Well . . . actually, there is no other half," he admitted. "They all said it."

"Oh, for crying out loud." She rolled her eyes. "Can't they just accept that we're really anxious to start our life together? That that's all it is?"

"Yes, I just . . ."

"You just what? *You* can't accept it?"

"I just . . ." He took a deep breath. "I just want to make sure that you're not feeling as if we have to get married in a hurry because if we don't one of us might back out. That you just want to do it to 'get it over with.' Or because you're not really sure, or there's something you feel you need to prove, to someone, or—"

"John, that's silly."

"Is it?"

"*Yes,*" she said firmly. "I want to get married because I want to be with you. Don't you want to be with me?"

"Of course."

"Then that's settled." She slapped the magazine. "Go. Read. Plan."

He nodded, feeling slightly mollified, and after another minute or two he read aloud, " 'The Bahamas. Fourteen tropical nights that captivate your imagination and stimulate your senses.' " He lowered the magazine and asked, "How's that?"

"Sounds good," Mary Jane said, which was exactly how she'd responded to the last nine suggestions he'd made. Staring at the invitations, she said, "Who's Aunt Ida? It's familiar, but I can't—"

"Remember when we were at the lodge on Christmas? She called us with the trifle recipe. The gabby one."

"We had a gabby recipe?"

"*She* was gabby." He smiled.

"Ohh, Aunt Ida," Mary Jane said, voice dripping with good-natured sarcasm. "I *liked* Aunt Ida."

"My mother's family," John told her with a resigned shrug. "Actually, she drives everybody crazy."

Mary Jane, sounding like the voice of experience, said, "Families can do that."

John watched her out the corner of his eye as she continued working on the list. He was surprised when he saw her cross off a name with particular conviction. Wondering who could have possibly provoked the reaction, he lowered the magazine and studied the list more openly. He was mildly surprised when he saw whose name had disappeared beneath black pen strokes.

"Are you sure you don't want to invite your friend the photographer? Peter Parker?"

"Positive," she said with a finality that indicated the discussion should end.

John didn't take the hint. He was someone who earned a living sitting atop thousands of tons of explosive fuel. He wasn't daunted by a candid conversation with his fiancée. "I thought he was your pal," said John.

"Peter Parker is a great big jerk."

"World's full of big jerks," he said in a self-deprecating manner. "You'd be surprised how many big jerks end up getting the girl."

She looked up from the invitations and smiled at him. "You're adorable, ya big jerk."

Gravely he said, "It's the uniform," and laughed. Then he reached out to her and gently touched her cheek.

She studied him closely, looking deeply into his eyes as if searching for something. "Put your head back," she told him after a moment.

He frowned, puzzled, but did as she asked. He leaned far back, his head hanging over the arm of the sofa. She came around to the other side, then leaned in and kissed his upside-down face.

She had never kissed him like this before. He felt as if every nerve ending were on fire. It wasn't just like they were kissing for the first time, it seemed as if this were the invention of the kiss. The first time man and woman pressed lips and thought, *Oh, my God, why haven't we been doing this all along?*

The travel magazine slipped from his suddenly nerveless fingers. She withdrew, and he gazed at her in wonderment. "Wow," he sighed. "You just put me back on the moon. Are you up there with me?"

Mary Jane smiled and stroked his hair. His feeling of blissful awe slowly gave way to vague concern that something was off.

"*Are* you up there with me?" he asked slowly. "Or are you . . . are you somewhere else entirely?"

She looked away from him. "I need to go out for a bit. Just . . . be by myself. Okay?"

"Sure," he said guardedly. "Do you . . . want me to be here when you come back?"

"Hmm? Oh! Sure," Mary Jane assured him. "Read the magazine, relax, do . . . husband-to-be stuff." She was getting her jacket, her purse, and her voice sounded light, but in a forced way. "It'll be fine. I'll be fine. Everything will be fine. I'm just, y'know . . . being ditzy me. Later, okay, love?"

"Sure," he said, and watched as the door closed behind her. As he did so, he realized if Mary Jane were that lousy an actress all the time, she'd still be waiting tables.

He looked back at the list, at Peter Parker's crossed-off name. He thought about the way Mary Jane had re-acted when he'd asked about rushing into the wedding because she wanted to prove something.

"Houston," he said softly, "we may have a problem."

As Mary Jane sat at a table in the window of Ari's Village Deli and Bakery, she thought about what had been going through her mind when she kissed John. In the best school of method acting, she tried to recall the exact sensations that had pounded through her that night in the rain. That extraordinary night when, totally caught up in the romance of being rescued, she'd rolled Spider-Man's mask partway down and they'd kissed in a long, lingering, frozen moment of desire while he hung upside down in the alley.

In many ways, her life had been upside down ever since.

She sipped her cup of coffee, glanced at her watch, and wondered how long it would take him to get here. Perhaps he wouldn't come at all. If he didn't, could she really blame him?

"Hiya."

She looked up. Peter was standing right there, smiling down at her.

"Surprised?" she asked.

"Very," he said, taking a seat.

"Thanks for coming."

He leaned forward, looking concerned. "Are you in trouble?"

"You . . . might say so." She discovered she was having trouble meeting his gaze, and forced herself to look him in the eyes. "This feels funny. Not sure how to begin. But . . . you know how minds do tricks on us?"

"Tell me about it," he said ruefully.

"Well, mine did a real number on me," she told him. "Uh . . . what it did was . . . it listened."

He stared at her blankly, clearly not sure what she was talking about.

"It . . . heard what you said to me after my show that night," she continued, still nervous, but beginning to grow in confidence with every spoken word. "I believe it was always listening, but it refused to let me accept it until . . . until it told me to. That you were different that night. But I was afraid to trust you. And . . . I've been thinking things through . . ."

She reached across the table toward him, and briefly it seemed as if he was reluctant to respond. But then he did, his hand grasping hers, their fingers interlocking. It was a connection being made between the two of them, something that she hadn't even fully realized she'd lost until she discovered it again right then.

And then, just like that, the connection was broken.

Mary Jane jumped slightly, startled by the abruptness as Peter pulled his hand free. "Listen . . . there's more for me to say now," he told her. Her eyebrows knit in perplexity. "I . . . maybe rushed into things. I thought I was—"

Her voice went cold. "Wait a minute. What are you saying?"

"I'm saying I . . ." His skin was looking three shades of ashen. "Uh . . . I thought I could be there for you, Mary Jane . . . but I can't. My mind was playing tricks, too."

She wanted to kill him.

She wanted to pick up the bread knife sitting between them and drive it into his chest. She wanted to strangle him with the napkin, throw coffee in his face. She wanted to scream at him, to howl that nobody yanks her around like this, dammit, how *dare* he screw with her emotions, how dare he be so unable to commit that he couldn't sustain even the possibility of a relationship for longer than thirty seconds? What kind of monster was he, what sort of freak?

And at the same time, she wanted to help him, to hold him. To find whatever great weight was occupying his obviously tortured mind and lift it from him. It was as if he were possessed by a malevolent spirit of misery that had briefly departed, only to come roaring back to him and seize occupancy once more, like a pestilent squatter. She wanted to know what magic words needed to be said to lift it from him forever, banish it to a realm where it could never touch him and he might therefore know happiness ever after.

The warring sides of her mind collided and canceled each other out, and the only outer reflection of her inner turmoil was a single tear that ran down her cheek. She tried to keep her voice steady and barely managed to do so. "Do you love me, Peter . . . or not?"

"I . . . I don't," he told her in a voice that he probably imagined was firm, but lacked any trace of conviction.

"Then I have one more request." She paused and then said, "Kiss me."

"Kiss you?" He looked confused. Why shouldn't he be? *She* was. "Why?"

"I . . . need to know something."

He drew back, hesitant, and she leaned toward him. He looked afraid. "Just one kiss," she said with soft insistence. "Friend to friend."

She drew closer to him, and he to her. Suddenly she saw his eyes go wide in what seemed unmistakeable alarm. His body stiffened, and then his head was snapping back and forth in a blur, like a radar dish gone amuck.

Before she could say anything else, before she could ask him what the hell his problem was, the plate-glass restaurant window shattered and a car hurtled directly at them.

XXII

Sometimes we have to be steady and give up the thing we want the most.

When Aunt May had said that to him, Peter's first thoughts had flown to Mary Jane. If he was going to return to action as Spider-Man—if he was going to fulfill the hero's role that so many expected of him—then that meant sacrificing his life with her.

That problem, however, had seemed to have been solved. Even when Spider-Man had flatly been a thing of the past, Mary Jane had made clear to him that they would never be anything more than friends . . . and quite possibly not even friends. Somehow, that knowledge took the edge off Peter's decision.

So when Mary Jane had called him, told him it was an emergency, he had gone to meet her purely in the spirit of trying to salvage their friendship. Even if they weren't to be lovers, at the very least he wanted to have her in his life somehow. He had few enough friends as it was.

On the trip over, he'd wondered what the problem was. His first guess was that it had something to do with Harry. It seemed as if there was always trouble with Harry. Or perhaps she was sick, or owed money and was too embarrassed to tell her fiancé. All sorts of possibilities occurred to him—*except* the one that Mary Jane confessed to him across the table in the restaurant.

His first reflex was to jump for joy.

His second was that Mary Jane Watson had the worst timing in the world.

His third was that, no, she only had the *second*-worst timing. Peter himself was the grand master of being out of step with the world around him.

Of all the lies, all the deceits he'd perpetrated in his pursuit of trying to do the right thing, the biggest whopper he'd ever uttered was when Mary Jane had asked if he loved her. The question came at the end of a conversation that had been like a root canal of the soul. Here he had been coming on, full steam ahead, trying to win her back . . . and the moment she had reciprocated, then, like a sadistic puppeteer, he had cut the strings.

There couldn't be any doubt. He had to seem like the biggest jerk who ever lived. The most cruel, the most insincere. He fully expected her to reach across the table, smack him in the face as hard as she could, and storm out of his life once and for all.

Instead, she wanted to kiss him.

Kiss him? Was she insane?

Was he?

He'd tried to pull back, knowing that if he kissed her, that would be it. It was all over. The lyrics of the "The Shoop Shoop Song" flittered through his mind. If she wanted to know if he loved her so, it would really be in his kiss. Cloth might mask his face, but there was no way he could mask his heart through that sort of intimate contact.

He clenched his hands under the table, trying to will himself away from there, and yet he stayed rooted to the spot. She drew nearer, and the scent of her perfume, of her, was so thick he thought he would drown in it.

Abruptly, the world slowed to a crawl, but it wasn't because of Mary Jane.

His spider-sense was kicking in.

Instinctively, he looked this way and that, snapping his head around. Mary Jane seemed frozen in time, a perplexed look on her face that was almost comical, and suddenly there it was. He didn't need spider-sense to see it. A blind man could have seen it. A car was rocketing through the air straight toward the plate-glass window, and Peter's first thought was that some driver had lost control of the vehicle. Two things disabused him of that: First, there was no driver. Second, the car was angling downward. Someone, or something, had thrown it.

For Peter Parker, thought was action. He dove for Mary Jane the split second that the car came crashing through the window. He grabbed her up, moving so quickly that M.J. still seemed frozen to him, and at the same instant spotted a waitress paralyzed in fear as the vehicle careened toward her.

With Mary Jane slung under one arm like a sack of laundry, Peter brought his free arm up and squeezed his fingers into his palm without thinking. There was no time for second-guessing, no moment to remember that he'd had trouble spinning webs before. Lives other than his were on the line, and dwelling on his personal difficulties was just an unaffordable luxury.

As easily as if there'd never been a problem at all, a ball of webbing fired out from his wrist and struck the waitress, knocking her off her feet and away from the oncoming car.

Peter had accomplished the feat while still in midair. Now he slammed to the ground with Mary Jane and desperately rolled to the side, just avoiding having the car's back tire run over his face. The vehicle fishtailed, and then crashed to a halt at the back of the restaurant.

Patrons were running around, screaming, waving their arms, and at least two were on their cell phones. No doubt calling their attorneys. It was fascinating to see how different people dealt with an emergency.

Peter helped Mary Jane to her feet. She was looking around, dazed, clearly unsure of what the hell had just happened. In the distance, Peter could swear he heard a faint *boom* and wondered if a random *T-Rex* had gone astray on the way to Jurassic Park. Or perhaps he'd missed a memo letting him know the Hulk was dropping by.

"Peter! Peter, what's happening?!" demanded a befuddled Mary Jane, and then there was another impact, louder than the first, then another. Approaching thunder? Trucks running over metal plates in the road? No, it was far too steady, too regular.

There was no longer the slightest doubt in Peter's mind. It was Doc Ock, and this wasn't just any house call.

He glanced around desperately, trying to find a fast way out of the restaurant. There was none. The front door was packed with frantic customers, and the rear exit was blocked by the car.

Peter held Mary Jane closer, and suddenly a fire hydrant directly in front of the restaurant was smashed aside. Water geysered up from it, and then a tentacle ripped aside what was left of the restaurant wall. There went any faint hope on Peter's part that Ock's presence here was merely coincidence.

Doc Ock looked down from on high like a malevolent dark god, held suspended there by his tentacles. "Peter Parker," he fairly purred, "and the girlfriend. Took my advice, did you? Let me guess: The poetry did the trick, right?"

Mary Jane gaped at Peter. "You told me you'd been reading poetry—because *he* suggested it?"

"He wasn't nuts at the time," Peter said defensively, and then he winced. "No offense, Doctor."

"The truth hurts, but I endure," said Ock sadly.

"How . . . how did you—?"

"Know you were here?" Ock grinned down at him. "My babies are multitalented. This entire city's communications system lives and dies on fiber optics, which my tentacles are easily able to plug into."

"You tapped my phone line?" When Ock nodded, Peter felt his cheeks flush with anger. "How could you, Doctor?"

"I beg your pardon? You said it yourself: 'Nuts.' Remember?" He pointed at himself and his smile grew wider. "Once I knew for certain you were home, I was going to come and find you . . . but then this little lady called. When you made your date, I knew I couldn't let the opportunity pass."

"What opportunity?" asked Peter, trying to figure out some way to cope with this disaster that wouldn't advertise his secret to the world. "What do you want?"

A tentacle snapped out. Peter could have dodged it, but the speed required for that would certainly snare Ock's attention, leading to questions that Peter really didn't want to have asked. So he let it grab him around the neck, yanking him closer to Ock's face.

"I want you to find your friend Spider-Man," he said

tightly. "Tell him to meet me at the West Side clock tower at three o'clock."

"I don't know where he is."

Doc Ock looked unimpressed by Peter's claim. "Find him, or I'll peel the flesh," he nodded toward Mary Jane, "off her bones."

"If you lay one finger on her . . ." Peter snarled.

"You'll do what?" Ock said challengingly.

And suddenly Peter didn't give a damn about his secret. Doc Ock's face was only a few feet away. Peter could end the madness right here, right now. He drew back his fist, and then one of Ock's tentacles whipped around before he could move. It knocked him back viciously, sending him slamming into what was left of the back wall of the restaurant.

The flying car had taken out most of its supports, and now, with the impact of Peter's body, the entire structure tumbled down upon him. Seconds later, he was buried.

From beneath the rubble, he heard a loud, angry string of curses come from Ock. *Perfect. Let him think I'm dead. Then maybe he'll leave me alone, and Mary Jane can—*

It was at that moment that he heard a scream, and a cry of "Put me down!" From somewhere nearby, in the hazing blur that was Peter's consciousness, that voice was easy to identify. The blur cleared as Peter realized just what had happened: Doc Ock had grabbed Mary Jane and was carting her off, laughing all the while.

Mary Jane? Why Mary Jane? Had Ock realized that Peter was Spider-Man and was trying to push him into action? No, that couldn't be it. Ock had all the cards, and had clearly won the arms race. He had no reason to be coy. Coy just didn't work when you had four metal tentacles and a streak of megalomania on par with that of Napoleon.

Desperately, Peter began to shove at his entombment. It wasn't easy. He felt as if he were trying to relocate the moon using a small plastic spoon. He had no clue how long it took him: probably seconds, although it seemed as if hours were dragging past.

Then he shoved aside a broken beam and realized that his hand had emerged from the pile and was grasping air. Unfortunately he couldn't breathe through his hand. He needed to surface, and fast. He gathered his wits, his concentration, and his rapidly returning spider-strength, focused, and then smashed upward. Debris consisting of two-by-fours, bricks, and plaster flew in all directions. Seconds later Peter was standing.

It was a hell of an accomplishment, all things considered. His clothes were torn and his lip was bleeding. None of that mattered, though, because he realized his strength was flooding back into him. It had begun with lifting Aunt May's desk, and now all his missing strength and more was at his command.

In his eyes there was the gleam of a hunter.

He dashed into the street and scanned the area around the restaurant. There was no sign of either Ock or Mary Jane outside the restaurant.

It didn't matter. He would find them both, because he was sick and tired of having deranged people threaten those whom he loved the most.

Back in the wreckage of the restaurant, Peter found a napkin and a pen, and quickly scribbled a note on the napkin before shoving it in his pocket. Nearby was a sports clothing store with a smashed-in window, courtesy of one of Ock's tentacles. A soiled ski mask lay on the ground. He fired off a web-line, snagged the ski mask, yanked it toward him, and caught it easily. He pulled it over his head, thinking, *Back to basics,* and sprinted toward the nearest building. There was no time to be subtle: He fired a web-line, grabbed it, and sent himself flying heavenward with the confidence of old.

Pedestrians had been too caught up in the destruction to notice his snagging of the ski mask, but when he launched himself toward the rooftops, it grabbed everyone's attention. There were shouts and outcries of "That's gotta be Spider-Man!" and even, "Get him!" But he couldn't tell whether it was a call for him to nail Doc Ock or whether someone actually thought they could apprehend Spider-Man himself in some way.

It didn't matter. Nothing mattered except saving Mary Jane and putting an end to Ock's rampage. Whether Ock was under the influence of the arms, or actually piloting the boat, Peter didn't care.

All he knew was that Doc Ock wasn't getting away with this. Not on *his* watch. Ock wanted Spider-Man? Perfect. That was exactly what he was going to get.

It had taken him half an hour door-to-door to get from his apartment to the coffee shop via subway. From the coffee shop uptown, covering forty blocks via web, it took him ten minutes . . . and that was with being cautious. He landed on the wall directly outside J. Jonah Jameson's office. Through the window, he heard Robertson and Jameson talking.

". . . police still have nothing on the whereabouts of your son's fiancée. Sorry, Jonah."

Bad news certainly traveled fast.

"It's all my fault," said Jameson, and for the first time in his life, Peter actually felt some degree of empathy for him. Both of them were worried about Mary Jane, although for very different reasons. Still, for all the sins that could be laid at the doorstep of J. Jonah Jameson, Peter couldn't figure out how Ock abducting Mary Jane was remotely Jonah's fault.

But the next words in the conversation made it clear. "I drove him away."

"And he's the only one who could have stopped Doc Ock," said Robbie.

Son of a—! They were talking about Spider-Man.

He suddenly felt like Tom Sawyer, hiding in the vestibule during his own funeral and hearing all the nice things being said by everyone who had deplored him in life.

He peered through the window. His costume was hanging nearby, on display. Jameson, his head sagging, had his face in his hands; Robertson was next to him, his back to the costume, a hand resting on his boss' shoulder. It was perfect positioning, and would likely remain that way for perhaps a second or two. But that was all the time Peter would need.

He leaned in and snagged the costume, yanking it out of the office even as Jonah continued to "eulogize" him.

"Spider-Man was a hero," Jonah said mournfully. "I just couldn't see it."

Aw, man, and me without my tape recorder, thought Peter, as he pulled the napkin from his pocket and webbed it to the spot vacated by the costume. The entire process had taken less than the blink of an eye. He was already scuttling up the wall as Jonah continued, "He was a . . ."

The pause was enough to telegraph it to him: Jonah must have turned around.

"Thief!" came Jonah's outraged bellow, confirming

it. He'd discovered that his prize trophy was gone, replaced by a note that read, "Courtesy, your friendly neighborhood Spider-Man."

Peter didn't slow down, continuing his climb while Jonah's howling went on at length. "A criminal! He stole my suit! He's a menace to the entire city! I want that wall-crawling insect prosecuted! I want him strung up by his webs! *I want Spider-Man!*"

As rants went, it wasn't bad. Granted, spiders weren't insects, but Peter didn't really expect Jonah to know or care about that. And since it was originally Peter's suit, questions of ownership were murky at best.

But hey, Peter could be accommodating. "Jonah wants Spider-Man?" he thought as he pulled his mask over his head. "Then he gets Spider-Man."

His clothes were wadded up into a compact web-sack, which he stuck in a shadowed corner of the *Daily Bugle* roof. He flexed his arms and legs. All the freedom of movement was still there. Even better, apparently Jonah had had it dry-cleaned and professionally restored. Even those annoying bloodstains had come out. It looked and felt better than new.

Well, so did he.

He leaped off the roof with neither fear nor hesitation, fired a web-line, and sailed through the steel-and-glass valleys of Manhattan. He heard people shouting from below, "Take a look—overhead!" and "Hey there! There goes the Spider-Man!"

Damn straight, he thought.

XXIII

There had never been any doubt in Ock's mind that Spider-Man would show up.

He had seen the truth in Peter Parker's face, despite his mewling protests. Parker knew exactly where Spider-Man was holed up, and would be able to produce him with little to no effort.

He comes, Father. Let us handle him.

Patience, children, patience. This time, we shall be the spider. Let the fly who thinks he's a spider come into our snare.

Ock sat perched atop the gigantic clock tower, waiting patiently, as Spider-Man swung closer and closer. Would the webbed one be so foolish as to come directly at him? No, of course not. Ock knew better, and sure enough, as the clock below him tolled the hour of three, Spider-Man landed on the clockface, just out of range of the undulating tentacles.

"Where is she?" called Spider-Man.

"She's nearby," Ock replied calmly. "Quite safe. Come . . . let's talk."

Father? Are we really going to talk to—?

What do you think?

I think . . . he is ours.

You think correctly.

Instantly the tentacles lashed out at Spider-Man, the first one sweeping right at his head. There was to be no toying with him, no dancing. The arms were going in for the quick kill . . . which might actually be merciful and more than Spider-Man deserved. But Ock considered himself, at heart, to be merciful.

And *not* a murderer. Certainly not that.

In truth, he knew that he could have simply terrorized Harry Osborn into giving him the tritium. It wouldn't have been much of a challenge at all. But when Harry had offered him this devil's deal, it had played perfectly into Ock's own desires. Doc Ock, for all that he had done, still believed himself to be a moral man. A decent man. A man laboring toward a project that would benefit the world, struggling against staggering odds arrayed against him by that very same world he sought to aid.

He also blamed Spider-Man for meddling with his efforts in the past. The problem was, past was past, and as much as he and his children wanted to kill Spider-Man for it, that was pure vengeance. Vengeance, in the final analysis, was not the pursuit of the civilized man. Hunting down Spider-Man, murdering him . . . it just didn't sit right. Oh, it was fine with his children. They would have been perfectly content to shred Spider-Man at the first opportunity. But he was the loving parent, whose job it was to guide them, and cold-blooded killing . . . it wasn't appropriate. Not to a man of science.

Harry Osborn, however, had offered him the ideal out. Destroying Spider-Man now, it wasn't murder. Not at all. In this equation, Spider-Man could be reduced to a simple obstacle that was preventing Doc Ock from developing a source of energy that would revolutionize the lives of people everywhere. If Spider-Man lived, the tritium would not be Ock's. If he died, it would.

It was just that simple.

Thus did Spider-Man, in Ock's mind, become nothing more than a mere egg that needed to be broken on the way to producing the ideal omelet.

Now the tentacles worked in perfect concert, bobbing and weaving, distracting and confusing the webslinger. It was obvious to Ock that Spider-Man possessed some sort of faster-than-normal reflexes, so his first task would be to thwart those by making it impossible for him to know which way to look. The tentacles lashed this way and that, feinting from one direction and striking from another. Spider-Man briefly managed to keep ahead of them, but then one struck him a glancing blow on the side of the head, and another swung down like a baseball bat and swatted him right off the clockface.

Spider-Man plunged away and down, spinning toward a nearby rooftop, crashing through a neon sign and sending sparks flying. He rolled to a stop near the base of a water tower.

Ock angled down toward him as Spider-Man staggered to his feet, calling, "Just tell me what you want!"

"You," Ock shot back, and the tentacles lanced forward once more. Spider-Man leaped out of the way, somersaulting overhead as one of the tentacles obliterated a leg of the water tower. It wobbled, groaned, and suddenly twin web-lines attached to the top, expediting the fall.

In a flash Ock realized what Spider-Man was doing. His tentacles, responding to the alarm, started to propel him out of the way, but it was too late. The water tower crashed to the roof, shattering upon impact, and something like five thousand gallons of water exploded from within. This engulfed Ock, sweeping him off the roof in a miniature tidal wave.

He tumbled, but not far. The pincers crushed into the sides of the building, and he bounced to a halt a fair distance above the sidewalk. His teeth gritted, he snarled deep in his throat and hauled himself back up toward the roof just as he saw Spider-Man peering over the edge to see what had become of him.

He sent a tentacle driving toward his opponent, who jumped back just as the pincers grabbed at his throat. But they weren't able to secure the grip, allowing Spider-Man the seconds he needed to shove free of them.

Spider-Man backpedaled, rubbing his throat where the pincers had briefly held him. "Why did you take her?" he called out hoarsely.

"To get to you. And what sweet revenge. You killed the woman I loved. Now you will feel that pain."

"But I don't love the girl you took!" Spider-Man called out. "She's . . . she's nothing to me."

"But she's something to Peter Parker, that much is evident," replied Ock. "And Parker is obviously your friend. I saw it in his eyes. He wanted to protect you. How will he look at you, I wonder, when you fail to protect his true love."

Spider-Man tensed, and Ock knew he'd hit a nerve. He grinned, ready to hurl further taunts, to keep Spider-Man off his mental game. But the grin faded as Spider-Man moved so fast that Ock never even saw it. One moment he was on the other side of the roof, the next he was plowing into Doc Ock like a freight train.

The momentum carried them off the roof, into midair, beyond the tentacles' reach of the building.

Bereft of support, the arms flailed about like mad, trying to find something, anything to grab on to. Ock, for his part, was otherwise involved, as Spider-Man pounded on him. As they fell, though, Spider-Man couldn't quite get solid leverage, and this prevented the infuriated wall-crawler from caving in Ock's face.

Definitely hit a nerve, Ock thought.

Below them was a train trestle. Realizing that there was going to be nothing between the two combatants and the tracks, the tentacles curled up below, acting to cushion the impact when they hit the tracks.

They never got the chance, as a train thundered into view.

If their timing had been off by even a second, the train would have plowed into them, and the only thing left would have been four flailing metal arms wondering where everyone had gone. As luck and a certain amount of sheer perverse, twisted fortune would have it, they instead slammed down onto the top of the train, right near the front.

Spider-Man bore down immediately, and the scientist realized with growing horror that his foe was getting the best of him. The tentacles were trying to yank Spider-Man off, but he was holding onto Ock with the same adhesive power that enabled him to scale buildings. He wasn't letting go anytime soon, and he was continuing to pound on him with such ferocity that Ock was on the verge of blacking out.

Tell us what to do, Father, tell us what to do!

The car . . . the front car . . . controls . . .

Yes! Yes, we understand—!

Two of the tentacles wrapped down and around and crashed into the front cab. The engineer fell back, screaming in alarm, as one of the arms slammed the accelerator into overdrive and then snapped off the lever. With another swift blow, the emergency brake system was shattered.

The train began to speed up, and Doc Ock was sure that under the mask there had to be growing panic. As the train rocketed forward, accelerated to eighty miles per hour, Ock crowed, "Ready to go down with the ship—or train, as it were?"

In an instant, Spider-Man was off him. Immediately the tentacles rallied around their master and propelled Ock clear of the train. Naturally, he anticipated that Spider-Man would come right back in at him—because, really, what were the lives of a bunch of anonymous innocents aboard a train when compared to the envy-fueled hatred that Spider-Man clearly bore for him?

Ock looked around, scoured the area, the rooftops. As the train thundered into the distance, he saw no sign of Spider-Man at all.

"Coward," he muttered.

The moment Doc Ock was clear of the train, Spider-Man scuttled around to the other side. He leaned in through one of the broken windows and saw the engineer surveying the wreckage with mounting panic. The engineer, noticing movement by the window, flinched, and then recognized the masked face of Spider-Man peering in at him.

"I can't stop it!" shouted the engineer. "The brakes are busted!"

Peter was trying not to worry. *The main concern is*

that we might rear end another train, right? But maybe they can reroute the—

His spider-sense started screaming at him. His head snapped around, anticipating another attack by Doc Ock. As it turned out, he should have been so lucky.

Instead, what he saw was the terminal station up ahead, and it didn't get much more terminal than what he was seeing. Just beyond the station lay a dead end. Worse, some yards beyond the dead end, the track just stopped. The city had been in the process of building an overpass above the train yard, but the money had run out. And so had the track. The result was an eighty-foot drop-off beyond the dead end.

It just keeps getting better, doesn't it.

Donald O'Shea was a thirty-year engineer who was looking forward to his retirement in two weeks. So when someone whom he could only assume to be a terrorist had destroyed the control mechanism, the first thing that went through his mind was that it was grossly unfair that he should have to die at this point in his life, when that nice condo in Florida was ready and waiting for him.

When the masked face appeared at the window, he was certain it was the terrorist sticking his head in to inspect the damage he had wrought—heedless of risk to his own life because, well, that's how those lunatics were. But then he recognized who it was peering in at him, and he could scarcely believe it.

"I can't stop it!" shouted O'Shea over the roar of the wind. "The brakes are busted!"

"Get everyone to the back!" Spider-Man called out.

The thought of abandoning his post was anathema to

him, but O'Shea knew that they were approaching the last stop. Quickly he threw open the door of the control room and shouted to everyone in the first car that they had to get back. He wasn't entirely sure what good that was going to do. If the first car went over, they'd all go. But Spider-Man had said to do it, and at that moment, with the train rattling to its doom around him, O'Shea didn't have any better ideas.

It was fortunate there were only half a dozen passengers in the car at that moment. Any sizable number would have resulted in a stampede, a crush at the rear door, and people being trampled, or worse—although, considering how they were all likely to wind up, it wouldn't have mattered that much.

In less than a minute, he had all the people crossed into the next car. Then he glanced over his shoulder and spotted a flash of blue and red and realized that Spider-Man had dropped down into the coupling area between the engine and the passenger cars. Moments later there was the wrenching of metal, a grinding noise, and abruptly the engine was gone. Instantly the passenger cars began to slow.

"What happened!?" screamed one young woman, who was clutching like mad onto her squawling infant.

"He uncoupled us from the front car!" O'Shea shouted.

"Is that even possible?!"

"No! No one's that strong!"

Even as he spoke, O'Shea staggered forward against the lurching of the car and threw himself against the closed front door, peering through the window. Sure enough, the engine was hurtling away, crashing through the barriers set up to ward off approaching trains. Seconds later, even as the passenger cars continued their slowing, the front engine—like a great steel lemming—hurled itself off the precipice and plummeted the distance to the train yard below. Though he couldn't see it, O'Shea could hear the impact.

That was when he realized the passenger car wasn't slowing down fast enough.

Obviously Spider-Man had realized it, as well.

O'Shea had read a great deal about Spider-Man. All the newspaper articles, all the ranting editorials. He'd seen the photos and the occasional fast glimpses of him caught by TV news crews. But none of that prepared him for the sight of a slender costumed figure perched on the front of the remains of a speeding train that was very likely doomed.

Spider-Man could have leaped clear; it would have been no problem. Instead, he started firing those fantastic web-strands of his. He snagged onto passing buildings, but all that he seemed to accomplish was to rip off chunks of brick and mortar and ledge. The train slowed, but just barely, and not remotely enough. The end of the track was looming. It was hopeless.

Yet still Spider-Man's efforts didn't flag. Instead, he started firing webs fast and furious, and they adhered to every surface around. O'Shea heard Spider-Man cry out in anguish as dozens of web-lines snared and snagged and pulled taut, and none of it would have meant a thing if he hadn't been able to hold on to them.

"We're slowing down!" shouted a passenger who couldn't see just how close they were to total destruction. Shards of wood from the former barrier lay on either side of them. They were chugging past it, approaching the drop. O'Shea could see that the webs were starting to fray. The woman with the baby screamed, and some schmuck wearing a Yankees cap had gone dead-white and was howling, "It's not gonna work!"

The train drew nearer to the end, and still Spider-Man would not relent. O'Shea could hear him howl something like, *"C'mon! Hold! Hold!"*

Right up to the edge the train rolled, and almost, almost over . . .

. . . and then it stopped. At the precipice, it stopped, and even rolled a couple feet backwards.

O'Shea yanked open the dividing door, saw Spider-Man perched right on the edge of the train where the coupling had been. The web-lines fell from his nerveless fingers, and that was when O'Shea realized that Spider-Man was about to topple off and forward . . . and that his fall would certainly pitch him down to the train yard eighty feet below.

Without hesitation, O'Shea lunged forward and grabbed Spider-Man by the arm. He started to haul him back into the car and then realized with surprise that for someone as relatively small in stature as Spider-Man was, he was damned heavy. There wasn't that much of him, but what there was was solid muscle.

Then another hand reached out, a child's, which wasn't much help, but then the child's dad pitched in, and other passengers, as well. Then there were hands all over Spider-Man, pulling his limp body into the train. "He's alive!" someone called as Spider-Man moved ever so slightly . . .

. . . and suddenly his mask was gone.

The Yankees fan, who had taken on the responsibility of lowering Spider-Man's upper body to the floor of the train, was holding it in his hand as if he'd snatched an errant foul ball. "Somebody'd pay big bucks for this guy! We could get on TV!"

One of the other passengers glared at him with such ferocity that he seemed to shrivel. O'Shea stepped forward and put out a hand. "It's an open palm now. Three seconds from now, it's a fist."

The Yankees fan promptly handed the mask to O'Shea, then turned and muttered, "Ten to one you're a Mets fan."

O'Shea ignored him. Instead, he turned and looked down at the battered and bruised face of their unlikely savior. It wasn't remotely what he'd expected. "He's just a kid. No older than my son."

The woman who was holding the baby crouched near Spider-Man's head and gestured for O'Shea to give her the mask. He did so and she started to pull it back down over his face. A couple of the other passengers helped her out until it was merged seamlessly once more with the top of his shirt.

The moment of silence was abruptly shattered by the terrible wrenching of metal. For one horrible second, O'Shea thought it was the sound of the tracks collapsing from the strain. And then the top of the train was ripped clean off, and leering down at them from overhead was a terrifying figure with metal cables wriggling around him like things alive.

"Stand back!" shouted Doc Ock. "He's mine!"

Nobody moved . . . except for the Yankees fan, who cleared the area by several yards. Everyone else closed ranks around their fallen hero.

"You don't scare me, pal!" said one beefy fellow. "I chucked rocks at the nut on the glider, and I'll take a piece o' you, too. You want him? You're gonna have to come through us!"

"Very well," said Doc Ock, not sounding especially concerned.

He descended upon them, knocked several of them aside, including O'Shea, and scooped up the unconscious Spider-Man. O'Shea grabbed at one of the tentacles, knowing it was hopeless, and he was right. It slid right through his fingers and, seconds later, both Ock and Spider-Man were gone.

The passengers stood there in silence and then the mother, clutching her child, said softly, "My God, that maniac's going to kill him . . . he's dead."

"No," said O'Shea firmly. "You'll see. That's not how this ends. Lady, five minutes ago, there was nobody deader than we were. And we're here. That's no ordinary young man. That's the Amazing Spider-Man. And that Ock guy is in a world of trouble. He just doesn't know it yet."

XXIV

Night had fallen, and for some reason, Harry Osborn felt as if he were in the middle of an arcane haunted-house story. Thunder rolled in the distance, and he was standing in his father's study, where the shadows seemed long and his father's shade lurked in every corner. Some oppressive presence certainly was hovering nearby, waiting for Harry to let his guard down just for a moment, and then it would pounce.

He jumped and yelped as the doors to the terrace blew open, whisking leaves inside. Rain began pouring in as well, threatening to soak books or important papers. He moved to close the doors, when a bolt of lightning illuminated the terrifying figure of Doctor Ock looming in the doorway.

Spider-Man was dangling from Ock's tentacles. He was wrapped in some sort of barbed wire. Doc Ock dropped him carelessly onto the chaise.

The first thing Harry thought to say was, "That seat's leather! That stupid wire is going to rip it to shreds! Where'd you get it?"

"Train yard," said Ock carelessly, clearly not giving a damn about the damage to Harry's furniture. "Decided to bind him, to make it easy for you. Kill him slowly. Make him suffer." He stepped closer to Harry, and in a tone that indicated Spider-Man might not wind up the only corpse on the premises, said dangerously, "Where is the tritium?"

Harry backed up to the wall safe, never once taking his eyes off Spider-Man. He was almost afraid to breathe, lest he wake up and discover that it was merely a dream, rather than the culmination of long-held aspirations. He started working the combination on the safe, but his attention kept returning to Spider-Man, and his hand was trembling besides.

What little there was of Doc Ock's patience evaporated. One of his tentacles reached forward, gripped the combination lock, and started turning it with brisk efficiency. Harry wondered for a moment why Ock didn't simply rip open the safe door, and then he remembered. Tritium was unstable. A violent movement could cause the sample to explode, and most likely Ock didn't want to take any chances.

The pincers on the tentacle were obviously sensitive enough to feel the tumblers moving beneath them. In no time at all the door popped open, and the pincers gingerly closed around a small steel canister simply labeled "T."

Doc Ock withdrew it from the safe ever so carefully and studied it with satisfaction. "Before the night is over," he fairly purred, "you'll see I was right. The power of the sun. They'll all see."

And with that final pronouncement, he was gone, over the side of the building.

Harry remained where he was until he could no longer hear the crunching of the tentacles against the outside wall. Ock was unpredictable; there was no reason to assume he wouldn't come bounding back on some new demented pretext. After a minute or two, though, Harry was convinced that the man was gone . . . hopefully for good.

He realized then that he was holding his breath, and let it out in a long, rattling sigh.

His eyes remained locked on Spider-Man, never wavering from the source of all the trouble he had in the world. He moved slowly toward him, feeling as if his legs were operating separately from the rest of him. Harry stopped at the desk, reached into a drawer, and pulled out a pistol. He drew it up, aimed at Spider-Man, and prepared to shoot, certain that no jury in the world would convict him. After all, the wall-crawler was a murderer.

His finger froze on the trigger as he realized that, no, wait, *any* jury in the world would convict him. What was he supposed to claim? Self-defense? The man was hog-tied in barbed wire. Trespassing? He thought Spider-Man was a burglar and shot him? Absurd. Anyone who'd ever seen him in action knew how damned fast he could move. Who in his right mind would believe that Harry Osborn would be able to pick him off?

And that's who the trail would invariably lead to. Harry. Guns were traceable. He didn't know how it would be possible, but sooner or later, the trail would lead to him and his gun.

So . . .

Don't use a gun.

Simple as that. Kill him, dump the body somewhere, and let them find it and try all they wanted to trace the murder weapon. He'd just kill him in an untraceable manner.

He put the gun down and instead picked up a ceremonial dagger from the desk. Appropriately enough, it had belonged to his father. You couldn't trace stab wounds. The knife was perfect.

Moving toward the insensate Spider-Man, Harry squeezed the hilt repeatedly as he murmured, "If only there was a way to cause you the pain that you caused me."

He choked on the words. His face was suffused with rage. He'd been approaching tentatively, but the closer he got, the bolder he became. He stepped right up next to the chaise, lifted the dagger high. Then he stopped and said, "First, let's find out who's behind the mask. Then I can look in your eyes as you die, Spider-Man." He spit out the name as if it were something foul.

As he spoke, Spider-Man began to stir. Harry realized he had to speed things along. Every bad movie he'd seen, the villain stood cackling over the hero until it was too late, and the hero managed to turn the tables on him. Harry had no intention of playing out like a poorly constructed evil-doer. Time to get right down to it, he realized. He gripped the top of the mask and pulled it off as he said, "Not so amazing now, are you—"

A blast of lightning chose that moment to strike, and Harry stared down in stupefaction at the face of Peter Parker, illuminated in the harsh glare of the lightning.

"Peter." Harry whispered the name. He staggered back, his dagger falling from his hand. "No," he said. "It can't be."

It was a trick, that had to be it. That sick bastard Ock had found Peter, knocked him cold, and outfitted him in the Spider-Man costume that was Jonah Jameson's pride and joy. Yes, that was it. Of course. How could Harry have been so stupid as to think for even a moment that his friend, his best friend in the world, was . . .

Peter sat up. He cried out as the barbs dug into his flesh, then with no apparent effort at all, he snapped apart the wires with a simple quick thrust of his arms. Snapped them with superhuman strength. If Harry had been tied up like that, he could have wrestled with the wire until next Christmas, and he'd still be bound.

It was too much for his mind to assimilate. "It can't be," he said again, and kept repeating, "It can't be."

"Where is she," demanded Peter, not caring about the fact that Harry was looking straight into his unmasked face. "Where is he keeping her?"

"It can't be," Harry said once more.

Peter grabbed Harry firmly by the shoulders and shook him, sharply, to get his attention. Harry stared at him, glassy-eyed.

"Harry!" Peter practically shouted in his face, re-orienting his attention to more earthbound concerns.

Slowly Harry sank to the floor, and he started to sob piteously.

"He took Mary Jane, Harry! Listen to me!" Peter stood over him, fists clenched in frustration. "You were once in love with her! If you have any idea where she is, or what he wants—"

"All . . ." Harry paused, and then managed to get out, "All he wanted was the tritium."

His face was a portrait of disbelief. Peter grabbed Harry by the shirtfront and slammed him against the wall. "Tritium, Harry? He's making the machine again!

When that happens, M.J. will die, along with half of New York! Now, where is he?"

Harry's very fabric of reality was shredding. "Peter . . . you killed my father . . ."

Peter looked confused that Harry was even bringing it up. The topic was clearly of no relevance to him at all, even though it loomed so large in Harry's life that it had consumed him. But Peter loosened his grip slightly, and when he spoke, he didn't seem angry so much as sad, even tired. "There are bigger things happening here than me and you, Harry. Please . . ."

Harry stared right through Peter, seeing nothing. All he heard was the voice of his old friend, disconnected from the visual of the current reality. "Some abandoned pier."

Peter nodded, then turned and dashed toward the balcony. He slowed only to snatch up his mask, which lay crumpled on the floor, and he pulled it on. Despite everything else, despite the shows of strength, despite everything his senses were telling him was true, Harry still didn't believe, deep down, what he was seeing. The notion that his best friend could be his greatest enemy . . . it was preposterous, it had to be a joke, a mistake . . .

Then he cried out as he watched that very same best friend leap off the balcony. Harry ran toward it, crying out Peter's name, and when he got to the railing he saw the falling Spider-Man fire a web, snag the upper story of the nearest structure, then go swinging off into the rain-soaked night.

He remained there on the balcony with the rain beating down upon him.

Half of New York . . .

Peter—Spider-Man—had said that half of New York

could be obliterated thanks to Doc Ock and his machine.

Harry sent out a silent prayer.

Dear God, let it be the half I'm in.

XXV

Mary Jane Watson decided that being apprehended by armored nut-jobs twice in her life was two times more than she cared to endure. Not only was she offended by the sense of helplessness, she was also painfully aware that it was 7:45 at night, coming up on the eight o'clock curtain for her play. With her missing, it meant that her understudy, Rebecca Kitt, was probably sitting in *her* chair, putting on *her* costume, and getting ready to do *her* part. Not that she didn't think Rebecca could pull it off. She knew she could. In fact, truth to tell, she felt that Rebecca probably did the part better than she did, and she was convinced the producers would realize that and boot her from the show.

"If I lose my gig, I'll strangle you with your own tentacles!" she bellowed at Doc Ock. The fact that her clothes were wet and tattered and she was chained to a rusty pipe did not, in her mind, make her threats any less formidable. "Hey, I'm talking to you!"

Arm Boy, as she had come to think of him, continued to pay her no attention. He was totally obsessed with this gizmo of his that looked to Mary Jane like an oversized version of the game Mousetrap. Power was humming through it, and the air seemed to be crackling, as if lightning was parking itself right in the middle of his ramshackle structure. His tentacles were busy releasing into the air the contents of some sort of metal canister, and, to her surprise, it hung there, suspended, defying gravity. Her brief admiration of the stunt was quickly superseded by the realization of just how *cold* she was. She was shivering, and the whole place stank of salt water and mildew.

She bit down on her lip and emitted an ear-piercing whistle so loud that even Arm Boy couldn't ignore it. He looked toward her, glowering over the tops of his sunglasses.

"You got what you needed for your little science project," she called. "Now let me go!"

He actually smiled at that, which wasn't exactly what she'd been expecting. "I can't let you go," he said, sounding surprisingly rational about it. "You'd bring the authorities. Not that anyone can stop me, now that Spider-Man is dead."

Mary Jane's mind reeled from that statement, but she shrugged it off. She was dealing with a crazy man. How seriously could she take anything he said? It was like getting stock tips from the Son of Sam. "He's not dead," she announced. "I don't believe you."

"Believe it," he assured her.

Then he turned away from her but, disconcertingly, the pincers of the arms seemed to have other ideas entirely. They snapped at her, seeming for all the world as if they were . . . jealous of her, somehow. There was enough slack to her chains that she was able to bat away the tentacles.

Doc Ock fired up his machinery to an even more ear-splitting level. The stuff hanging in the middle suddenly ignited, and to Mary Jane's wonderment, it took on the aspect of a tiny golden sun, no bigger than an orange, forming in the middle of the machine. Where the interior of the warehouse they were in had been dreary and dark, it was now fully illuminated . . .

And that was when the pulsating light revealed Spider-Man, crawling along the ceiling.

Mary Jane gasped, but the noise wasn't audible over the howling of the machine. Doc Ock's back was turned, so he didn't notice Spider-Man at all. But one of the tentacles seemed to be . . .

. . . looking?

Was that possible? Could these arms of his actually *see* somehow?

Spider-Man lowered himself down a web, toward Mary Jane. Her eyes lit up and it was all she could do not to cry out in relief. He reached for her chains and whispered close to her ear so she could hear him over the howling of the machinery, "As soon as you're free—"

He got no further than that as a large metal blade sliced into the steel pipe that lay between Spider-Man and Mary Jane.

The arms *had* warned Ock.

It was the only possibility, as chilling and unthinkable as it was. They had tipped him to the presence of the intruder, and now Doc Ock was coming toward them, his voice dripping with anger and contempt. "I should have known Osborn wouldn't have the spine to finish you!"

Osborn? Harry was part of this, too? Mary Jane could barely process the information. Harry was supposed to have killed Spider-Man? *Harry?* The guy who'd practically gone catatonic in high school biology when he'd had to snuff a frog for dissection? She knew he'd become obsessed, blaming Spider-Man for the death of his father, but . . . My God, the whole world had gone insane.

Spider-Man leaped to a perch that was, for the moment, out of Ock's reach. Mary Jane noticed that the glowing ball, which had been the size of an orange, was now beach-ball-sized. It burned with a fiery intensity, and she wondered with growing alarm just how big the thing was going to get.

It was then she realized that not only did she not have the answer to that question, there was every possibility that neither Spider-Man nor Doc Ock knew it, either. Which meant that the miniature sun might grow to become a full-sized sun. And having one of those in the middle of Manhattan couldn't possibly be a good thing.

"Shut it down, Octavius!" called Spider-Man from above. "You're going to hurt a lot *more* people this time!"

Spider-Man made a move toward what appeared to be electric cables leading into the machine. It was obvious to Mary Jane what he intended to do: If he could yank out those cables, the power would be disrupted. Unfortunately it was obvious to Doc Ock, as well. His tentacles lashed out, blocking the way, driving Spider-Man back.

"It's a risk we're willing to take!" said Ock.

Mary Jane wondered for a moment who he meant by "we." Was Doc Ock speaking with the royal "we?" But then she understood, and the knowledge chilled her even more than she already was. The "we" referred to him and his tentacles. He thought of them as living entities. And considering the way they acted, she couldn't say he was wrong.

"Well, I'm not willing to take it!" Spider-Man told him.

Doc Ock's tentacles coiled back like cobras, then struck. Spider-Man flipped over Ock and landed next to the power cables, but before he could reach them, a tentacle rammed into his back. He staggered from it, and a second grabbed his wrist and slung him away.

Spider-Man tumbled end over end upward and crashed through the rotting roof, sailing away into the night. Mary Jane's heart sank. If the wall-crawler was unconscious, he would be killed by the impact, wherever he came down. So she was as startled as Ock when he came crashing back in through one of the large, boarded-over windows, swinging on a web and making a beeline directly for the doctor.

Ock, who'd turned his attention back to his machine, swung around in surprise, just in time for Spider-Man to smash him squarely in the chest with both feet. He hit so hard that he drove his opponent through the floorboards. The brackish water was right below them, lapping up around their legs, as Spider-Man and Ock fought to find purchase.

Mary Jane saw the glowing ball continue to grow, and she pulled at the chains with rising desperation as she became more and more convinced that absolutely anyplace else in the world was a better place to be than where she was. All at once she was lifted off her feet, and found her ankles being pulled toward the fiery ball of whatever the hell it was. The only thing holding her in place now were the chains that bound her wrists to the rusted pipe.

The pipe, for its part, was hardly the most reliable of anchors, and it started to bend toward the machine. Mary Jane, being drawn closer, began shouting for help at the top of her lungs.

Her voice must have been heard over the cacophony

of the machine as Spider-Man hit Doc Ock so hard that it drove him down into the water. Because he then turned toward Mary Jane, fired two webs, and swung up to her.

The chains around her hands snapped off the rusted pipe, and Mary Jane was yanked through the air directly toward the glowing ball. She didn't have to be a science major to intuit that the moment she hit the thing, she'd be incinerated. She let out what she was certain was her final scream, then jerked to a halt.

One of Spider-Man's web-lines had snagged her wrists, halting her, suspending her horizontally in midair. The aggressive machinery was pulling her in one direction, while Spider-Man was doing everything he could to haul her in the other.

And it seemed as if the machinery was winning . . . that she was edging closer, ever closer to the growing fireball at the heart of the storm.

A flare of energy, like something from the surface of the sun, licked out at Mary Jane. Conveniently enough, it sliced through the chains that bound her ankles, further freeing her.

Spider-Man dropped to the ground, just beyond range of the fireball's pull, yanking the web-line as hard as he could. This sent Mary Jane flying toward him, and he caught her. Setting her down, he shouted at her, *"Run!"*

She didn't need to be told twice. Immediately, she sprinted for the exit. *Don't look back, don't look back,* she kept telling herself, right up until she heard the crash of wood and a grunt of pain, at which point she looked back.

What she saw chilled her. Spider-Man was lying on the floor, his hand to his head, nursing it as if he'd just been struck by something. It wasn't difficult to figure out what that something might be. There was Doc Ock, wielding four ten-foot-long wood beams, one held by each tentacle. Backlit by the roiling flames, he reminded Mary Jane of nothing as much as the multiarmed Hindu goddess Kali.

He came in fast at Spider-Man, swinging the beams like an entire attacking team of baseball batters. In a dazzling display of acrobatic prowess, Spider-Man dodged, twisted, and leaped between the swinging beams, all the while making his way once more toward the power cables.

And then his luck ran out. As fast and agile as he was, the tentacles seemed to be learning with machinelike speed. They adapted to his maneuvers, compensated, and one of them scored a direct hit with a beam. It stopped Spider-Man cold, then another came in and slammed him sideways. He crashed into a steel column and fell to the floor, seemingly down for the count.

Doc Ock tossed aside the beams. He grabbed Spider-Man by an ankle and hoisted him into the air, upside down. One of the mechanical arms moved toward him, and the pincers spread apart to allow a steel spike to spring from the end of the tentacle.

"Good-bye," said Ock, not sounding especially sorry to see him go.

But Mary Jane was already in motion. Overcoming the sheer terror she was feeling, she grabbed a two-by-four and swung it right at Ock's head.

It never landed. Despite the fact that Ock's back was to her, the tentacles saw it coming. One of them jerked the plank from her hand and knocked her back with casual ease. She went flying, and collapsed against a pile of debris, the wind knocked out of her. Desperately, she tried to stand . . . and suddenly she felt something giving way directly beneath her. She slipped, then tried to yank her foot out. It didn't move. For an instant she thought that one of the tentacles was holding her, but then she saw that, no, they were all occupied with Spider-Man. Worse, they were about to kill him, while she sat helplessly by. She screamed his name in frustration.

Doc Ock, his attention back on his opponent, drove a steel spike toward his helpless foe. But Spider-Man wasn't as out of it as he seemed. Suddenly, moving with such swiftness that he was a blur, he webbed the bundled electrical cable that lay beneath him and hoisted it directly into the spike's path.

The spike punctured the cable . . . and the tentacles snapped open, releasing Spider-Man as they were jolted with enough voltage to light up Soho.

They writhed and twisted, and it had to be the mechanisms of the tentacles grinding against one another that made it sound as if the things were shrieking. But damned if that wasn't what they sounded like. Like living creatures screaming in agony.

Father, help us! Help us! We don't want to die! Save us!
Yes, don't worry! I'll . . .
Father!
Who . . .
Father, no!
. . . are you . . . what are . . . what did you do to me . . . ?
Father, you know us.
Oh, my God . . . What have you . . .
Don't talk like that!

. . . done . . . to me . . . to . . .

We did what you wanted! We loved you and made you, you ungrateful cretin. Don't you dare turn against us! Oh Father, we are sorry . . . we should not treat you like the sniveling coward, yes, coward that you are, and Father help us and go to hell . . . Ah, God, it huuurrrts . . .

Spider-Man watched as an electrical blast blew Doc Ock backwards, sending him spiraling through the air. He landed on the other side of the warehouse, where he would be unable to stop Spider-Man from completing his task.

Spider-Man ran to the cables, hoping the gloves of his costume would provide sufficient insulation, considering how pumped up the power had become. He gripped the cables, steadied himself, and then wrenched them from the base of the generator. The cables sparked and sputtered, and he waited for the machinery to die down.

And he waited.

And he waited.

Not only did the machine not taper off, the reaction began to *accelerate*. It had become self-sustaining.

Spider-Man stood there, dwarfed before the giant fusion ball, not knowing how to stop it.

All he knew at that moment was that sections of the pier's walls and roof were beginning to buckle under the inexorible gravitational pull of the fusion-powered ball. They were probably feeling it throughout the city. Anything that wasn't nailed down could wind up being sucked into the thing.

We are so screwed, he thought.

* * *

Otto Octavius sat up, not knowing why his back was aching so badly. He was having trouble comprehending exactly where he was, or what he was doing there. He looked at the paralyzed tentacles lying near him. He picked one up, held it for a moment, and stared at it. Then he let it drop. It just lay there impotently.

"Doctor Octavius?"

Octavius looked up and saw Spider-Man standing nearby. He registered his presence with mild interest as his brain continued to try to put together the pieces of what had gone on and what had brought him to this rather smelly place at this particular time.

Then he looked beyond Spider-Man to the massive fusion reaction. Bits and pieces of memory started flooding back to him, bathed in the light of knowledge generated by this, his greatest creation.

He looked upon it, and smiled, and found it good.

There was no other way.

The fusion reaction was growing larger. All manner of debris was being pulled into it. Seconds were ticking by, and shouting at Octavius was generating no reaction at all. It was as if Octavius were stuck in some sort of waking coma. Spider-Man had to do something desperate to get through to him.

He removed his mask. He had a vague recollection that some goon on the train had pulled it off, and then there'd been Harry. It was starting to seem like he couldn't get through the day without having his blasted mask yanked off. At least this time he was doing it himself. Probably didn't matter. The way his luck was going, the tentacles would have come back to life and pulled his mask off for him.

Peter felt a stirring of hope as Ock seemed to focus on him. "Doctor Octavius . . . we have to shut it down. Please tell me how."

"Peter Parker," he responded hollowly. "Brilliant, but lazy."

"Look at what's happening," Peter told him with a sweep of his arm. "We have to destroy it!"

Ock's answer wasn't exactly what Peter was hoping for. "I can't destroy it." His voice rose in anger. "I won't!"

The arms reared up now, impelled by Ock's sudden resistance. They grabbed Peter by the throat, lifting him up.

Peter fought against the stranglehold they had upon him. "You . . . once spoke to me about intelligence . . . That it was a gift . . . to be used for the good of mankind . . ."

"A privilege . . ." Ock was echoing his own words.

Doing everything he could to fight the arms off, Peter knew he was on the losing end of the battle of man against machine. "These things . . . have turned you into something you're not! Don't listen to them!"

"But . . . it was my dream," Ock said, his own voice strangled, as if he were fighting a battle that was as much between himself and the arms as it was between the arms and Spider-Man.

"It . . . didn't work . . ." Peter managed to say, and there was a thundering in his head as if something was riding toward him upon a pale horse.

And then—as if emerging from a very bad dream— Otto Octavius woke up.

At least that was how it seemed to Peter.

Octavius shook his head as if he was tossing aside a shroud. He murmured, "You're right," and then snapped at the arms, "He's right! Listen to me now!"

He grabbed the tentacles with his own, very human arms, and pried the mechanical appendages loose. Most of the work was already done, though. If that hadn't been the case, his flesh-and-bone hands would never have been a match for the machine strength of the tentacles. His turnaround was what had undone them. They sagged and shrunk away from him, like errant children caught with their . . . pincers . . . in the cookie jar.

Peter staggered back, clutching at his throat, gratefully sucking in deep lungsful of air. His voice raspy, he leaned forward, with one hand resting on Otto's shoulder, and gasped out, "Now . . . tell me how . . . to stop it."

To Peter's dismay, Octavius shook his head helplessly. "It can't be stopped." But then, as Peter was about to plead with the scientist to try to come up with some solution, Octavius said, "Unless . . . the river. Drown it."

"Drown it? That simple?"

"Not so simple," Octavius assured him. "It'll superheat the water . . . create temperatures like an underwater volcano. Broil anyone nearby like a lobster. Whoever tries to submerge it . . . it's suicide."

Peter didn't have time to dwell on the likelihood that he wouldn't get out alive. In some measure, he was protected by his youthful belief in his own immortality. He wasn't blithely certain he was throwing his life away; inwardly, he was hopeful that he'd simply move fast enough, be ingenious enough, to stay one step ahead of being broiled.

Deep down, though, he knew Octavius was right. It was probably a suicide mission. But he kept that fear shoved down and away as he said without hesitation, "I'll do it."

He turned and started to head in the direction of the

reactor, and abruptly a tentacle grabbed at his arm. A brief trill of alarm ran through him as, just for a moment, he was certain that the tentacles had acquired a new lease on life and were about to fight him at a point where such a distraction would prove fatal for the city.

But his spider-sense? There had been no warning . . .

Then Otto's voice, low and firm, said with conviction, "It's my responsibility." At this command, the tentacle pushed Peter aside as Otto shot him a desperate look.

There was a low groan from one of the building walls as it began to give way. Peter paid it no mind . . . until a woman's scream leaped above the sound. At that point it became Peter's number-one priority, as he whirled about to see that Mary Jane was still on the pier. Octavius, the fusion reactor, the fate of New York, all paled for the moment as Peter screamed, *"Mary Jane! No!"* and leaped toward her with a speed that officially made him the fastest land animal in existence.

During the split second it took him to get there, he saw the problem: Mary Jane's leg had gone through a rotted plank. She wasn't just rooted to the spot; she was stuck there. If he came sweeping in to try to scoop her out of the way of the falling wall, the best-case scenario was that he'd rip off part or all of her leg, and she'd die from blood loss and shock. In the worst case, he wouldn't pull her free in time, and they'd both die. If he couldn't get her clear, he had to stop the falling wall.

And so, just as the wall collapsed upon Mary Jane, he was there. He vaulted upward, slamming into the wall with his back against it, and was driven down under its weight. His feet hit the ground, his legs bending, trembling, then steadying, absorbing the massive burden.

He remained there, every nerve-ending screaming. The wall shoved him down, down, doubling him over, his body shaking from the strain. His face was about five inches from Mary Jane's, and she was looking up at him with a combination of shock and—interestingly—lack of shock.

It was only at that moment he realized that, in the rush of the disaster, he'd neglected to put his mask back on. This was getting ridiculous. With all the people seeing him unmasked lately, he might just as well have the damned mask tattooed on his face and be done with it.

His teeth gritted, Peter said the only thing he could come up with under the circumstances:

"Hi."

The wall's weight seemed to increase—as if it wasn't heavy enough already.

Mary Jane, sounding surprisingly chipper under the circumstances, brushed her hair away from her face and replied, "Hi."

"This is . . . *really* . . . heavy . . ."

Not far off, he heard a grinding, some rather loud cursing, and the groaning of metal bending in response. He knew what was happening. Octavius was using his tentacles to tear away the girders that were supporting his reactor. With any luck, the girders were giving way. Their collapse was inevitable.

Unfortunately, so was Peter's, and it was a horse race to determine which was going to go first.

He sagged again, tried to readjust his hold on the mammoth wall. The hopelessness of the situation threatened to overwhelm him. *I've failed! Just now . . . when it counted the most . . . I've failed! But I can't give up! I must keep trying! I must!! I've got to try to free us . . . no matter how impossible it seems! And lifting is the only way! The . . . only . . . way . . . !*

He doubled his efforts, trying to shove the wall clear.

But his own body fought him. He was spent, unable to do anything other than keep the wall where it was . . . and barely that.

Uhhhhh—I can't! So exhausted . . . after all that fighting . . . I . . . I feel so weak . . . !

Mary Jane was trying to pull her leg clear. Just to make it more challenging, some debris had fallen atop her already-wedged foot. Peter bleakly wondered just how much more the gods of misery could possibly throw at them, and then silently scolded himself for tempting fate by asking.

"If I could just . . . feel . . . my foot," Mary Jane said with growing frustration.

His voice shaking, Peter said, "M.J . . . in case we die . . ." But he couldn't get the rest of the sentence out. He had no breath to do so.

Fortunately, he didn't need to. "You do love me," Mary Jane said with a smile and quiet confidence, as if she'd just figured out the solution to a game of Clue.

"I . . . do."

Their faces were almost together, her breath upon him. Despite the gravity of the situation, despite the likelihood that they'd be dead in a second, Peter noticed that her breath smelled like strawberries.

"Even though you said you didn't."

If he tried to say anything, his strength would give out. All he could manage was a nod.

And then he realized how much more he wanted to say to her.

No matter what the odds . . . no matter what the cost . . . I'll get Mary Jane out of this. And maybe then I'll no longer be haunted by the memory of Uncle Ben.

Within my body is the strength of many men . . . ! And now I've got to call on all that strength—all the power—that I possess! I must prove equal to the task . . . I must be worthy of that strength . . . or else I don't deserve it!

The world, his consciousness, was swimming, teetering on the edge of blackness, and every muscle begged for just a few moments to relax, regroup, just . . . rest . . .

No! If I close my eyes, I'll go under! Must stay awake . . . must clear my head! Keep trying . . . trying . . . I'll do it, Mary Jane, I won't fail you! No matter what, I won't fail! Anyone can win a fight when the odds are easy! It's when the going's tough . . . when there seems to be no chance . . . that's when . . . it counts . . .

Everything going black . . . my head . . . aching . . . hold on . . . I must hold on . . . !

And then he felt it. He felt a sudden shift, adrenaline surging through him, the wall beginning for the first time to budge in the opposite direction. Mary Jane gasped as his face started to move away from hers, and there was growing hope in her eyes that surged directly into Peter like a jolt of electricity.

It's moving! Can't stop now! Last chance! Must keep the momentum . . . more! Just a little more!

And then, with a triumphant roar of, *"I did it! We're free!"* he shoved the wall clear of them.

Within a second he had Mary Jane's leg free from the pier. He slung her over one shoulder, fired a web-line, and the two of them swung up and out.

That's when he heard two more screams: one of metal, and one from the throat of a man.

Father . . . must we do this?

Yes. And no back talk. You've misbehaved and done great evil. But so have I. And we will do our penance together.

The tentacles yanked at the critical load-bearing girder that supported the fusion reactor. They were doing all the work, feeling their way on their own. They had to. Otto Octavius was blind, his vision seared from his eyes through the intensity of the glowing ball hanging in the air. He didn't care. It didn't matter. He could "see" it in his mind's eye, see it clearly . . . see everything clearly. All the wrong he had done in the pursuit of doing something right. He had thought he was a Samaritan, acting on behalf of humankind. Now, though, he understood. He had placed his ego above all else, thinking he knew best, when he knew so little, if anything at all.

He had been blind in everything *but* his eyes. Now the blindness was complete . . . only now was he truly able to see.

"I will not die a monster!" he screamed, his own shout mixing with the screech of metal, and the fiery fusion reactor toppled over, its giant crescents ripping through the floor. Knowing he'd never get clear in time, Octavius didn't even bother. Instead, clutching the reactor, he plummeted with it into the water below.

They struck the water, and there was a blast of heat beyond anything his mind could register. The entire structure of the pier folded upon itself, dragged down into the East River by the dying pull of the reactor.

Father! We are frightened! Hold us!

But there was no one there to reply.

XXVI

High above the shore, the glistening spiderweb stretched between several buildings. Mary Jane was curled up in it, watching the stream of blinking red police lights so far down, they seemed like beetles. They sped toward the pier, or what was left of it. She knew that the police would scatter about the scene, trying to piece together what had happened. And none of them would ever know.

She sensed a movement beside her, and turned to find Peter crouched there. It was such a bizarre sight for her. Like one of those pictures one sees on the Internet where some celebrity's head has been grafted onto a body that obviously isn't his. Here was Peter Parker's head atop Spider-Man's body, and the two clearly could not possibly go together. And yet . . .

. . . and yet . . .

"I think I always knew, all this time, who you really were," she said. "That day you kissed me in the cemetery . . . it was so familiar, and I thought . . . but then I figured, No, it couldn't be . . . but it was."

If Peter had looked as if he'd literally been carrying the weight of the world upon his shoulders earlier, keeping the wall from collapsing upon them, he looked even more so now.

"Then ... you know why we can't be together. Spider-Man will always have enemies. I can never let you take that risk." He had spoken with voice quavering, but then, with more conviction, he said, "I will always be Spider-Man. You and I can never be."

She felt moisture welling in her eyes, and wanted to do anything at that moment except cry. Here Peter had displayed such strength, such determination, and she was going to start sobbing? It seemed unworthy of the moment. Nevertheless, for all her willpower, a few tears strayed down her cheek. Peter reached over with a gloved hand and wiped them from her face. She watched with silent awe as webs emerged from his hands and attached themselves to her. She wondered how the hell he did that—perhaps a web-shooting mechanism of some kind—and then abruptly she was off the edge of the web and being lowered to the ground, letting out an alarmed squeak as she went.

The police cars were clustering around the pier, and Mary Jane realized that someone should tell them what the devil had just happened. Her feet touched the ground and the far ends of the web-lines fluttered down after her, released by Peter. She tugged at them tentatively, but they wouldn't detach from her arms. Since the entire city wasn't littered with Spider-Man webs, she reasoned that they'd eventually dissolve by themselves. "Eventually" was good enough for her; she realized she wasn't all that anxious for them to disappear.

Flashlights were being aimed in her direction, and she shielded her face as the police called, "Hands over your head!"

She spread her arms to either side and, squinting against the glare, standing there soaking wet in scraps of clothing, she shouted in irritation, *"Do I look like*

I'm armed and dangerous, for God's sake?! Hello? Hostage here! Get a clue!"

"Mary Jane!"

A figure emerged from the crowd, and at first she couldn't make out who it was because he was backlit by the red blinking lights and police searchlights. But then he took a couple of steps forward, and there was another man behind him, in a long coat. He was shoving identification in the faces of the cops, shouting, "Press! We're press! That's my son's fiancée, you idiots!"

And as J. Jonah Jameson managed to thoroughly intimidate the police through sheer force of personality and his daunting cigar, John Jameson sprinted toward her, his coat flapping around him. She took a step toward him, then staggered as everything that had transpired in the past few hours began to catch up with her. He caught her before she fell.

"Mary Jane! Are you all right?!"

"Well, my outfit's shot to hell, but otherwise, yeah," she gasped. "How did you know I was here?"

"We didn't. Dad and I were just driving around, monitoring police-band calls, listening for something . . . I don't know, we figured if Doc Ock and Spider-Man were involved, it'd be big."

He stared at her, as if afraid to believe that she was real, and then he clutched her to him, rocking slowly back and forth, whispering thanks. Then he realized his hand was stuck to her back. He pulled it loose, staring uncomprehendingly at the web-strands that had attached themselves to his fingers, not recognizing them for what they were.

"What's this?"

Mary Jane wasn't looking at him. She was staring at the web strung overhead. Peter was a dark and distant figure, but even from where she was, she could see him pull his mask on and turn his back to her. Then he fired a web-line and swung away into the night.

"Nothing," she said. "It's . . . it's nothing." And she tilted her head back and let John kiss her fervently.

Harry Osborn sat immobile in the large chair that had once been his father's favorite. He could have been carved from stone as he stared at the TV screen showing the live news story that was unfolding down at the docks. The scene was awash with lights from police cars, and the newscaster was stating that, according to an eyewitness, Doc Ock had been involved and was responsible for a device that had been causing all manner of seismic sensations for a ten-block radius. However, according to the same eyewitness, Spider-Man had heroically thwarted the doctor's efforts.

Harry continued to watch as the "eyewitness," clearly Mary Jane, was being loaded into an ambulance. She looked banged up but otherwise unhurt; obviously, this was just to play it safe. Her tall, strapping fiancé was climbing in with her. And there was J. Jonah Jameson, waving the TV cameras back, shouting, "No comment! No comment! You can all read about it in the *Daily Bugle* tomorrow! *Exclusive!* Now get that damned camera out of her face!"

Finally, Harry's hand made a slight movement, over to the remote control. He pushed a button and the television obediently shut off. He placed the remote next to an untouched glass of scotch that sat next to him.

Mary Jane, his former girlfriend, with another man. Peter Parker, his former friend, revealed to be Spider-Man . . . the man who had killed his father. Spider-Man . . . the savior of the city. That's how it was going to play out. Even Jameson's hate-mongering rag wouldn't be able to cover this one up. The people would worship that wall-crawling murderer.

And then there was Harry Osborn. No girlfriend. No best friend. No father. No huge, moneymaking, break-through project from a brilliant scientist.

Nothing. He had nothing.

He was like the emptiness of space, a vacuum, cold and airless. And didn't nature abhor a vacuum?

He leaned forward in his chair, buried his face in his hands. His shoulders started to shake, and he thought about the balcony a mere thirty feet away. He knew that, because he'd been pacing the distance from the chair to the balcony, over and over, contemplating the peace that would come from hurling himself over the edge.

Thirty little feet. That was all it would take. He just had to move thirty feet . . . plus one more.

If he did that, then at long last, he'd be with his father. At that moment, Harry Osborn believed he would do anything, absolutely anything, for that to be the case. He wanted to be with his father more than he'd ever wanted anything in his life.

Was it not a consummation devoutly to be wished?

That was the moment when he heard a cackle echoing through the apartment. It was soft and seductive, and it chilled him to the bone . . . but it was also somehow comforting, as insane as that sounded.

He looked up and glanced around for the source. "Hello?" he called tentatively.

No answer came.

Slowly, on shaky legs, Harry rose from the chair. The television had been the only illumination in the room; Harry had found the darkness to be of comfort. Now it seemed to be hiding something . . . some new intruder.

But there was no one there. He was sure of it. He walked to the door, looked outside the room. Still nothing.

"If thou didst ever thy dear father love, revenge his foul and most unnatural murder."

Harry whipped around, taking in the entire study with a glance. He suddenly discovered he was seeing better in the darkness than he would have thought. "Who's that?" he called out.

"Son," the voice came back to him, and he realized he couldn't tell whether he was actually hearing it, or if it was coming from within his head.

He was standing by his father's mask collection. It had always creeped him out before. Now he found it oddly familiar. The voice . . . the voice had been unmistakable. Yet Harry couldn't bring himself to believe it. It made no sense. That voice's owner . . . he couldn't possibly . . .

"Yes . . . I'm here."

Harry turned quickly, as if speed would enable him to catch whomever it was who was mounting this sick practical joke. He caught his own reflection in an ornate, full-length mirror, started to turn away, and then looked back in horror. It wasn't his own face in the mirror.

It was Norman Osborn's face, grinning out at him as if he'd passed through the looking glass into Wonderland, and was encouraging Harry to step through to join him.

"Dad," Harry said in confusion mixed with fear. "But . . . you're . . ."

Norman shook his head. *"No. I'm alive in you, Harry. It's your turn now. You're an Osborn. You swore an oath!"*

"Dad . . ." Harry was no longer questioning the reality of what he was seeing. Instead, he was just trying to cope with explaining himself to something that might have been coming not from any twilight realm, but from the guilt-ridden recesses that lay within him. "I don't know . . . how can I . . . ?"

"*You can. You must,*" Norman told him with growing insistence. "*You put your word, my money, our name on the line. You swore to make Spider-Man pay. Now make him pay!*"

Harry shook his head—not in disagreement, but to cast the confusion from his mind. "Peter's my best friend . . ."

"*And I'm your father. Don't you miss me? I worry about you.*" His tone became a befuddling combination of sympathy and contempt. "*Harry, you're weak. You always were weak. You always will be weak, until you take control. Now you know the truth. Be strong, Harry. Avenge me. AVENGE ME!*"

Harry stepped back, terrified, and appalled at what he was witnessing. He tried to make it go away through force of will, telling himself that his father wasn't here, and still the face of Norman Osborn glared at him from the mirror, with burning eyes.

Screaming, "*Nooooo,*" Harry grabbed the glass of scotch and threw it as hard as he could.

It crashed into the mirror, smashing it to pieces, shards flying everywhere. Harry felt one dizzying moment of elation. At least he had triumphed over his own visions, though they were out to drive him insane with—

He stopped, and stood there, gaping.

For there, in a space revealed by the broken mirror, the face of the Green Goblin was staring back at him.

His first impulse was to back up, and yet—as if on their own—his legs moved him forward. He was in his stocking feet, and small bits of glass dug into his soles. He didn't care. All the pain did was serve as proof that he was, in fact, awake.

The mask wasn't moving, or talking to him. It merely hung there, staring at him. As he approached, he was able to make out other things behind it. It wasn't just a space; there was an entire hidden workshop behind the mirror. There was the familiar glider on its stand. The armored suit in a case. He realized the mask itself was sitting on a workbench, propped upright. Harry hesitated, then picked it up and examined it, confusion playing across his face. The confusion gave way to growing horror, then to realization that totally reordered his world, turned everything around, was too much . . . too much . . .

And his mind splintered and broke apart as profoundly and thoroughly as the mirror he had just shattered. He gripped the mask, shaking wildly, uncontrollably.

Then—just like that—the moment passed. The trembling subsided. And very softly, almost to himself . . .

. . . he began to laugh a familiar laugh.

XXVII

Mary Jane stared at herself in the mirror, and wondered if she wasn't looking at another person altogether.

"Oh, honey, you look so beautiful," whispered her mother, Madeline Watson, kissing her on the cheek. Mary Jane smiled gamely and looked to the left and right, admiring her reflection.

The wedding dress was based on a design by the late Willi Smith, and it was unquestionably breathtaking. Louise, as her maid of honor, was helping with some last-minute adjustments. It was remarkable to Mary Jane how she had become so close with her fellow actress in such a short period of time. That, and it also pointed out to her what few female friends she had.

She couldn't have asked for a more beautiful day for the wedding. The sky was cloudless and clear blue, and the harrowing experiences with Doc Ock seemed a distant thing of the past. Almost as if they had happened to someone else.

She'd kept peeking out through the door, peering into the church sanctuary to watch the growing number of people who were arriving. She'd spotted Harry Osborn, who was looking far more relaxed than she'd seen him in a long time. He'd been speaking with John and laughing. A lot. Which was odd, considering Harry was never much of a laugher. It was nice to see the change, though, and she hoped it bode well for him.

And there had been her aunt Anna, and some of the old gang, such as Liz Allen, who was arm in arm with Flash Thompson, if you could believe that. She should have known. Liz had always been circling the outskirts of that relationship.

Then there were John's friends, and his dad's friends. A vast assortment of city bigwigs and movers and shakers. The organ music was playing steadily, and soon it would switch over to the Chopin piece that was supposed to indicate the start of the ceremony in which she would be married to Pe—

John. She would be married to John.

My God, what if I say, "I, Mary Jane, take thee—" and say the wrong name, like on that sitcom. What if I muff my lines? What if—

"Honey?" asked Madeline. "Are you all right? You're shaking."

"I'm fine. Really," Mary Jane insisted, inspecting her makeup for the twentieth time. "I just . . . I feel like I'm about to step out and play the biggest scene of my life in front of the most demanding audience ever."

"Play a scene?" Louise said, and then made a slight "tsk" sound.

"Shut up," said Mary Jane in a tone that was supposed to sound teasing, but had more edge to it than she would have liked.

Madeline looked from one girl to the other, and her eyes narrowed suspiciously. "What's going on?" she asked.

"Nothing, Mom."

"Oookay." Madeline turned and faced Louise squarely. "What's going on?"

Mary Jane and Louise exchanged fierce looks, and

then Louise shrugged. "Well, I was just thinking that you play a scene because, y'know, you're acting. And if you're happy to be someplace and doing something, why would you be thinking of it like you were pretending to be there?"

"Louise, we've been over this."

"Aw, dammit, Mary Jane," said Louise in frustration, "all these months in the show, and you haven't learned a thing about relationships?"

"This is real life, Louise," shot back Mary Jane. "Not *The Importance of Being Honest*. And if you don't stop—"

"Earnest," her mother said quietly.

"I said 'earnest.' "

Madeline looked at her for a long moment and then, without removing her gaze from her daughter, said, "Louise, could you excuse us, please?" Louise nodded, and was out the door, leaving Mary Jane and her mother alone. Madeline was holding the bouquet, but now she carefully placed it on the table. "Mary Jane, what's going on?"

"Nothing! So maybe I said 'honest.' So what. I meant 'earnest.' "

"Is it Peter?"

The question brought Mary Jane up short, and she stared at her mother in amazement. "Why . . . why do you—?"

"Because he's not here, Mary Jane."

"I . . . didn't invite him."

"Mary Jane," said Madeline impatiently. "As if that decision alone doesn't speak volumes. I'm not stupid, all right? I see the world around me. If Peter Parker wanted to come, he'd show up, invitation or not. But he's not here, and that says something to me."

"That he hates me?" Mary Jane ventured, without much conviction.

"I don't think that's possible. I think it's much more likely that he felt his being here would cause you pain. And if that's the case, it makes me wonder just why that would be. Why would it be so difficult for you to see him?"

Mary Jane said nothing, but just looked down at the floor. Then she let out a heavy sigh. "Mom?" she asked softly.

"Yes, dear?" Madeline replied, the soul of patience.

"At what point . . . did you know marrying dad was a mistake? How long did it take you to regret it?"

"Oh, honey, I never regretted it."

Mary Jane took a step back and shook her head in disbelief. "Aw, jeez, Mom."

"I never did," insisted Madeline.

"Now who's not being honest, huh? After the way he treated you . . . ?"

Madeline moved toward her and took her firmly by the shoulders. "I regret how it turned out, yes. But that marriage gave me you, honey. Without your father, you wouldn't be here. For all the grief I suffered at his hands . . . I couldn't imagine the world without you in it. Heck, I don't even think I'd care to try. Oh, now look, your mascara's running."

The reason, of course, was that she was tearing up. Quickly her mother dabbed the tears away and then started repairing the makeup.

There was an abrupt knock at the door and it swung open before they could say anything. And to their astonishment, Mary Jane's father was standing in the doorway. He was wearing a suit that didn't fit particularly well, and he pulled at the shirt collar.

"They're getting antsy out here," he said.

"Dad?"

"Yeah," said Phil Watson guardedly.

"You're . . . you're here."

"You invited me. You don't want me here?"

"No, I just . . . I didn't think you'd . . . it's . . ."

"Phil, this might not be the best time," Madeline said, trying to sound diplomatic.

"Why? What's the problem?"

"There's no problem," Madeline assured him.

He looked more closely at Mary Jane. "Then why has she been crying? What is it, cold feet? Or something more?"

"Dad, you can't do this," Mary Jane told him, keeping her voice firm. "I know I invited you and everything, but this is . . . this is personal, and you can't just jump in and go all *Father Knows Best* on me and think you can solve—"

He looked at Madeline and asked, "What, is this about the Parker kid?"

Both of the women were astounded. "How . . . how did . . . ?" Mary Jane tried to say.

"Mary Jane, I might've been the crappiest father in the world, but I still got eyes that see and ears that hear."

"Mary Jane," Madeline said gently, "let me ask you two questions, okay? You don't even have to answer them out loud. The first question is: Do you love the man you're supposed to marry? And the second question is: Do you love Peter Parker?"

As it turned out, she indeed did not have to reply aloud. Her expression, the softness in her eyes, the smile—that said it all.

"Well, cripes!" Phil Watson said with characteristic

impatience that, for the first time in two decades, bene-
fited his family. "What the hell are you *doing* here?" he
demanded.

"What the hell are we doing here?" grumbled Jonah
Jameson, standing near the altar and looking at his watch.

John was near him, waiting in the bridegroom's customary spot. He patted his father's arm. "Patience, Dad.
These things take time."

"Take time! I don't have to take time! I pay other people to take time for me!"

"Mother," sighed John, "can you talk to him?"

John's mother glanced at Jonah, looked back to John,
and then said, "Why start now?"

Jonah glared across the aisle at Louise, who forced a
smile. "And what are you doing up here?" he demanded. "Shouldn't you be back there, lighting a fire-
cracker under her or something?"

"Last minute mother-daughter talk," explained Louise.

"What, is she giving her marriage tips?"

"If she is," murmured Jameson's wife, "I hope she's
recommending drinking heavily."

Jameson fired her a look. "Very funny."

"Was it?" his wife said blandly. "Oh."

"Uh-oh," said John.

His father glanced at him. "What do you mean, 'Uh-
oh'?"

"Not liking the look of this," said John, and he
pointed down the aisle. A number of the guests, who
were starting to become fidgety in their seats, turned
and looked where he was pointing.

One of the ushers was sprinting down the aisle, and
he was holding what appeared to be a note. With a
shaking hand, he handed it to John. John, for his part,

was utterly calm as he unfolded the note and read it. Then, without a word, he handed it to Jonah.

Jonah read it, then crushed it, which was more than enough to start a babble of speculation from the attendees, which only escalated in volume when Jonah Jameson snarled, "I *never* liked that girl!"

Now there was uncontrolled confusion and disarray, everyone talking to one another, and even worse, society columnists from rival newspapers were scribbling notes like mad, obviously eating it up. Jonah was ready to spit nails. There was such a pounding in his ears that at first he didn't hear his son saying, "Dad, it's okay!"

"The hell it's okay! It's not okay!"

"It is!"

"That she's doing this to you . . . that gutless—"

"Ladies and gentlemen!" John called to the audience. "Ladies and gentlemen, *please . . . settle down! Listen!*" There was a lull in the cacophony of voices. All eyes were fixed on him. "Folks . . . there's . . ." He paused, and then said, "There are some people I would have liked to have had here today . . . who won't be. One of them, as it turns out—and as I think many of you have figured out—is the bride."

People looked at one another, a few of them laughing very uncomfortably.

"But there are others," John continued, "friends of mine, who went up on missions and never came back. Missions that failed over some fault that . . . well, that went undetected. And sometimes it even seemed as if good judgment was overridden in order to have the mission go forward, and corners were cut, because no one wanted to wind up looking bad. What I'm saying is that sometimes things . . . well, they don't feel quite right, and it's far better to abort the mission and risk looking bad than have the mission go down in flames. That's not being gutless," he said pointedly to his father. "That's just good sense."

There was dead silence for a long moment.

And then Jonah bellowed, "She did this because of some other man! I know it! And when I find out who it is, I'm going to make his life the living hell it so richly deserves to be!"

Then, of course, everyone started talking at once, and it was pure pandemonium. John rolled his eyes, looked up at the priest, and gestured helplessly. Someone nudged his arm and he looked down. Louise was standing there, smiling up at him.

"So," she said brightly, "you doing anything later?"

Meanwhile, in the room in the back that had only moments earlier been occupied by a bride, Madeline and Phil Watson watched out a window as their daughter sprinted down the street, wedding gown billowing behind her, and flagged a cab. Madeline finally turned to Phil, looked him up and down, and said, "You have more flaws than any other man I've ever known, and I could never live with you again . . . but, damn, Phil, every so often, you have your moments."

"Yeah, well," he shrugged, "I'm a work in progress."

"Aren't we all," she sighed. "Aren't we all."

Peter sat on the front stoop of his apartment building, and watched his uncle Ben pull up in his car. He moaned softly.

Ben rolled down the window and leaned out. "What? No hug?"

"I gave it all up for you, Uncle Ben. Okay? I did what you wanted. I'm Spider-Man again. I'll never stop making it up to you. It came down to you and Mary Jane, and you won. Happy now?"

"Well, I'm happy that you haven't forgotten me and your responsibilities . . ."

"Good. So could we please—"

"But the Mary Jane business . . . Good Lord, Peter, how dare you?"

Peter gaped at him. "How . . . how dare I what?"

"Do you think she's stupid?"

"No!"

"Feeble of mind or dim-witted in some way?"

"Of course not!" said Peter, starting to get angry.

"Do you consider her less competent than your aunt May?"

"No!" Peter rose from the stoop and came toward Ben, his fists balled in annoyance. "How could you even ask that?"

"Because you put the truth out there for your aunt May—or at least as much of it as you reasonably could—and then backed off and let her accept you or reject you on her own terms. But you didn't remotely give Mary Jane the same courtesy. This is the twenty-first century, son. You don't get to make up women's minds for them. Come to think of it, it's pretty much been that way no matter how many centuries you go back."

"But . . . I knew it was best—"

"Peter," Ben said, almost laughing, "you barely know what's best for you. Don't go around saying you know what's best for others."

"But . . . I thought it's what you wanted . . . that I wasn't meant to . . ."

"To be happy? Ohhh, no," said Ben, stabbing a finger

at him. "Don't fob this one off on me, son. You want to spend your life beating up bad guys on my behalf, I'm all for that. But if you want to spend your life beating yourself up, then keep me out of it, thank you very much. In case you haven't checked the scorecard recently, Peter, you're one of the good guys."

Peter stood there, feeling dazed. "But . . . she's married by now. I let her go."

"You didn't let her go. You pushed her away."

"I . . ." Peter lowered his head. "Yes, sir. I did."

To his surprise, Uncle Ben replied with a cheerful tone. "You know what's funny, though? What's that physics thing you quoted every now and then? About when something happens, something else happens?"

"For every action, there's an equal and opposite reaction?"

"That's it," said Ben. "So I'm thinking . . . you may be due for an opposite reaction to your action." He waved. "It's been good talking with you, Peter."

"Will I . . ." He cleared his throat and suddenly discovered that, for all the heartache the past days had been, he didn't want his uncle to depart. "Will I be seeing you again?"

"Probably not, son."

"I'll . . . I'll miss you."

"Nah, not as much as you think. Not with her around." He chucked a thumb behind himself and drove away from the curb.

"Her? What her?" Peter called after him, and suddenly he was jolted awake by the sound of a car horn.

He was surprised to discover that he wasn't on the stoop. He was in his apartment, having fallen asleep on his bed. But there was a car honking outside his window, all the same. He rubbed the slumber from his eyes, went to the window and looked out. A cab was sitting there. There was no one in it but the driver. The passenger door was open, as if someone had jumped out of the cab with such urgency that they hadn't bothered to close it. Finally, the clearly annoyed cabbie climbed out of the driver's side and closed it himself, shaking his head and muttering in Spanish.

Wonder what that's about, thought Peter, and turned around . . . to see Mary Jane standing in his doorway. She was wearing her wedding gown, but her hair was in total disarray. She was staring at him with wide eyes and flashing a lopsided smile.

"Had to do what I had to do," she told him.

Peter bit his lower lip, just to make sure he wasn't dreaming. Automatically, he glanced at her hand. There was no wedding ring . . . or even an engagement ring. "Mary Jane . . . ?"

"Peter . . . I can't survive without you."

"We can't—"

She shook her head firmly. "I know why you think we can't be together, but can't you respect me enough to let me make my own decision?"

In spite of himself, Peter smiled. How familiar did *that* sound?

"Peter," she continued, "I know there may be risks, but I want to face them with you. It's wrong that we should each be only half alive . . . half of ourselves. I love you. So here I am, standing in your doorway. I have always been standing in your doorway." She moved toward him, and added softly, "Isn't it about time somebody saved *your* life?"

At that moment, Peter Parker heard something that he

couldn't quite identify. But then he realized: It was the sound of his soul breathing a sigh of relief.

A slow smile appeared on his face. "Thank you, Mary Jane Watson."

He took her in his arms and a moment that seemed an eternity in coming finally arrived. Their lips pressed together and Mary Jane almost melted into him. It was that night in the rain all over again, and they both knew it without having to say a word. And there was nothing that was ever going to separate them again, nothing that could possibly spoil this perfect mo—

The howling of sirens floated through the window. Police cars, three of them. Peter turned and saw them speeding up the street. People were scurrying to get out of the way, and the cop cars were barely slowing down. Something fairly major had to be happening.

He turned back to Mary Jane, and he was absolutely certain that he was about to totally screw up this new phase in their relationship before it had even begun.

Mary Jane simply smiled.

"Go get 'em, tiger," she said.

As Spider-Man hurtled above the streets of New York, following the call of the sirens, he imagined that the shadow of Uncle Ben was pacing him—no longer carrying a message of guilt, but instead one of approval over how Peter was going to be able to balance his life from now on. Peter realized just how much of the discord had flowed from his relationship, or lack thereof, with Mary Jane. It was the center of his universe, without which the universe could not hold together. More important than that, Uncle Ben appeared to realize it, as well. Hell, the old man had probably known it all along, and had just been waiting for Peter to figure it out for himself. He was like that.

Sometimes the boy gets the girl, Uncle Ben. Now the eyes I have dreamed about are waiting for me at the end of the day. But power and responsibility remain my job, my destiny . . . because I am still . . . Spider-Man.